WENCHE
ST

'My, but that's a fine sight,' Jankin drawled. 'Not many like that.'

Rosanna wiggled her bottom and looked back.

'See,' she said, 'and I'm ready too. Goose grease that is, Peter Jankin, so you may think yourself lucky.'

'Oh I do,' he assured her. 'Best thing for buggering girls, is goose grease, I always say.'

WENCHES, WITCHES AND STRUMPETS

Aishling Morgan

Nexus

This book is a work of fiction.
In real life, make sure you practise safe sex.

First published in 2002 by
Nexus
Thames Wharf Studios
Rainville Road
London W6 9HA

nexus-books.co.uk

Typeset by TW Typesetting, Plymouth, Devon

Printed and bound by
Clays Ltd, St Ives PLC

ISBN 0 352 33733 8

Mistress Perfection

Sarah poured herself a glass of wine and glanced to the clock. It read ten minutes after ten, which gave her enough time. David had said late, which meant eleven o'clock or more. At least, it always had before. The knowledge did nothing to diminish her nervous thrill, part apprehension, part anticipation, as she completed her preparations.

With a glass of wine by her side, the television on, in a loose robe with nothing but panties beneath, she felt secure enough to start. From the pocket of her robe she pulled a rag, an off-cut of bright red pigskin. She caught the scent of leather, faint, yet enough. Relaxing back into the armchair, she put the leather to her face, closed her eyes and let her imagination run.

The noise of the television became lost, her surroundings irrelevant. In her thoughts she was in a bar, somewhere, anywhere. Men surrounded her, rough, muscular men in black leather, their faces set in expressions of bestial lust as they watched her. She was dancing. She had been forced to dance: to pay for a repair to her car, for enough petrol to get her home, even out of raw lust, it didn't matter. They told her she had to dance – striptease.

She'd been taken into the back of the bar and made to dress in two pathetic scraps of soft leather. She'd been chivvied out by a big, hard-faced woman, all bright red lipstick and dyed blonde hair, a really big woman, huge, powerful enough to handle her physically. The men had clapped as she appeared, and helped her up on to a table, more than one hand touching her bottom. Now she was dancing, flaunting herself, wriggling her breasts and bottom for them like a little slut.

She was trying to hold back from the deeper indignity of exposing herself, but their patience was wearing thin. They were calling for her to show her breasts, a few at first, then more, until it was a rhythmic, urgent chant and she could no longer resist. She pulled off the tiny leather bra, showing her naked breasts, the round, pink handfuls of sensitive flesh only David had seen since they'd been married at nineteen . . .

Sarah tugged open her robe to bare her chest. Her hands went to her breasts, stroking her nipples until both had popped out, hard beneath her fingers. With her topless the men became more urgent still. Several had erections, and as she cupped her breasts in her hands and held them out to show how full they were, she realised that she was not going to get out of the bar without at least sucking cock. If she resisted, they'd just make her, and if she let her panties down, they'd fuck her as well.

As if reading her mind, the brassy blonde barmaid called out to the men, urging them to take her into the back room. She was grabbed, pulled down from the table, carried squealing and wriggling into the back room. A huge, black motorbike was propped up to one side, old and dirty with oil. Despite her protests, she was thrown over the seat, her leather panties torn off and stuffed in her mouth to shut her up . . .

She pushed the scrap of pigskin into her mouth, chewing on it to get the rich, musky tang into her senses. Her hands went down, pushing at her panties, then off. She spread her legs, her fingers going straight to her pussy, to delve between her sex lips and find her clitoris.

Chewing on the leather in her mouth, back arched in pleasure, Sarah began to masturbate.

It was what the bikers would make her do, rub her pussy in front of them as they readied their cocks. She'd be over the bike, her breasts . . . no, her boobs, big fat pillows of girl flesh, would be spread across the petrol tank. Her bottom would be up, on the pillion seat, raised and spread, her legs cocked apart, her pussy gaping, her bottom hole showing. The sour, bestial taste of leather would be thick in her mouth, as it really was, and the air full of it, along with oil, and sweat, and the smell of cocks. She'd masturbate, because she had to, because she'd been told to, rubbing at her pussy in an utterly lewd display before they just took her and fucked her and fucked her and fucked her . . .

Sarah came, her teeth clamped hard on the scrap of leather in her mouth as a long, glorious orgasm swept through her body. It held beautifully, a plateau of exquisite pleasure as she imagined how well the bikers would use her; how long, and how many times they'd make her come before she was left slumped on the old bike, exhausted but happy, and probably pregnant.

Her orgasm hit a last peak at the thought of being impregnated and never knowing who had done it. She spat out the leather and let her body go slowly limp, her fingers still in the wet mush of her sex, her face setting into a happy, sleepy smile, reflecting her contentment at the way she'd come.

Eventually she got up to retrieve her panties and wash, before settling back into the chair to finish her wine. On the television, a woman dressed from head to toe in black leather was talking seriously about her work as a dominatrix, making Sarah smile for her own shy fantasies.

'With me,' the woman was saying, 'men come to realise their true nature. To submit to the power of a woman is natural for men, all men. Sadly, few women

3

have the courage or ability to express the natural dominance that is a reflection of male submission.'

'How about submissive women?' the presenter asked.

'Yes, there are women who need to submit,' the dominatrix continued, 'and I cater for them too. Many feel unfulfilled by their partners, even those partners who are willing to correct them –'

'You mean spank them?' the presenter interrupted.

'Perhaps spank them,' the dominatrix went on. 'There are many forms of correction. Very few men do it at all well, simply because it is in their nature to submit, and not to dominate. True dominance is a female thing, and rare even then.'

'And you are a true dominant?'

'Completely.'

'What does that mean exactly?'

'It means a great deal. For one thing, I am in touch with my inner Goddess. There is a measure of divinity in me, something all men need to worship, at heart. Few women can achieve that. Because of that, my body is sacred, untouchable, not that my slaves would dare to try.'

'So you never strip off for them, nothing like that?'

'Never. No man is allowed to see my naked body.'

'And you never fancy a good spanking yourself?'

'Never, absolutely not. I express pure, absolute dominance. I could never be punished. You shouldn't even say that.'

'Stuck-up bitch,' Sarah remarked to herself.

The shot changed and Sarah realised that the dominatrix was sitting on a man. He was near naked, dressed only in tight rubber pants and a rubber hood.

'So, Mistress Perfection,' the presenter went on, 'perhaps you would give us a demonstration?'

'Certainly,' the dominatrix answered.

Sarah reached out for her glass, wondering vaguely if she should change channel. The dominatrix had stood up to select a whip from a rack of implements on one wall. Her slave had followed, dog-like at her heels, and as he turned he revealed a lemon-shaped birthmark on the back of his leg, a mark horribly familiar to Sarah. The slave was David.

Sarah had stared, dumbstruck, as she watched her husband being whipped. The dominatrix, Mistress Perfection, had done it with one booted foot on David's back, the spike heel ground into his flesh. He had gasped with pain, but been told to shut up, and afterwards had grovelled at her feet, begging to be allowed to lick her boots. She had denied him the privilege, and ordered him back on to his knees as a seat.

As Sarah watched, her feelings of betrayal had grown gradually stronger. At first she had tried to cling to the hope that it might not be him, despite knowing full well that it was. When he had spoken, even that last thread had been broken, leaving her in tears of anger and frustration. Even then, she was trying to tell herself that the problem lay with her, that she should have answered his need for domination. But she knew this was unjust. In eight years, he had never mentioned it.

The final insult came at the end, when it was revealed that Mistress Perfection charged two hundred and fifty pounds for an hour of her time. By then Sarah had worked out which of David's supposed late nights at work were in fact visits to the dominatrix. They were regular, weekly, which meant that over a thousand pounds a month was going into the woman's pocket.

She thought of his refusal to buy a second car for her use, of the holiday she had spent redecorating, of the cheap red nylon underwear she had received on her last birthday. All of it she had accepted on the grounds of economy. For the last six months she had been working as a part-time typist for a balding, greasy-haired Italian who not only failed to keep his hands to himself, but seemed to expect her to be grateful for his attentions.

As the programme faded to an advert she stood up. Thoughts of revenge boiled in her head, of taking a knife to his collection of suits, of smashing his squash trophies, even of setting light to the garden shed. Nothing satisfied. Every choice, short of murder, would leave her feeling small, and cheated, and ineffectual. It wasn't even as if it would make him angry. She could imagine his response: denial, and hurt, days of sulking and resentment, being told that the money would have to come out of her earnings. Leaving was no better a solution, representing defeat, while the odious Mistress Perfection would still be getting her husband's money and attention.

For a while she stood in indecision, before going to the bathroom. She stripped and showered, shaved the stubble beneath her armpits and trimmed her pubic hair. In the bedroom, she applied powder and scent, before dressing in the tarty red underwear David had bought her, and which she had refused to wear. She completed her make-up, now hurrying, and slipped into stockings, a tight dress of deep red velvet and the highest heels she could find.

She left, walking away down the road even as David's BMW came the other way. He failed to notice her, and she continued down to the high street. A bus took her towards the city, to a pub outside which she was sure she'd seen motorbikes, and not the sleek, colourful machines she saw in her own neighbourhood. There were none there, but she went in anyway.

Two hours later she was in the back of an old Mercedes, sucking on a man's cock. He was black, something she knew would infuriate David almost as much as her being with another man at all. So were his friends, who watched from the front seats, one fondling her naked breasts, one with his hand up her panties, rubbing at the wet crease of her sex.

They had her, much as the men in her fantasies did, only without the indifference to her feelings she always imagined. At first they had vied for her attention, and it had taken an open invitation and the removal of her dress in the car to get them to accept the idea of sharing her. Even then they had been polite, asking for their cocks to be sucked, and again when the time came to pull down her panties and fuck her.

It was done on the back seat, with Sarah mounted on the lap of the man she had sucked hard, bouncing up and down on his cock with her bottom spread to the others' attention. One spanked her as she was fucked, bringing back memories of her husband at the dominatrix's feet. At that, she asked if one of them would like to try and get his cock in her bottom hole, something she had always denied David, despite his whining requests.

She was buggered. Her anus was greased with the car's dipstick, prodded in and out of her rectum until she was slimy and open. As she was held spread by the man in her vagina, another climbed behind her, to force his impressive erection into her back passage. Both came in her, after she had taken her own orgasm with their cocks in her holes. The third had her in her vagina, kneeling on the back seat, his friends laughing at him as he tried to come in her already sperm slick hole. His solution was to bugger her and to come in her mouth, with Sarah gagging on his dirty cock until she got her mouthful.

They dropped her outside her house. Her make-up was smeared, her mouth full of sperm, also her panties. David had waited up, and stared in astonishment as she came in. Her answer was a cold silence and the slam of the spare-room door.

Her night of dirty sex did little to soothe Sarah's feelings. Some of her pride was restored, but very little of her hurt. David denied everything, accusing her of using his supposed misdemeanour as an excuse for her

own unfaithfulness. She had failed to record the programme, and she found herself increasingly frustrated
and angry, as he first began to sulk, then to stay out late
more frequently.

Twice more she went out for sex herself, first indulg-
ing a pair of dirty-minded youths on a railway siding by
letting them watch as she peed and then take turns with
her bent across a rusting oil drum. A week later she
realised her biker fantasy, to return home oily, sore and
stripped of her underwear. The only effect was to drive
David further away.

Realising that she was likely to lose him, and that
despite everything she didn't want to, her resentment
began to focus on the dominatrix. On the programme
the woman had come across as insufferably superior,
proclaiming herself a natural dominant. With her own
submissive fantasies, Sarah found it hard to imagine
herself as the woman's equal, especially when it was
obvious that David worshipped her. Much easier was to
imagine the woman laughing at her, before putting her
down across a knee for a bare-bottomed spanking.

Mistress Perfection, the woman had called herself,
and Sarah found it hard to deny that it was a suitable
name. The dominatrix was tall, slim, elegant, also cool
and poised, as Sarah knew she could never be. Sexual
arousal made Sarah feel like a slut, wanting to spread
her thighs or lift her bottom so that she could be
penetrated. Mistress Perfection, she suspected, would
remain imperturbable even at orgasm.

Despite her hatred, she found it increasingly hard to
keep the woman's image out of her fantasies. She would
be masturbating, her thoughts running on some group
of rough men using her for their sexual amusement,
when Mistress Perfection would intrude on the scene,
breaking Sarah's concentration, or spoiling her orgasm.
When she suspected David was with the dominatrix, the
feelings were worse, until at last her resistance broke.

David was out, with Mistress Perfection. Sarah was drunk, the bottle of wine from which she normally took a glass before restoring the vacuum stopper standing empty by her side. She was feeling aroused, and wanted to masturbate, but every time she tried to fantasise she found herself thinking of the dominatrix and her husband. He would be on his knees, in nothing but the tiny rubber pants, and only those because the cock and balls which had so long delighted Sarah disgusted Mistress Perfection. Sarah would come in, full of righteous indignation, only to be laughed at, to be told to strip, to get on her knees . . .

Sarah dragged herself back from the edge. She had already allowed her robe to slip open, and her nipples were shamefully erect. Her panties were wet too, and she had been on the verge of slipping her hand down the front, to relieve herself of the agonising need to come over her own degradation. She swallowed what little wine remained in her glass and once more closed her eyes, forcing herself to concentrate on a favourite fantasy.

She was on a building site, a typist in one of the portable cabins, outside which muscular young men worked, topless, their smooth skin gleaming with sweat as they worked in the hot sun. Some would tease her, others would be polite. One, the biggest, would have a standing joke, that as they had their tops off during work, so should she. She'd try and laugh it off, pointing out that she had a lot more to show off than he did, but he would persist, and the joke would catch on.

One day her boss would be out. After lunch, the big man would come into the cabin, with others, drunk. He'd have a black leather waistcoat on, and he'd tell her he was going to take it off, and that she'd have to take her top off too. She'd refuse, trying to sound stern, but giggling despite herself. They'd realise she was willing. They'd force her to strip, or strip her themselves,

9

topless, then nude. The pungent, sweaty leather waist-coat would be wrapped around her head so that she couldn't see who was doing what, and she'd be fucked . . .

Sarah had her leather rag in her mouth and a hand down her panties, rubbing firmly at her clit. She was at the edge of orgasm, her muscles already tightening, when the scene in her head changed. It was still the cabin, but Mistress Perfection had walked in, in full leather, whip in hand. The big, powerful builders immediately cowered down before her, as they might if faced with an angry Goddess. The naked Sarah was snatched by the hair, thrown on the floor, thrashed as she grovelled and squirmed in her pain, and masturbating her wet, juicy pussy even as she was beaten . . .

With an unbearable shame mixed in with her ecstasy, Sarah came. The orgasm was short, her head rebelling the instant she regained control of herself. She had done it though, and as she slumped down in the chair she was sobbing hard and mumbling David's name to herself over and over.

Two days later she rang Mistress Perfection. The number had not been hard to find, posted on a lurid card in a city phone box. A quick check in David's electronic notepad showed the same number, listed among his clients as Ms G. Prefect. It was hard to ring, but she forced herself. A female voice answered. Sarah, with a lump in her throat, replied, explaining that she had seen Mistress Perfection's piece on television and understood that women were accepted for discipline as well as men.

The woman on the other end of the line responded, first with surprise, then with suspicion. Sarah was obliged to answer a string of questions, but eventually the woman agreed to accept her as a client, so long as they met first, on neutral ground. Sarah accepted, and put the phone down with an address in the city and a date for an afternoon later in the week.

On the day she dressed carefully, in large, secure bra and panties, jeans, a thick sweater and boots. It did little to help with her nervousness, which grew by the minute as her train drew her towards the city.

The area proved less glamorous than she had expected, an enclave of shops among offices and squat concrete blocks of flats. The address was a pub on a corner, beside a fishmonger. Glazed tiles of rich brown, cream and sea green advertised wines, beers and spirits, while the frosted windows gave the name of a long-merged brewery. The image created was very different from the smart city bar she had been imagining, and more so within. There was a worn red carpet, covering most of the linoleum beneath it, pool tables, a dartboard, and seats upholstered in tatty crimson plush. The barman was smoking.

Sarah ordered a vodka and lime, taking a swallow before she chose a seat from which she could keep an eye on the door. Ten minutes after the appointed time a woman came in – Mistress Perfection.

It took Sarah a moment to recognise the dominatrix, and then mainly by the black leather coat and spiked collar. Otherwise, Mistress Perfection was as far from Sarah's expectations as the pub. For one thing, she was shorter than Sarah herself, and that with at least three inches of heel to her smart black boots. She was also younger, and the look of dominant certainty Sarah remembered now seemed simple malignancy.

Mistress Perfection looked around, and met Sarah's eye. Sarah responded with a nervous smile. The dominatrix turned to the barman to give an order and jerk a thumb in Sarah's direction. The barman nodded and turned to draw a double measure of Southern Comfort. Drink in hand, Mistress Perfection came over to Sarah's table.

'So,' the dominatrix said, sitting down opposite Sarah, 'you're the girl who wants her bottom smacked.'

Sarah shrugged, unable to produce the words she had intended to say. Mistress Perfection laughed.

'How sweet. You can't even get the words out, can you?'

'What I want to say,' Sarah managed, 'is that you should stop seeing David Walsh.'

'What are you talking about?'

'I'm asking you to stop seeing David Walsh.'

'Who's David Walsh?'

'You know who David Walsh is! He comes to you every week.'

'Look, what is this? I thought you wanted to be a client.'

'No. I just want you to stop seeing David, that's all.'

'Look, girl, I don't even know who you're talking about. I've got loads of clients. Most of them don't give their surname. Now –'

'He's about six foot, slight build, dark hair ... No, you must know. He was the guy you were on telly with.'

'Oh, you mean Turdball. So what do you care? You're not his girlfriend, are you?'

There was so much contempt in the response that Sarah found herself blushing, but she managed a reply.

'I'm his wife.'

'Oh dear,' the dominatrix sighed, 'the little woman's come round because hubby's been unfaithful. Look, girl, I can't help it if you can't give him what he needs, so fuck off and leave me to make my living.'

She swallowed her drink and got up, leaving Sarah speechless with anger and humiliation. At the door the dominatrix stopped, to give Sarah a last look of amusement and disdain, and left.

Sarah got up slowly. She made for the door, fighting back hot tears.

'Hey, what about the drink?' the barman demanded as Sarah reached the door.

She barely heard. Outside, the dominatrix was standing by the fishmonger's, obviously so indifferent to

Sarah that she hadn't even bothered to leave quickly. Sarah made to go the other way, only to rebel at her own cowardice. Turning back, she walked past the dominatrix, who didn't even bother to look round. Sarah began to cry.

'Oh, and you can tell Turdball to wash properly next time he comes to me,' the hated voice sounded from behind her.

Sarah stopped to look round at the dominatrix, her vision hazy with tears. Her emotions were bubbling up inside her, so strong that she couldn't speak. She took a step towards Mistress Perfection, who looked back at her, the strong, stern face showing only amusement at Sarah's distress, then back to the display of fish. Knowing she had to say something, Sarah reached out, pulling at the dominatrix's shoulder.

'How dare you touch me!' Mistress Perfection spat.

The dominatrix lashed out, faster than Sarah could react. The smack landed hard, full across Sarah's cheek, and with the pain her anger burst through all her other emotions. She snatched at the dominatrix, her hand locking in the leather coat. Mistress Perfection gasped in surprise and anger, off balance for an instant, before driving a knee up towards Sarah's crotch. It missed, hitting Sarah's leg. Sarah screamed, wrenching the dominatrix into her, snatching and clawing in a wild frenzy. They went down, on to the pavement, Sarah's body striking the leg of the fish stand to send a cascade of ice and fish over the pavement and the glazed tiles in the shop doorway. A male voice sounded in anger, but the women ignored it, struggling together on the ground, kicking, scratching and tearing at each other's hair, faces and clothes. Sarah was on top, but Mistress Perfection had her wrist, forcing it back. Only it wouldn't go, and as Sarah pushed back she realised that she was stronger, much stronger. Her free hand snatched out at Mistress Perfection's head, catching the dominatrix's hair, to tear it loose from its tight bun. Sarah gripped it, wrenching. Fingernails raked her face, but she kept her hold, forcing Mistress Perfection over, face down in a mess of spilt cod's roe.

'Fuck off! Get off me, you mad bitch!' Mistress Perfection screamed. 'I said get the fuck off me! Help!'

'Get off her, you fucking psycho!' the fishmonger shouted.

Sarah ignored them both. She was on Mistress Perfection's back, pinning her down, to force her face further into the mess of crushed ice and fish. They were half in the shop, the owner staring at them from a few feet away, hesitant.

'Just you stay out of this!' Sarah shouted at him.

The man backed away. Squatting over Mistress Perfection's body, Sarah dragged her victim further into the shop, indifferent to her struggles and protests. A roll of tape stood by the till. Sarah snatched at it, braced her knee in Mistress Perfection's back to stop her from escaping.

'What are you doing, you stupid little bitch!' the dominatrix screamed. 'Just fuck off!'

'Shut up!' Sarah screamed, and smacked the dominatrix in the face with all her force.

Boiling with rage, indifferent to the scratches on her face and neck, Sarah straddled her victim. She grabbed one arm, to twist tape around the wrist, and the other, forcing them together to link them, and again to bind them tight, fixed into the small of the dominatrix's back. Mistress Perfection still fought, kicking and cursing, wrenching against the tape, screaming threats. It didn't stop her being tied, Sarah's anger and strength were simply too strong. With her arms bound, Mistress Perfection finally went limp.

'You cannot do this to me!' she said, her tone now icy. 'Get off me, now. I'm ordering you!'

'I said shut up!' Sarah responded, and twisted her wrist hard in Mistress Perfection's hair.

The dominatrix cried out in pain, starting to kick again, and resist. Her head was forced back and held in place. A big tub of jellied eels had burst open near them. Sarah scooped up the contents from the floor, along with sawdust and a few stray whelks, to push the revolting handful at her victim's mouth. Mistress Perfection saw what was going to happen and shut her mouth tight, thrashing her head from side to side and kicking wildly with her feet.

'Open it!' Sarah screamed, wrenching at Mistress Perfection's jaw and crushing the wad of eel meat, jelly and sawdust against the reluctant lips.

Wrapping her arm around the dominatrix's head, Sarah tightened her grip. Finger and thumb went to the perfectly proportioned nose, squeezing the nostrils shut. Still Mistress Perfection refused to open her mouth, squirming in desperation beneath Sarah's body. Her face began to colour, flushed pink, to red, to puce, and her mouth sprang open, to gasp in air an instant before being filled with the fishy mess in Sarah's hand.

Sarah laughed, and tightened her grip on the dominatrix's head still more. Holding the muck into her victim's mouth one-handed, she got hold of the tape with her fingers, to pull it open and force it across the writhing, frantic girl's mouth. Mistress Perfection gave a last pained squeal and went quiet as her mouth was sealed, the tape shutting her half-open lips. Sarah pulled at the roll and wound it around Mistress Perfection's head as tight as it would go.

Scratched, bloody, but victorious, Sarah stood up. On the filthy floor, Mistress Perfection still struggled, writhing in the mess, her hair full of bits of cod's roe and jellied eel, her face slimy with it, her clothes soiled. She managed to roll over, to look up at Sarah with raw fury in her eyes. There was no hint of defeat, let alone remorse, and once more Sarah felt her anger boil up.

Mistress Perfection's coat had come open in the fight, revealing a leather mini-skirt, fishnet tights and a leather bra top, all black, and all slimy with bits of fish. Gritting her teeth, Sarah sank down over her prone victim and took a firm grip on the bra top. New shock showed in Mistress Perfection's eyes for an instant, then panic as the garment was wrenched up over her breasts. Sarah grinned to see the sudden fear in the dominatrix's eyes, the first show of vulnerability. She had meant to smear the woman's breasts with mess and leave her bound and topless on the pavement. It was not enough, not with the savage delight she had felt at breaking the woman's armour of cool.

With her face set in a rictus grin, Sarah shifted her weight on Mistress Perfection's legs. Her hands went to the little leather skirt, wrenching it up, as the dominatrix began to struggle, eyes wide with consternation and fury as her body slipped and splashed in the mess of fish and water on the tiles. The skirt came high. The dominatrix's slim hips came into view, with a pair of tiny black panties showing beneath the fishnet.

Sarah put her hands to the button of the mini-skirt, only to realise that a seam had begun to come loose. She gripped it hard, and tore. The threads burst, the seam split. Laughing, Sarah tugged the ruined skirt out from under Mistress Perfection's bottom, and as she did so she caught the scent of leather. It was mixed with fish and the dominatrix's scent, but it was enough. As she dug her fingers into the holes of Mistress Perfection's fishnet tights, there was a new element to her feelings: sexual sadism.

'What was that crap about no man being allowed to see your naked body?' Sarah snarled, and looked up to the wide-eyed fishmonger. 'Here, you, how'd you like to see the great Mistress Perfection's bare cunt?'

The fishmonger said nothing, but there was hope in his eyes. Sarah pulled. The tights tore wide, exposing the dominatrix's panty crotch. At that, Mistress Perfection went wild, thrashing crazily in the mess, but succeeding only in adding to what already plastered her hair and

16

coat. Sarah took hold of the little black panties, her fingers well down, and pulled. They came down, showing off a neat, shaved vulva, only a hint of crease showing in the tightly clenched V of the girl's thighs.

'Show it, bitch!' Sarah spat, and wrenched again.

The panties descended further, taking the ruined tights with them as Mistress Perfection writhed her now naked bottom in the fishy slime of the shop floor. Sarah stood, bent-kneed, to wrench at the panties. Mistress Perfection kicked out frantically, her body slipping on the floor. Sarah pulled harder, bracing herself, with a foot on Mistress Perfection's belly. The panties came, jerked high and off, along with the ruined mess of tights and the dominatrix's boots.

Mistress Perfection was left squirming on the floor, naked from the waist down, trying to turn so that she could hide her sex. Sarah ducked down to catch hold of the wildly waving legs and pull them high. Mistress Perfection managed another outraged squeak as her legs were rolled up, to display the heart of her sex, with the fleshy pink folds of her inner lips sticking out from between the outer. Sarah rolled her higher still, to show the neat little bottom and the puckered brown anal star.

Sarah snatched at a tray of mackerel, scooping up the slime that coated the fishes' slippery bodies, to slap it between the writhing buttocks. Mistress Perfection gave another muffled squeal of rage, also disgust. Sarah took no notice, smearing the gelatinous mess over the girl's sex and up between the trim buttocks, over the tight brown anus and into the open pink hole of the vagina.

Snatching at the mess on the floor, Sarah began to smear Mistress Perfection's sex. First were handfuls of the revolting mixture of jellied eels, whelks and sawdust, squashed out over the wet pink pussy. Cod's roe followed, Sarah laughing in demented glee as she stuffed two fingers into the woman's sex to push up some of the slimy mess.

'Here,' the fishmonger said.

Sarah looked up, ready to scream at the man, only to find him holding out a large squid. She took it, and they shared a smile. Mistress Perfection's teeth had finally got the better of the tape, making a hole in the middle. She was making odd bubbling noises as her vagina was prepared, Sarah fingering the little hole to push up lubricating fish slime. Sarah just laughed, pulled out her fingers, tightened her grip and pushed the bulbous, turgid body to the slimy vaginal hole.

It squeezed up, slowly, helped by the mackerel slime and its own coating of mucus. Mistress Perfection thrashed crazily as her hole filled with squid, but could do nothing. In no time the entire animal was inside, just the head and tentacles protruding from her vagina, like an insane beard. For a moment, Sarah enjoyed the view. Looking up, she found the fishmonger offering her another squid, and grinning.

'On your face, bitch!' she ordered.

Mistress Perfection made no effort to obey, but was turned anyway, and her coat pulled up to expose her neat little bottom, the cheeks clenched hard to protect herself. She was trying to look back, and screamed in outrage as she realised what was about to be done to her, kicking up her legs in an effort to get at Sarah's face. The gag had torn wide, and the dominatrix was screaming abuse.

To no effect. Hooking one leg between her victim's knees, Sarah began to force the slim, elegant thighs apart. They came, to show the squid in the dominatrix's cunt, then the dirty brown spot of her anus.

'No, not that, not there, fuck off!' Mistress Perfection wailed, and there was panic in her voice. Sarah pressed the pointed end of the squid's body in between the quivering buttocks.

'Are you ever going to touch my husband again?' she asked.

'No. I swear. I won't,' Mistress Perfection babbled.

'No, you won't,' Sarah answered, and pushed.

Mistress Perfection gave a single, long wail of despair as the fat, rounded squid was forced against her anus. She was clamping her buttocks, but her skin was too slimy, her anus too well greased to resist. It went in, slowly at first, stretching out the little hole, wider and wider. All the while she babbled and shouted, not threats, but promises and apologies. Sarah paid no attention whatever, cramming the squid all the way into the woman's rectum, before she at last let go.

With a mollusc in both holes, Mistress Perfection finally gave up. She lay limp on the floor, beaten, and when Sarah began to smack the slimy pink bottom, she took it with squeals of pain, but no anger. Even with her buttocks bright red she made no attempt to roll away, and when the squid in her vagina squeezed out at a sudden contraction, Sarah realised she had made her victim come. At that she laughed, and stopped the spanking.

Mistress Perfection was rolled on to her back once more. The tape was peeled from her head, freeing her mouth. Sarah climbed on board, to ease down her jeans and settled her bottom on her victim's face. There, in front of the astonished shopkeeper, she allowed the beaten woman to kiss her anus, before masturbating by grinding her sex into the dominatrix's face. By then the shopkeeper was also masturbating, with a fat pink cock sticking out from his overalls. Sarah paid no attention, letting him spunk over the dominatrix's sex and belly before she climbed off.

After that there was no resistance at all. Sarah cut away the tape that bound the now docile woman's wrists. The coat was pulled off and the late Mistress Perfection fled naked down the street, the squid's head protruding from between her reddened buttocks as she ran, the tentacles waving wildly behind her, the eyes staring back in an expression of frozen surprise.

Virtual Tramps

'So is it good?' Jersey asked.

'Is it good?' Chanel echoed. 'Believe me, girl, it's the best. It's so real; it's unreal.'

'So what happened?'

Chanel didn't answer immediately. A pair of men had passed them, young, in smart black suits and the narrow-brimmed, sharply creased hats which were just coming into fashion. Both girls looked pointedly forward, then turned once they were sure the men would have had a chance to take in their own rear views.

'Bite,' Jersey commented.

'Believe me, once you've been on the machine, they wouldn't be in it,' Chanel replied. 'Let's go through the park, yeah? It's quieter.'

Jersey nodded agreement. They turned in at a gate, to start down a long aisle of scarlet and yellow tulips, their steel-tipped heels making staccato clicks on the faux-stone path.

'So it went like this,' Chanel began, taking Jersey's arm. 'Four guys, firemen, bodies like they'd been carved from stone. Alpha prime bonus meatfeast. Muscles? You've seen nothing.'

'So what did they do?'

'What didn't they do? I had them every way there is, and I do mean every way. And they don't tire. They come back for more, and more, and more . . .'

Chanel finished with a wistful sigh.

'Twenty-two times the monitor said I hit high. I never did that with a real man.'

'Twenty-two times! In how long?'

'One solitary hour. That's heat.'

'That's heat, no question. Tell me about the meat.'

'Four, like I said. The first one's a daddy; so hard, cock like a log . . .'

Chanel trailed off. They had reached a fountain, a great semi-circular bowl of carved granite into which water gushed from a goat's head set in an ornate back. Several men were seated around it, a drinking school: bearded, ragged, stinking, bottles of Pear Jack or cans of HiGold clasped in grubby hands.

'Hey, black pussy!' one called. 'Where'd you get that ass?'

Both girls quickened their pace, looking away with their noses turned high, Chanel blushing.

' 'Cause it don't fit in your panties!' the drunk called after them, to a chorus of laughter from his friends.

'Look at 'em roll!' another called.

'Mine's the white bitch,' a third sang out. 'Hey, pussy, wanna suck my cock?'

'How dare they!' Jersey hissed, blushing in turn as they hurried on.

'Disgusting!' Chanel agreed.

'As if they could possibly imagine we could be interested in them!' Jersey exclaimed. 'I mean, would we ever!'

'Not in ten billion. Disgusting.'

'I'm surprised the authority allows it.'

'They can't do a thing,' Chanel said. 'Didn't you read the case? It's their right, the judge said. What about our rights, yeah, our right not to get cheeked by scabbies?'

'Or worse,' Jersey answered.

Both girls turned uneasy glances backwards, but the drinking school had lost interest, two of them arguing while the others shouted encouragement or abuse. Jersey slowed her pace, relaxing as a uniformed authority man joined the path they were on, tipping his cap respectfully to both.

'So the black prime,' Chanel continued where she had left off. 'He does a strip routine, yeah, right down to the bare . . .'

Jersey held a smile as her friend described the encounter with the four muscular firemen, trying to concentrate, but with her mind wandering back to the ugly, abusive drunks who had dared to accost them. She was in a designer split-midi, her accessories perfectly matched, her blonde hair in a tsunami wave, each perfect fingernail a different shade of blue. It was the height of fashion, a look that put her far above them, impossibly far. What they'd said had been outrageous, so utterly disrespectful that she could only assume that they had no idea of their own social position.

They had reached the gate at the far side of the park, and turned to follow the side until it ended at a cluster of buildings, old red brick and concrete mixing with the more modern glass and fauxstone. One, its front fashioned in the form of a high, black glass mask, bore a great, scarlet V. They crossed to it, the mouth opening to receive them.

Within was a round room of the same black glass, with a single keyhole desk at the centre. A young woman sat behind it, smiling as they entered.

'I have an appointment to see Robert Anster,' Chanel announced.

The girl spoke quickly, nodded.

'M Anster will see you directly, M.'

A moment later a door swung back, admitting a small, neatly dressed man. His face broke into a smile as he saw them, and he came forward with quick, precise steps.

'Chanel, pussy, back again? So soon, and with a friend.'

'This is Jersey,' Chanel explained. 'Jersey, meet Robert, my personal V-space pilot.'

'Divine,' Robert responded, bowing to Jersey. 'Do come.'

He turned, leading them back through the door and up a flight of stairs.

'Choice?' Jersey whispered.

'Naturally I am,' Robert answered, making Jersey blush. 'I mean, who else would you trust? With me, there's no fear of fiddling, I assure you.'

'I see what you mean,' Jersey admitted.

Robert had reached a landing, which opened on to a long passage set with doors.

'Together?' he asked.

'Yes,' Chanel replied.

'Paired or Mastered?'

'Mastered, please, Robert.'

'Room three then. Come along in.'

He pushed open the door wide to reveal a room, devoid of equipment save for two large chairs upholstered in black leather, each on a raised circular platform, one central. He gestured as if at some invisible assistant, at which the platforms became illuminated and the walls of the room changed to banks of screens showing various titles and images.

'And so what will it be today?' he asked.

He pointed at one of the illusory screens, which grew larger to show a selection of pictures as he went on. 'We have just the most prime historicals in – Jane Eyre, Oswald and Cynthia, even a new Monroe bioxperience if you ask nicely.'

'Erotica, I think, Robert,' Chanel replied.

'Bold girls!' Robert said, moving his fingers to change the screens, to display a range of erotics.

'Can I tempt you to a fantasy world? We have Cave of Txacalin, fresh in. Sex with an octopus God? Sublime!'

'I don't think so,' Chanel answered, with just the touch of cold his familiarity warranted. 'Just the Well.'

'Well it is the favourite. Ha, ha! Who's for the Master?'

'What's the Master?' Jersey queried.

'The controlling forma,' Chanel explained, nodding to the central platform. 'My friend will take the Master, Robert.'

'It's a new system,' Robert explained. 'Rather than sharing a mutually balanced fantasy, the Master forma slaves the others to the mind of its user.'

'Wouldn't it be better for me to be ... er ... slaved, the first time?' Jersey asked.

'No,' Chanel answered her. 'I want to see what goes on in your little pussy head.'

Jersey blushed, and shrugged.

'You haven't tried the Well?' Robert asked.

'No,' Jersey admitted.

'Then follow carefully,' he said. 'As I'm sure you know V-space erotica draws on your own fantasies. That way, you don't get what we give you, you get what you want. With the Well it's a bit different, simpler really, but not always so easy to handle. Most programs create a world for you, the Well draws on your own. Nothing will seem to change, which is what makes it so real.'

'And so good,' Chanel added.

'Does this get recorded?' Jersey asked.

'Absolutely not,' Robert assured her. 'If there's one thing we are, it's discreet. Can you imagine the suits if we sold recordings of appointments? I mean, we get some prime people in here, the sort who'll sue you if you look at them.'

'Sit down,' Chanel urged. 'It's safe.'

Jersey complied, lowering herself into the comfortable embrace of the chair. As she settled the illumination dimmed. Sensation changed, her body registering gentle pressure, as if a warm, viscous fluid was enveloping her.

'Immersion initiated,' a voice spoke from nowhere, calm and level.

Jersey saw Robert clasp his hands together as the last flicker of illumination faded. Again the voice spoke.

'Welcome to the Well, M Jersey Challoner.'

The blackness dissolved, to restore her view of the room, with Chanel in the neighbouring chair and Robert standing smiling by the monitor wall. She stood, gingerly, wondering if she was in the fantasy, or if the simulator had failed.

'Nice outfit,' Robert remarked.

Jersey glanced down, to find that her split-midi was now a deeper shade of red, heavier and bore an excitingly familiar logo.

'Chanel! This is a Marco Marri dress!' she exclaimed.

'Naturally. It's your fantasy,' Chanel answered. 'Take a glimpse at your panties, and don't mind Robert. He's not really here.'

Jersey quickly opened the split in her dress, revealing a pair of briefs that barely covered the mound of her sex. They were heavy scarlet silk, a triple panel of lace picking out the letters NYG.

'Oh my God! NYG! I must be wearing a million euro!'

'Maybe. That's fantasy.'

A hurried glimpse down the front of her jacket top showed a matching bra, and more.

'My boobs! And yours! Chanel!'

'Most girls have bigger breasts in fantasy,' Chanel answered. 'Yours are nice. Look in the mirror.'

Jersey moved across the room in excitement, Chanel coming to stand beside her, to stare back at their own reflection. Both had changed, their breasts bigger, their waists slimmer, their legs longer, their faces more delicate, more feminine.

'Animay or not!' Jersey exclaimed.

'Prime look,' Chanel agreed. 'Won't the boys just eat us!'

'They'll have to!'

'Bet on it, girl! Come on, no time like now.'

They ran from the room, giggling as they descended the stairs to the foyer, where in place of the girl a muscular young man now sat, apparently naked.

'Bite!' he said, showing two rows of perfect teeth.

'Later, maybe,' Jersey replied coolly, and followed Chanel out into the street.

'Now for the sex!' Chanel announced.

Jersey turned towards the park, looking around her as she walked. The pavement was crowded, mainly with men, perfect men. Some were black, others white, and every shade between, yet all were taller than her, muscular and with impressive bulges in their trousers. Most looked rich, city men or sportsmen, along with a scattering of rugged workers. All had the look she most prized on handsome men: tough, yet looking subtly balanced by sensitivity.

'Meatfeast,' Chanel sighed, 'double meatfeast. Who's it to be, Jersey?'

'They . . . they'll choose us,' Jersey admitted.

'An old-fashioned girl!' Chanel laughed. 'I always guessed!'

Jersey blushed and smiled at her friend. As they walked, every man was turning to admire them, most frank, some shy, but all turning their eyes to first her, then Chanel. They had beautiful eyes too, deep, intense, rich brown or piercing blue, even green or violet. None approached, to her increasing surprise, as she reached the park gates. She turned in, Chanel beside her.

'Outdoors?' Chanel questioned. 'Naughty pussy! No, I know your bite, Jersey girl. It's going to be those two we saw, yeah?'

'I'm not sure,' Jersey admitted. 'Hey, look!'

Ahead of them was the fountain. A group of ragged, ill-kept drunks were gathered around it, if anything uglier and more repulsive than before. Beyond them a girl was approaching, young, blonde, busty, in a yellow split-mini which revealed a glimpse of thigh with each step. Her jacket top was equally short, buttoned tight at her waist, to flare above and below, showing a deep slice of cleavage and the rounded bulge of her bare tummy.

'Hey, pussy!' one of the drunks called. 'Where'd you get that ass?'

The girl quickened her pace, lifting a pert nose disdainfully into the air.

' 'Cause it don't fit in your panties!' the drunk called out, his companions immediately bursting into laughter.

For a moment the girl paused, only to walk on, faster still. One of the drunks stuck out a foot, tripping her. She stumbled, almost caught herself, only for one of her bright yellow spike heels to snap, sending her tumbling into a flower bed. Slowly, she got up. Her jacket top had burst, revealing her bra. It was ample, but hardly ample enough, with the catch at the centre obviously under strain and her huge breasts lolling forward and down despite their support. One stocking was laddered and dirty at the knee, her tiny skirt now high enough to give a glimpse of fleshy thigh. She rounded on the drunks, spitting a piece of earth from between painted lips.

'How dare you!' she demanded.

'Nice boobies,' one said, staring lecherously at her chest.

The girl pulled the sides of her top together with a single, angry motion. She was furious, her face red, her cheeks blown out in rage. One of the drunks stepped forward, an older man, with white in his matted beard and a bald dome surrounded by a fringe of long, greying hair.

'You need a wash there, pussy cat,' he said, pointing.

'Oh just ... just go and bother yourself!' the girl shouted.

'Bother myself?' the man echoed. 'Did you hear that, boys? The lady says I should go and bother myself. Now I am offended.'

Some laughed. Two more jumped down from the edge of the fountain, one moving behind her, another on to the path. Quickly adjusting her skirt, the girl began to back away, her anger gone.

'Tell you what, boys,' the white-bearded man said. 'I reckon she needs a bath, and to wash that dirty mouth out.'

'Yeah,' another answered, the youngest and dirtiest of all, with a red cap worn sideways on his matted hair.

'Now just leave me alone,' the girl said, casting a worried glance towards Jersey and Chanel who had stopped to watch.

She turned, now desperate. The drunks were already round her and closing in, Red Cap directly in front of her, White Beard behind. Red Cap reached out, as if to take hold of her breasts. Instinctively she stepped back, straight into White Beard's waiting arms, which closed around her waist. She screamed as she was lifted off her feet, kicking out, one yellow shoe flying away to land on the lawn. Immediately Red Cap darted in to catch her bare foot.

'In the fountain! Give her a wash!' called another drunk, gesticulating with his bottle of Pear Jack.

'No!' the girl screamed. White Beard swung her around, half-dropping her, his grubby hands clutching briefly at fat breasts before he snatched her up once more, beneath her armpits. Red Cap already had her other foot, and together they swung her up, off the ground.

'One!' the fattest drunk called, his great pale belly appearing beneath the hem of a tatty jumper as he staggered back in laughter.

'No!' the girl screamed again as she was swung back.

'Two!' the drunks called.

'No!' the girl screamed a third time, her second shoe flying loose.

'Three!' the drunks called.

White Beard and Red Cap let go.

This time the girl's scream was wordless as she was sent flying into the air, arms and legs waving wildly, but only for an instant before she hit the water with a splash. She disappeared beneath the surface, to come up a moment later, floundering in the water, legs kicked up in a display of stocking tops, suspender straps and panty crotch. At last she recovered herself, her head emerging, blowing water from her mouth and nose, her blonde hair plastered around her head.

Chanel had started forward and Jersey followed, quickly reaching the fountain, where the drunks had gathered to enjoy their victim's plight, pointing and roaring with laughter as she struggled into a sitting position. She tried to stand, only to slip on the slimy bottom of the fountain and sit heavily down in the water. At that her bra catch gave up the unequal struggle and snapped, spilling out two fat globes of pale pink breast flesh, each the size of her head. She gasped, covering what she could of her breasts with her hands, a ridiculous gesture that drew further laughter from the drunks.

'Here, let me help you,' Chanel said, reaching out a hand.

The girl hesitated, pausing to pull the sides of her sodden jacket top together across her breasts before reaching out for Chanel.

'Here, she's spoiling the fun!' the fat drunk protested.

'Just go away, you horrible men!' Chanel spat.

White Beard, who was nearest, backed off a pace. Chanel stretched further to grip the blonde girl's hand, bending across the fountain. Immediately Red Cap ducked down, caught Chanel beneath the cheeks of her bottom and heaved, lifting her, to send her toppling forward with a scream, face first into the fountain. For a moment only Chanel's legs were visible, kicking frantically above the surface of the water, before she managed to turn over. Her head appeared, mouth wide in outrage, eyes blazing fury.

The blonde girl had fallen too, and now turned on to all fours as she rose. For a moment she was bottom up, her mini high, to expose the taut white seat of a pair of minuscule panties, absolutely bulging with chubby, globular bottom, and pulled tight against the wet folds of her sex. Fatso blew his cheeks out. Pear Jack took a hasty swallow from his bottle. Jersey stepped nervously backwards, and screamed as powerful arms closed around her waist.

She was hauled into the air, just as the blonde girl had been, kicking and squealing in surprise, shock and horrified anticipation of what they were going to do to her. It did her no good. The man who had caught her was big, and held her easily until Red Cap and Fatso could get a grip on her arms and legs. Only when he let go did she even see him, and then only as a leering face in a great bush of red hair an instant before she was swung into the air.

'One!' the drunks called.

'No!' Jersey screamed. 'Not this! No!'

'Two!' the drunks called.

'No!' Jersey screamed again. 'No! This is a Marco Marri! No!'

'Three!' the drunks called and let go.

Jersey screamed again as she found herself flying through the air, high, to land bottom first, right in the centre of the fountain, and go down, under the water, her open mouth filling, dirty brown-green water swirling around her.

For one horrible moment she was in blind panic, with no sense of up or down, until she hit the slime of the bottom. She pushed up, broke surface, gasping and coughing, to spit out a goldfish. Chanel was beside her, kneeling, the blonde girl a little further away, also kneeling, and with her ruined jacket top clutched miserably across her bare breasts. The drunks were around the fountain, hemming them in. There were now six, including the bushy-haired man and a squat, ugly newcomer. Everyone was looking at the girls, and they were no longer laughing. Jersey and the blonde girl backed hastily against the sold back of the fountain. Chanel rose up in the water, her hands on her hips.

'Let us out, right now!' she stormed.

'Let us out, right now,' Pear Jack echoed. 'City bitch!'

'What if we don't want to?' Fatso demanded.

'You ain't in no position to make demands, black pussy,' Red Cap answered her.

'No,' White Beard added. 'We're the ones what are in a position to make demands. Ain't we, boys?'

'Yeah, right,' Red Cap said. 'They wanna come out, they gotta get their tits out. That's fair, ain't it?'

'Sounds fair to me,' White Beard agreed, and turned to look at the girls.

'No way in hell, boy!' Chanel exclaimed. 'And who in hell do you think you are anyhow? You've got no right to order us, you dirty alleynappers . . .'

'OK,' the blonde girl said suddenly. 'If you promise to let me go, yes?'

There was a moment of silence, six pairs of bloodshot eyes turning to the girl.

'Yeah, we promise,' White Beard said. 'Don't we, boys?'

The other drunks answered, agreeing with sincerity, even gratitude, in their voices.

'Peel 'em,' Red Cap demanded.

Very slowly, carefully, the blonde girl stood. She was smiling, but a little tic at one side of her mouth betrayed her nervousness. Her breasts seemed enormous beneath her ruined clothes, great fat globes of flesh, straining out the wet material, twin humps marking her nipples. Then she opened her top and there they were, bare, bulging, huge and pink and wet, quivering slightly, the rose pink nipples now poking high.

The drunks stared. Fatso licked his lips. A trace of drool escaped the corner of Pear Jack's open mouth. Red Cap squeezed his crotch, where his dirty trousers hid what appeared to be a truly monstrous erection.

'That's what I call meat,' Bushy breathed.

'Imagine your cock between them,' Ugly added.

'I could fuck 'em for a week,' Red cap agreed.

'May I . . . may I go, please?' the girl asked.

'Yeah, you can go, pussycat,' White Beard said. 'Go on, fuck off before the boys decide to spunk you up.'

She went to the side, Fatso making way for her, and even offering his arm to help her out of the fountain. For a moment she met his eye, the tic in her cheek fluttering for a second until her feet found the ground. She ran, abandoning her shoes, off across the park, hands clutched tight to her ruined top, bottom wobbling under her sodden miniskirt. The drunks watched her go before turning back to Jersey and Chanel.

'Yours now,' White Beard demanded. 'Come on, out with 'em.'

'No,' Chanel answered. 'Now this has gone far enough. Let us out this moment or I shall call authority.'

As she spoke she pulled her interface from her pocket, deliberately holding it so that they could see how slim and expensive it was as she prodded at the keys. Nothing happened. Again she tried, squeezing her thumb hard into the recognition print, then shaking it. Still nothing happened.

'It's the water,' Red Cap informed her. 'Don't like water, those fancy AEAs.'

Chanel threw down the interface, glancing desperately around the park. Jersey did the same. It was empty, while the stream of people beyond the gates were paying no attention whatever. Chanel began to move towards the side. Ugly, Pear Jack and Fatso clumped together in front of her, grinning to show off their horrible teeth. Chanel stopped.

'Looks like you're going to have to get them big black boobies out after all,' Ugly leered.

'Let us out, now!' she demanded. 'I'm telling you!'

'You don't tell us nothing,' Red Cap answered.

'Boobies out, you come out,' White Beard said.

Chanel's face set in angry defiance.

'Boobies out!' Pear Jack called. 'Get them boobies out!'

'Boobies out!' they chorused, chanting. 'Get them boobies out! Big black boobies out! Boobies out, get them boobies out, big black boobies out! Boobies out, get them boobies out, big black boobies out! Boobies out, get them boobies out, big black boobies –'

'You want my titties? Here are my titties!' Chanel suddenly screamed, and tugged the button of her jacket top wide. 'These, yeah, these what you want to see, you dirty perverts? A pair of big black titties? Yeah, well, get a good eyeful, because you're never going to see them again, nor anything like them, and you are never going to touch, not your sort, not ever!'

As she spoke she had opened her bra wide across her abundant chest, to show off her huge, firm breasts, the rich brown skin glistening wet from her dunking, her ebony dark nipples straining to erection. The men gaped, now silent, their eyes lingering on her glorious chest. Eventually, White Beard spoke.

'You, the other one,' he demanded. 'The same.'

Jersey stood, reluctantly, aware that there was no way she was going to get away without showing her breasts, and keen to avoid the humiliation of being chanted at the way Chanel had been. With her face red with blushes, she opened the button on her jacket top, letting the sides loose to reveal the scarlet silk of her bra. Her nipples were shamefully erect, with the lacy NYG logo across each cup hinting at their colour and shape. She swallowed as her hands went to the clip, fumbling with the tiny catch until it sprang open. Eyes shut in furious embarrassment, she pulled the cups wide, displaying her naked chest to the leering men.

'How would you know which one to fuck first?' Bushy breathed.

'Or which hole to fuck 'em in,' Ugly added.

Jersey opened her eyes, alarmed by what they were saying. All six were staring, eyes fixed to the abundance of firm breast flesh on display, and all six had painfully conspicuous bulges in their trousers.

'Well, boys, that was nice,' White Beard said. 'Do we let them go?'

The others remained silent.

'No,' Red Cap said suddenly. 'I want her to ask nice first, the fancy black pussy. I think she reckons she's better than us.'

'Yeah,' Pear Jack agreed, the others immediately adding their voices.

'I think I'm better than you?' Chanel echoed in anger and astonishment. 'Are you blind? Are you stupid? I mean, look at you. What have you got? You've got nothing!'

'Chanel,' Jersey said softly.

Chanel turned, her eyes blazing. Jersey shook her head.

'Don't make them cross,' Jersey urged.

'Cross?' Chanel demanded. 'They don't know what cross is!'

She rounded on the tramps, ready for a fresh spate of invective, only to stop. Red Cap had his cock out, a huge, gnarled thing, the dirty brown trunk thick with veins, the foreskin a great fleshy mass, almost black, the scarlet head glossy with pressure and wet at the tip.

'Show us your panties,' he demanded. 'I wanna spunk.'

'Yeah,' Ugly agreed. 'We want a panty show!'

'Panty show, yeah!' Pear Jack called. 'A dirty one! Pull 'em down, nice and slow.'

'Jerk 'em up your arses!'

'Wiggling your bums about!'

'Show us your cunts!'

'Show us your shit holes!'

'Best give 'em what they want,' White Beard said. 'Show us your panties.'

Chanel was backing away, red-faced, Jersey too, until they met the back of the fountain, pressing to the granite on either side of the pillar supporting the goat's head. Pear Jack had got his cock out, a fat brown thing, the head purple, wider than Red Cap's, if not so long. Ugly was burrowing in his fly, Fatso too.

'We'd better do it,' Jersey whispered to Chanel.

'No, girl, not in a billion!' Chanel hissed back. 'Titties are one thing. Panty show is rude!'

'They'll come quick . . . they'll lose interest . . .' Jersey insisted, babbling. 'Just pretend it's not for scabbies . . . that it's for some prime meat . . . you'd do it for meat, yeah?'

Chanel pursed her lips, glancing at the row of fat cocks waiting for her beyond the wall of the fountain, and spoke.

'You . . . you promise you'll go away if we do panty show for you?'

'You know where this is going if you don't,' Red Cap answered, bouncing his cock in his hand.

'Promise?' Chanel asked.

'Oh, I promise,' he answered.

Chanel swallowed, exchanged a glance with Jersey, and abruptly turned, sticking her bottom out towards the men. They cheered in response, and began to wank at their cocks. Slowly, Jersey got into the same lewd pose as her friend, her bottom stuck out, with the wet material of her split-midi taut over her bottom.

All the drunks had their cocks out, six thick shafts of eager male meat, every one pointing at the girls. Jersey shut her eyes, trying to imagine that she was showing off to some smart, rich young city man. It was impossible, as was resisting the opportunity of watching Chanel give a panty show. As her hands went back, so her eyes once more came open.

Chanel's were shut, firmly, screwed up in furious embarrassment as she gave a display girls usually held back until a man agreed to be faithful, even to become engaged. Her bottom was stuck out, wiggling as she inched up the rear of her skirt, to show the backs of her thighs, and stocking tops, and twin rings of soft, bulging flesh and panties. They were white silk, the material bursting with cheeky black bottom, Chanel's big cheeks filling them to capacity, her pussy a plump pear of girl flesh, blatantly wet, and not just with water.

Jersey had followed her friend's action, easing up her skirt to show off the seat of her bright red panties, and she knew she looked just as lewd, and just as ready sexually. Six stiff cocks agreed. She pushed her thumbs into the waistband of her panties, as did Chanel, only to stop. They looked at one another, faces hot with blushes, hesitating. Jersey was wondering if she dared be so rude, in a public park, with six hard-cocked drunks eager to see what they had, their rear views, their full, cheeky bottoms, their tight anal stars, their ready pussies.

'Down!' Red Cap called.

'Yeah, down,' White Beard added.

'Down, down!'

'Down, down, pull 'em down!'

'Down, down, pull 'em down! Show us your bums!'

'Down, down, pull 'em down! Show us your cunt holes, show us your bums!'

'Down, down, pull 'em down! Show us your shit holes, show us your cunts!'

'We'd better,' Jersey managed. 'And most of it's showing anyway.'

It was true. Her sodden panties concealed very little, and even as she spoke she had begun to pull them down.

36

So had Chanel, the two girls gradually exposing their bottoms, black and white, chubby cheeks flaunted and wiggling, open, the panties gliding down. Slowly, two broad, female rear views were revealed, fleshy cheeks wide to show off dimpled bumholes and puffy, ready pussies.

Panties held down, Jersey kept her pose, listening to the obscene slapping noise of six filthy drunks jerking their cocks over the sight of her naked bottom. They were going to come over her, over her bare rear view, over what she liked to show to clean, eager, complimentary young men, and was now stuck out for the filthy enjoyment of drunks.

There was a chuckle. The wanking noise stopped. Puzzled, Jersey opened her eyes, and screamed.

The drunks were clambering on to the fountain wall, and into the water, faces leering, erect cocks waving. She snatched her panties up an instant before they reached her. Three were on her, three on Chanel, both girls screaming in surprise and struggling as they were grabbed. Fatso snatched Jersey her by the hair, pulling. Her balance went. She was in the water, and under it, her mouth filling. One had her jacket top, pulling it hard down her back, to trap her arms. She came up, to have Ugly grab her by the hair and dunk her.

They held her down, laughing at her struggles, groping at her body and tearing at her clothes. Her skirt went, torn off, to leave her panty-clad bum thrust up out of the water, the rest of her beneath. A hand closed in the waistband, lifting, to pull them hard up into her crotch, between the lips of her sex. Her head came above the surface.

'No! Not my panties!' she screamed, gasping. 'They're NYG, you . . .'

For a moment she hung by her panties, then they tore. Both sides snapped as one, to pull free in Red Cap's hand and leave her bare bottom and the lips of her sex on show to him.

'Cunt! I see cunt!' he sneered. 'I smell cunt too.'

'No, please,' she managed.

Immediately her head was pushed back under the surface. She was held under, air bubbling from her mouth, her legs kicking, her arms splashing in the water. Something nudged her face, Ugly's cock, and she was pulled up, to be presented with it, fat and dirty, the shaft crooked, the head a glossy ball of purple meat. She shook her head, her mouth tight closed. Immediately she went under, held thrashing beneath the surface as hands closed on her boobs and bum, groping, fondling.

Again she came up. Again the fat cock was thrust at her face. Her mouth came open, and was filled with penis. They cheered as she started to suck.

'See, she wants it!' Ugly called. 'Let's fuck her, boys!'

Jersey tried to deny it, but she was already sucking cock. Fatso took her by the boobs, groping them. Red Cap grasped her thighs, positioning her for fucking, his cock pressing to her leg, sliding up the crease of her bum, nudging at her pussy hole.

It went up, deep into her. They began to fuck her, front and rear, Red Cap and Ugly rocking her body between them, their cocks easing in and out as Fatso pawed at her boobs with stubby, greasy fingers. She had given in, resigned to being thoroughly used, unresisting as they amused themselves with her body. Sucking, she watched Chanel from the corner of her eye, fascinated by what was about to happen to her friend, but with little sympathy, as it had already happened to her.

Chanel had not given in. White Beard, Pear Jack and Bushy had her bent over, top gone, heavy breasts swinging under her chest as she struggled, her tiny, white silk panties her sole garment. She was clinging to them, desperately trying to keep them up as Pear Jack tried to pull them down with equal determination. Neither would give, but the panties did, ripping at the crotch, to hang loose, a pathetic scrap of torn silk that did nothing to hide the full, rounded black globes of her magnificent bottom. Her sex showed, the dark lips pouting out between her thighs, shaved bare, as was the fashion, with the tiny gold ring of her clitty hood piercing showing among the rich pink flesh at the centre. Her anus also showed, a dark star of flesh, virgin tight.

'Fucking look at that!' Pear Jack swore, pointing to Jersey. 'Come on, black pussy, give us the same as what your mate's giving!'

'Yeah, suck on this!' White Beard demanded, even as he pushed his cock at Chanel's mouth.

She resisted, tight-lipped. Bushy tightened his grip on her waist, holding her firmly in place. Behind her, Pear Jack was trying to get his cock to her hole as she writhed in a desperate attempt to stop it happening, wiggling her bottom and shaking her head to stop either getting a filling of cock.

'Hold the bitch still, will you?' Pear Jack demanded.

'I'm fucking trying!' Bushy answered.

'Well, try a bit fucking harder!'

'Maybe she don't want yours. I bet she stays still for me.'

'I will not!' Chanel managed in outrage and had her mouth filled with White Beard's cock.

Her eyes went wide, with shock and disgust. Her cheeks bulged out, but he had a firm grip in her hair and was soon fucking her mouth. Seeing her suck, Pear Jack doubled his efforts, catching her up under her thighs, to hold her thrashing in the water, until he could get his cock to her hole. It was about to go in, his head in the mouth of her sex, when it stopped. So did the two men in Jersey, who turned, pulling free of Ugly's cock. An authority man stood by the fountain, his dark green park keeper's uniform showing the double chevron of a corporal. Chanel's head drew slowly off White Beard's cock. For a moment a string of saliva joined mouth to penis, to break as she spoke.

'And not before time!'

Jersey was released, Red Cap's cock pulling from her vagina.

'Bathing in the municipal fountains is prohibited,' the park keeper announced.

'So's giving us a hard time,' White Beard answered him. 'Judge said so, didn't he?'

'Well, yes . . .' the keeper answered, suddenly doubtful.

'It's our right, it is,' Red Cap said.

'Yeah,' White Beard said, 'to "freely enjoy the city's facilities without prejudice on grounds of sex, race, religion, income or housing status", I learnt that, I did. It's our right. Overriding, it is.'

'Well, yes . . .' the keeper repeated.

'That doesn't mean they can just fuck us!' Chanel swore.

'No by-law against sex in the parks, M,' the keeper said. 'Same law. Sorry to have troubled you then, gentlemen. Have a good day.'

As the park keeper turned away, twenty centimetres of thick, dark cock was pushed unceremoniously up Chanel's vagina. She gasped and her mouth was filled too. Jersey was pulled back down by her hair on to Ugly's erection as Red Cap's slid back up her sex. Once more they began to fuck her, mouth and vagina, laughing as her flesh wobbled to their thrusts. It was getting faster too, and Red Cap's ball sack was slapping on her pussy, the coarse hairs touching her clitoris. Her nipples were out too, the sensitive flesh brushing on the rough wool of Fatso's fingerless gloves as he groped her.

She realised she was going to come, even as it happened. The orgasm hit her, a sudden jolt of pleasure as her vagina contracted on Red Cap's cock. At that, both Red Cap and Ugly came, spunk exploding in her mouth and up her vagina, to spurt out, over her abuser's balls, in her face and down her thighs. Neither stopped, pumping into her sperm-slick cavities, to make her come again, and a third time, in a welter of sperm and saliva and the juice from her sex.

Fatso took one plump breast and began to rut on it, rubbing his cock and balls on the creamy skin and in the ruins of her bra, until he too came, spraying sperm over her boob and side. She reached up to take Ugly's balls, squeezing them to make him spurt again, and fill her mouth with an impossible quantity of spunk. Some she swallowed, more sprayed from her lips and over his balls and her hand.

He continued to fuck her mouth, his erection as hard as ever. From behind her she could hear the slopping, squelching noises Red Cap's cock was making in her vagina, and Pear Jack's in Chanel, telling her that her friend's hole would be as full as her own. She pulled her head around, in time to see White Beard come in Chanel's mouth. Spunk exploded from the black girl's nose and around her lips, while her bottom and breasts were already heavily soiled, with thick white clots of come on the brown flesh. She had given in though, utterly, sucking diligently on White Beard's cock and helping Bushy on one fat breast.

The girls were used, comprehensively. Jersey was fucked repeatedly, by all six of the men, sometimes with two cocks in her vagina at the same time. She was also buggered, her anus forced by White Beard as four others held her still. So was Chanel, wriggling madly in a desperate attempt to avoid her fate, only to be lifted bodily to have her sperm-slick anus impaled on Red Cap's erection.

They were buggered head to tail, each watching as the other's bottom bounced to the drunk's anal thrusts. Others groped and pawed at their bodies, masturbating them until both came, and with their orgasms drew off the men in their bottoms. With their rectums full of spunk the girls abandoned even the pretence of decent

41

resistance. Jersey allowed herself to be fed the cock which had just been up Chanel's bottom, massaging sperm into her nude breasts as she sucked on it. She came on her own fingers, even as Chanel was fed White Beard's erection.

By then other drunks had begun to gather round, or to chase other girls through the flower beds and bushes for their own amusement. A pretty, dark-haired girl was caught and thrown in. She screamed in outrage as she hit the water, to fall silent as she went under, scream again as she came up, and fall silent once more as a thick cock was stuffed in her mouth. A moment later a man was behind her, her skirt was up, her panties were down and his cock had been pushed deep into her body.

Another girl was picked up from behind as she tried to escape, and put in the fountain. There, strong arms took her around the waist. She was lifted, her legs kicking wildly, to splash water in every direction, an erect cock pressing between her buttocks. Up she went, pushed face-on to the fountain, forcing herself to cling on to it as her legs were lifted and spread to his cock. Her breasts squashed out around the goat's head, so that the water gushed out between them and down over her belly, even as he found her hole, his huge penis filling her in one smooth motion. She was fucked, her man humping merrily away as she clung desperately to the fountain, water spilling out over her chest, her breasts and bottom squashing and bouncing to the rhythm.

Two sisters were caught at the gate and dragged back, to be tossed in with the others. Their captors quickly had them stripped and on their knees, sucking cock in the nude, until first one, then the second had her mouth filled with sperm. Made to kneel, they were fucked from behind, face to face, with their big breasts swinging in the water, until they lost control and began to kiss, open-mouthed together, sharing the drunkard's sperm.

A group of nuns tried to cross the park, and were given the same undignified treatment: caught, thrown high into the water. Others followed, city girls, two nurses, a mother and daughter, until the fountain was a mass of struggling girls, stocking-clad legs, wet panty seats, fat breasts, fatter bottoms, cunts furry or shaved. The drunks fucked them, indiscriminately, using mouths, pussies and bumholes, spunking in them, and over them, tireless, insatiable.

Jersey was floundering in almost pure sperm, with more in her womb, her belly and rectum. Red Cap was up her bottom hole, holding her legs with two fingers in her sex and his thumb on her clitoris, to make her come over and over again. She was near fainting, utterly exhausted, yet still jerking weakly at the fat cocks she held in either hand, and sucking on a third.

The man in her mouth pulled out, laughing. Others approached, carrying Chanel, smeared in sperm from her ruined hairdo to her painted toenails. She was kicking and writhing, pleading faintly, but the men just laughed. Jersey was held up, supported, her fat breasts wobbling to Red Cap's thrusts, her nipples poking up through the crust of sperm. She saw what was to happen, and groaned, a moment before Chanel's body was laid on hers, head to tail, her friend's slimy, sperm-smeared sex was inches above her face.

Jersey struggled to resist but a drunk pressed down on Chanel's bottom. The soft, sticky mess of Chanel's sex was pushed to Jersey's face, and an instant later she was licking. Her mouth filled with sperm and pussy juice, her hands closing on Chanel's bottom. Not knowing what she was doing, unable to stop herself, she buried her face in the mess. Her tongue went up Chanel's pussy, lapping up spunk and juice, her nose pressing into the black girl's open, sopping anus. At that Chanel began to lick in turn, her tongue lapping between Jersey's clitoris and the straining, cock-filled anal ring. Jersey came, instantly, jabbing her tongue at Chanel's anus as the orgasm peaked, unable to breathe as her mouth filled with a great gush of slimy, filthy tramp's mess . . .

. . . and she was on the soft black chair of the simulator, gasping for air, her muscles locked in orgasm, but with no drunks, no fountain, only Chanel beside her, and Robert, looking down at her with a wry smile on his lips. He made a motion in the air, the illumination grew stronger.

'You are one wild pussycat!' he remarked.

'I . . . I . . . never,' she managed, panting.

Chanel sat up, slowly, to stare, glassy-eyed, at Jersey.

'I couldn't . . . I never!' Jersey managed. 'That wasn't my fantasy! I couldn't possibly have a fantasy like that! You must have been hacked!'

'Hacked?' Robert queried. 'My dear girl, this is an isosystem. It can't be hacked. I'm afraid to say, your dirty little fantasy is all your own. Don't worry, I won't tell, I'm not allowed to, and I'm sure Chanel won't.'

Jersey nodded weakly.

'You have to try, it's just the best,' Jersey remarked. 'It's so real; it's unreal.'

'Well, I'm not sure, really,' Sally replied.

'Be brave, girl,' Chanel put in.

'It . . . it's just that I've never tried anything like it,' Sally said. 'There was a mobile place at a fair near the farm, and some of my friends went, but I never did. I was scared Mum would find out, and . . . Oh, I don't know!'

'Just go with it,' Jersey urged. 'I promise I won't mention it to anyone.'

'Yes, but . . .' Sally stammered. 'I mean, what will you think? I mean, my fantasies can be pretty rude.'

Chanel laughed. 'Rude? Girl, you ain't seen nothing! Wait until I tell you what your cousin hits high on! Your sweet little farm-girl fantasies are not going to shock us, please believe me!'

'You've got to try,' Jersey insisted. 'Come on. Robert, a room for three please, Mastered.'

'The Well?' Robert queried.

'The Well,' Jersey confirmed. 'Come on, Sal, I'd love to see what gets to you, I'm sure it's ever so sweet! Nice meaty farmboys? Maybe a big old lady, to spank your little tush?'

Sally had gone pink, but she allowed them to lead her down the corridor. Minutes later they were in their chairs, Jersey relaxing at the now familiar feeling of immersion. Blackness surrounded her.

'Welcome to the Well, M Sally Chancellor,' the voice spoke, and once more Jersey could see.

They got up, Sally staring in wonder at the fashionable split-midi which had replaced the plain dress she had been wearing. Her hair had changed too, set in a fashionable tsunami wave, while her make-up was richer and more colourful.

Jersey and Chanel shared a glance and a nod. Quickly pulling up Sally's skirt, they revealed lacy French camiknickers in a style thirty years out of date.

'Kinky girl!' Chanel remarked. 'So there are hidden depths to you after all.'

Sally blushed and smiled.

'So let's see what you like!' Jersey teased, and took Sally by the hand.

They went outside, finding the street much as it was in Jersey's fantasies, the men bigger, and generally older, but similar, and mostly city men.

'So you like the city men?' Chanel asked. 'I suppose they seem pretty meat to you.'

'They do,' Sally admitted, blushing pink.

'And you like them big and rough, by the look,' Jersey stated, 'and not too gentle, I'll bet, cousin Sally. What's your favourite posi? Plenty says it's not on top.'

'From ... from behind,' Sally answered, her voice little more than a whisper. 'Like ... like animals do it.'

45

'Oh my!' Chanel put in. 'What is it with you white girls? Bums in the air, always your style!'

Sally responded with a nervous giggle.

They had reached the park and turned in. Jersey looked around, to bite her lip in disappointment. There was no group of meaty city men waiting for them. No dirty, lecherous drunks hung around the fountain, nor were there any of the green-uniformed keepers visible. It was empty, or almost so.

A pig was rooting among the scarlet and yellow tulips, a large, black and white boar, quite obviously a boar, from the vast scrotum that hung behind and the huge, corkscrew penis that jutted out beneath its belly – erect.

Jersey looked quickly at Sally, who was smiling. Beyond her was Chanel, mouth open wide in shock, further still was the park lawn, across which more pigs were trotting, boars like the first, each erect and ready.

A Lady in Church

'. . . and heed the words of our Lord! Do not dismiss them, for they apply as surely today as yesterday, and as surely tomorrow. "It is easier for a camel to pass through the eye of a needle than for a rich man to enter the Kingdom of Heaven", so sayeth our Lord, and so say I!'

The Reverend Thomas Annaferd paused in his sermon, to look out across the congregation and judge the effect it was having on each. Towards the back, those in service, the day labourers and their wives, gave back the same expressions of stolid good nature they invariably wore to church. Annaferd reflected that if they were listening at all, they obviously felt his words irrelevant to their daily lives. Further forward, the artisans of the parish showed little more interest, with one or two of the younger wives at least attentive, if apparently unworried by his threats of hellfire and damnation. Even the wealthier farmers seemed undaunted.

Only in the front row did his words appear to be having any effect. Squire Glanvil himself, easily the richest man in the parish and any among its neighbours, was looking distinctly worried. His wife, the best-fed woman in the church as much as she was the best dressed, seemed positively scared. The same was true of the elder daughter, who was clutching her mother's arm and biting her lip. Even the rakish son seemed nervous, leaving only the younger daughter, Alice, apparently unaffected. She, in sharp contrast to her family, wore an expression of beatific content, with her eyes closed and her hands folded lightly in the lap of her embroidered skirt, where the crinoline rose up.

From the corner of his eye the Reverend Annaferd saw his verger make a meaningful gesture towards the wooden collecting box. Ignoring the man, he began to speak again, determined to press home his point.

'Reflect!' he boomed. 'Lest we think that these strictures do not apply to us. In the time of our Lord few men in Judea were wealthy as we count wealth. The Romans ruled, taxing as they pleased, the wealth of the country taken abroad. To them, we would have seemed a society rich indeed. Our thrift would seem to them profligacy, our hovels fine houses. All of you should fear God, unto the most needy among you, and fear him now, for who knows when life may be cut short? None know, not even the most youthful among us!'

Again he paused, drawing himself up to his full height and staring down his nose at his congregation. He suppressed a smile as he saw the change he had effected, with more than one of the farmers' wives looking distinctly worried, and there was nervous fidgeting even among the artisans. Mrs Glanvil and her eldest daughter looked terrified, the Squire and his son shifty. Alice alone remained calm. If anything her smile had grown broader, and there was a subtle tension evident in the set of her mouth. Raising his voice to a righteous thunder, he continued.

'Is there one among you who can say they have not tasted cream this last week?' he demanded. 'Who has not supped ale or cider? Who has not eaten good lean meat? These things are wealth! Palaces, carriages and ships also, it is true, but no less what you take for granted. Indeed, the very fact of taking such wealth for granted shows your sin in true light! I see wealth all around me, even now, in velvets and satins, pearls and jewels! Who can deny this? Who can say they might hope for heaven, when they go clad in embroidered silk?'

He stopped, looking pointedly at Alice Glanvil, whose dress was a voluminous affair of yellow silk embroidered with an extravagant pattern of flowers and birds. She took no notice whatever, her eyes still closed, her smile broader than ever, her mouth now twitching distinctly. He stared, puzzled, as what appeared to be a spasm of violent emotion crossed her delicate features, to vanish as quickly as it had come. Her eyes came open and she met his gaze with a look entirely free of guile or guilt.

Sighing under his breath, he turned to the verger and nodded. The collection box began to go round, most giving at least moderately under his hawk-like stare. The sermon over, he continued the service, with prayers, hymns and pieces of ritual in their ordained order, until the final Amen. As usual, Annaferd went to the church door, where he stayed as the congregation left, to exchange conversation, remarks, smiles or simple nods according to the status of his parishioners.

Alice Glanvil passed in her usual place, the last of her family, but rather than walk to the waiting coach, she detached herself from the others. Annaferd watched from the corner of his eye as she walked slowly away among the gravestones, to disappear around the corner of the church. If she had seemed unnaturally serene during the sermon, now the opposite was true, her walk awkward and her expression nervous.

With a final all-inclusive nod to the remaining members of the congregation, mainly servants, he returned to the interior of the church. His long gait took him quickly to the vestry, out of the door at its side, and so to the back of the church. As he peered around a buttress he caught a glimpse of yellow. It was Alice, her

49

back to him, standing beneath the shadow of a yew and otherwise hidden from view by a high mausoleum.

Alice threw a last nervous glance in the direction of the road and reached down for the hem of her skirts. Annaferd's expression set in both guilt and indignation as he realised she was about to relieve her bladder. He watched anyway as the silk dress was hauled high, the cage of her crinoline inverted, her elaborate petticoats lifted, to reveal lace, well-shaped legs clad in silk stockings, a bare, rounded bottom, and a dwarf.

Virago

Chi-Mai looked up at the elegant, metallic green spire above her. To either side, similar constructions stretched away along a strip of some hard, black material, in differing colours, but all in the same style. In front of them, in the arched doorway of the near building, the Learned Juilla Tia had paused in her lecture to admire the structure. Other than their teacher, Chi-Mai herself and her fellow scholars, no other living thing was visible.

'Albion Surity,' Juilla Tia stated, pointing up to the letters visible above the door. 'A company already in existence for three hundred years when this building was put up. And quite a building it is. There is an elegance to the late Neo-Perpendicular, an elegance we miss. Look, art, in a building purely functional.'

'Why would they trouble, Learned?' Xui asked from beside Chi-Mai. 'Is it art for the sake of art?'

'Far from it,' Juilla Tia answered. 'Here we see art for the sake of function, which was an essential element of capitalism. These structures were built not for accommodation, but for work. Without being able to transport solid matter save by actual physical displacement, the people were obliged to group together in order to perform their tasks. Each group, a company, or frequently a section of a larger company, would occupy a single building. As I explained yesterday, many groups

51

would have been in competition with one another, to a greater or lesser extent. Hence the need for beauty, to draw in those people from whom they hoped to take money, to themselves rather than to a competitor.'

'It seems wasteful of resources,' Mia Ki commented. 'Yet you say their energy was limited?'

'Wasteful, yes,' Juilla Tia admitted. 'Yet their productivity was notably higher than rival systems, such as Communism, allowing a larger margin of waste. As to the limitations on their energy, this is true only in relative terms. As you will see, some of their artefacts still function, after more than six hundred years. Come inside.'

She turned to the arch, stepping through. The scholars followed, into a high elegant room. Twin spiral staircases rose to either side, following the walls in an interlocking double helix. Doors showed along their lengths, some open, more closed. Juilla Tia crossed the room, taking a slim object of bright metal from the pocket of her tunic as she went. Beneath the point at which the staircases met was a high, arched door. She pointed the device, pressing her thumb to the centre. There was no response.

'There is energy,' she remarked. 'The primary control system is certainly functional. It is possible, I suppose, that the mechanisms have actually corroded through sheer age. The tallest door, I suspect, opens to a refectory, and it may well be that old or low value food gynoids were abandoned. I have known older ones to be functional.'

She turned to her right, pointing to a second door, marginally lower. Again nothing happened. A third door also remained firmly shut. The fourth swung open.

'As I said,' she announced, 'still functional. I know it is fashionable to imagine our ancestors as crude primitives, but it was really not the case. Even the males, I sometimes suspect, were less disruptive than we are led to believe.'

Chi-Mai shared a glance with Xui, amused by the idea of the huge, hairy males as anything other than beasts, their drive to mate too strong to allow rational behaviour. They followed as Juilla Tia entered the room, the door sliding shut as the last of them entered. It was radically different from the first room, low beneath arches, painted in a brilliant array of primary colours. A circular rug occupied the centre of the room, an open space around which stood structures of bent metal and moulded plastic. Boxes stood against the walls, each filled with a jumble of brightly coloured objects. At the far end was a row of terminals. Among them sat a woman.

'Gynoid,' Juilla Tia remarked with satisfaction and stepped quickly forward.

'Is this a museum, a gallery perhaps?' Que-Li asked.

'Neither, it is a nursery,' Juilla Tia responded, 'a crèche to be exact, a place at which adults would leave their children during the period assigned for work. The gynoid is the supervisor, or "Nanny", an early version of the Virago model, I think.'

'Virago 4, cheeky Miss,' the gynoid replied, and stood up.

Chi-Mai stepped back, nearly tripping over her own feet. The gynoid towered above her, to nearly twice her height. It was heavily built too, massive, with broad shoulders and hips, great, round breasts and powerful limbs. No less alarming was the face, round and red beneath steel-grey hair pulled up into a bun, the mouth small and firm, the eyes big, and formed to seem kindly, yet lifeless. Juilla Tia had also stepped quickly back at the unexpected activation of the gynoid, but recovered herself, to perform a polite genuflection before speaking again.

'Good afternoon,' she began, smirking slightly. 'I am the Learned Juilla Tia, Reader in the History of Political Systems at the Laig Teaching Facility. May I ask who I have the honour of addressing?'

'Nanny will do very well, young lady,' the gynoid replied. 'Oh dear, what have they sent me now? Nine of you, and all girls? No nappies either by the look of it. Tut, tut, as if I didn't have enough to do. I shall need fresh supplies, I'm afraid, soon enough. Oh dearie me. Well, to work, I suppose, and as there are no nasty little boys to watch today the rug will do very well. Line up, girls, line up!'

'You are perhaps mistaken,' Juilla Tia replied as the massive gynoid advanced on her. 'We are not charges. I am a teacher. These are my scholars. We are all adults.'

'My, what nonsense you do talk,' Nanny replied, 'and you no more than knee high to a grasshopper!'

'There has been some loss of height among humanity in the last six centuries,' Juilla Tia hastened to explained. 'A deliberate choice, to reduce individual consumption. Albion Surity is six centuries gone. Your primary control system has energy, but is moribund.'

'Fairy tales and taradiddles!' Nanny exclaimed happily. 'Plenty of time for that later, Miss Julia. For now, on the rug with the lot of you. There'll be no nasty little messes, not while I'm in charge.'

Behind Chi-Mai, the twin sisters, Sui-Ei and Sui-Vei, giggled. Juilla Tia turned them a look of admonishment, then spoke to the gynoid once more, her tone carefully level.

'Check your recognition programs, Virago 4. I suspect they have become corrupted. As you will then clearly see, we are adults.'

'A proper little madam, I see,' Nanny declared. 'A Director's daughter, I'll be bound. Well, Miss Julia-Director's-daughter, you know what happens to little madams, whoever Daddy may be.'

'I am an adult,' Juilla Tia insisted, 'note . . .'

Her hands went to her tunic, easing the belt before lifting it to display her breasts as she continued.

'As you see, I am physically mature, capable of lactation.'

'My oh my!' Nanny exclaimed. 'A proper little show-off, and such long words! Now I don't wish to warn you again, but I will simply not tolerate this sort of behaviour. Now come along, on the rug with the lot of you.'

She clapped her hands as she stepped forward to the rug. Three girls, Que-Li, Ana and Lui Zei moved on to it, shooting apprehensive glances at the huge gynoid. The others hung back, behind Juilla Tia, as the teacher took out her control device and pointed it at Nanny.

'Now we'll have none of that!' Nanny snapped, one great arm snatching out with astonishing speed, to grab the control. 'You know you're not allowed your own toys in the nursery, Miss Julia. It only causes arguments. Now that's the third time I've had to warn you, young lady, in as many minutes. There won't be another!'

Juilla Tia made to speak, opening her mouth, only to shut it again. Nanny slid the control into some hidden recess and walked to the centre of the rug.

'Enough nonsense,' she said. 'Time you were in your nappies. Who's first?'

None of the scholars moved.

'Now, now, there's no cause to be shy,' Nanny declared. 'There are no boys to peep, and *we* all know what girls have between their legs, don't we? Now come along. What's your name, my dear?'

'Ana,' the nearest girl said, stepping back.

'Well, Miss Anna,' Nanny answered. 'You shall be first.'

The great arm snapped out, catching Ana's arm. She squealed, struggling as Nanny drew her in.

'Do not fight her,' Juilla Tia said quickly.

'Just so,' Nanny stated, sinking to a kneeling position. 'My, but what a fuss, and all over nothing. Really, I don't know what things are coming to. Such airs you girls do give yourselves. Imagine not wanting to have your nappy on, at your age!'

'I'm nineteen years!' Ana squealed, still kicking until Nanny took her ankles, both gripped easily in one massive hand.

'Be calm, Ana,' Juilla Tia urged. 'She is unable to hurt you. It will be the most basic tenet of her programming.'

Ana's reply was a whimper. She had been laid down, helpless, Nanny still holding her by the ankles.

Chi-Mai watched in horrified fascination as Ana was put in a nappy. It was done briskly, Nanny moving with quick, sure movements, and humming as she worked. First Ana's tunic was pulled up, revealing tight black panties, which drew a tut of disapproval from Nanny, and were removed summarily despite squealing protests and a brief struggle to cling on to them. Pantiless, Ana's legs were rolled up, showing off her little pink cunt and the brown dimple of her anus.

She was cleaned, her sex and anal area wiped with a moist tissue. She was dried, a big powder puff dabbed to her bottom and sex. She was creamed, one thick finger exuding a pale yellow lotion and rubbing it firmly over her vaginal lips and around her anus.

Still holding Ana by the legs, and indifferent to the girl's embarrassed wriggling, Nanny produced a large pink nappy from the front of her dress. It was opened, slid under Ana's bottom, pulled up between her legs and fastened at the sides. Nanny let go.

'There we are, all done,' Nanny said kindly. 'Was that so bad?'

Ana stood up, red-faced and sobbing with embarrassment. Her stolen panties had vanished somewhere inside Nanny's voluminous garments, and while her tunic had fallen back into place, the bulk of the nappy left it pushed out at back and front, revealing the bulge of puffy pink material between her thighs. Several of the other girls giggled at her discomfort, but there was no mistaking the nervousness of the sound.

Hidden behind the other girls, Ana pulled up one side of her tunic to tug at the nappy. Chi-Mai bent to help, but the seal had fused in some way, making a tight belt around Ana's middle, beyond their strength to break.

'I can see you, Miss Anna,' Nanny chided. 'And you, young lady. We'll have none of that!'

Chi-Mai stood back quickly. Ana dropped her tunic.

'Good girls,' Nanny said. 'Let's not forget that my behavioural program is Golden Afternoon, shall we? Now, who's next?'

The girls had backed away, clear of the rug. Juilla Tia alone held her ground, to address Nanny.

'We wish to leave now, Nanny. The day is at an end,' she stated. 'Please return my controller.'

Nanny's reaction was instantaneous. One great arm shot out, grabbing Juilla Tia by the leg. The teacher jerked back by instinct, but too late. She was drawn in, not trying to fight, but with her face working in alarm and embarrassment. As Chi-Mai watched, she realised that the teacher's emotion were entirely appropriate.

Calmly, without fuss, at least on Nanny's part, the Learned Juilla Tia was spanked.

It was done with the same brisk efficiency Nanny had shown putting Ana into a nappy. The teacher was placed across Nanny's knees and held firmly in place. The tunic was lifted, to show a small, firm bottom encased in plain white panties. Protests and demands for release were ignored, as was the instinctive cry of shock and dismay that came when the panties were pulled unceremoniously down and off.

With Juilla Tia's panties off and her neat pink bottom bare to her class, she forgot her own admonition not to struggle. She kicked and writhed, squirming her body in Nanny's powerful grip, but succeeding only in providing a view of her sex lips and the little pink hole of her anus to the class.

The spanking was given regardless. Firm, purposeful slaps were applied to the crest of the teacher's bottom and beneath the tuck, to make the cheeks dance and spread, quickly leaving her red-bottomed and gasping. As Nanny spanked, so she lectured.

'This is what happens to naughty girls, Miss Julia. It's panties down and across Nanny's lap for spanky-pankies. Director's daughter or not, it's what you deserve and it's what you'll get. And don't say you weren't warned. Now, that's your botty warm, so let me see what you deserve. Trying to sneak out! Just plain foolish, that is, as well you know. A round dozen should cure you of that . . .'

Twelve hard smacks were delivered to Juilla Tia's bouncing bottom.

'Playing with gadgets! And you know it's forbidden, I'll be sure. A dozen again, would be appropriate . . .'

A second dose of twelve spanks was administered.

'Showing off your little chest! What a disgrace. Two dozen, and think yourself lucky I'm not fetching the paddle . . .'

Juilla squealed in protest at the sentence, to no avail, as a full twenty-four slaps were applied, turning the noise of protest to pain.

'And to top it all, saying I'm an old model!' Nanny finished, and laid into the teacher's bottom with a furious salvo, delivered with the full weight of her massive arm.

Juilla Tia took them badly, in a flurry of kicking legs and a spat of piping squeals, her legs wide to show both cunt and anus, her head shaking in her pain and misery. The girls watched, some shocked at their teacher's fate, some giggling in nervous amusement, hands to mouths or clasped over their own tender bottoms.

'. . . and one for luck!' Nanny declared, planting a final smack, to leave Juilla Tia's bottom a ball of scarlet flesh, thoroughly and precisely spanked.

Released, the teacher tried to rise, only to be taken firmly by the hand.

'And where do you think you're going, Miss Julia?' Nanny demanded. 'With no nappy on?'

Juilla Tia sat down, her head hung in defeat. Nanny took hold of her. She was rolled up, her cunt and anus cleaned, powdered and creamed. Her bottom was creamed too, a thick white ointment applied to the smarting cheeks with her legs rolled up to her chest, held still, with everything showing in detail. Only then was she put in a nappy and released. She stood and rubbed at her bottom through her nappy, her face set in consternation.

The girls had formed into a huddle on the rug, aware of the consequences of resistance, and none eager for a spanking. Nor were any eager to be put in nappies. They hung back, each reluctant to be next but not one daring to show real resistance. Nanny smiled up at them and patted the floor in front of her knees.

'Honestly,' she chided, 'what shy girls you all are. Now come along, enough nonsense, or do I have to spank the seven of you? You, girl, what's your name?'

'Lui Zei,' the reply came, a frightened whisper as the others drew aside to leave her standing alone.

'Come along then, Miss Lucy,' Nanny ordered, her voice firm and full of the unspoken threat of spanking.

Lui Zei went, dropping to her knees. She was taken, stripped of her panties, cleaned, put into a nappy, released to stand shame-faced with the others, hands folded over the conspicuous pink bulge that protruded from below the hem of her tunic. Deciding that it was best to get it over with, Chi-Mai stepped forward. Strong arms took her to lay her down, and lift her ankles. She shut her eyes in shame as her panties were twitched off, thankful that while every intimate detail of her sex and bottom was on show, at least it wasn't in the course of a spanking.

A gentle finger touched her sex, cleaning, to wipe her lips and burrow briefly into her anus. Powder was applied, dabbed on, and cream, rubbed directly on to her sex, the big, soft fingers touching her clitoris to make her twitch in involuntary reaction. The twins giggled, and again as Chi-Mai's anus was creamed. Her bottom was lifted, the nappy put on and fixed in place, leaving her to scamper back to the others.

Xui followed, and Que-Li, then the others. Each in turned was rolled up for the display of neat pink cunt and tiny anus, each given the same shame-filled routine, until all nine girls were in the same sorry state, nappied and blushing.

'It really is most inconsiderate,' Nanny declared as she stood, her voice tetchy, and directed not at the girls but at the ceiling of the room. 'Two more and I'd have run out of nappies. Really!'

Nanny stopped, her expression set in a stern frown, still directed at the ceiling.

'She's trying to contact the primary control system,' Juilla Tia said quietly. 'With luck it will tell her there's not supposed to be anybody in the crèche.'

Nanny clapped her hands.

'Very well, girls. Time for Free Expression.'

Several of the girls exchanged worried glances, which turned to relief as Nanny walked not towards them but back to her place among the monitors. Juilla Tia sat down on the rug, her face registering a touch of chagrin at the feel of the nappy. Chi-Mai followed suit, and the others. Nanny paid them no attention, apparently attempting to activate one of the monitor screens.

'How will we get out, Learned?' Mia Ki asked.

'It shouldn't be too difficult,' Juilla Tia responded. 'Her first concern will be our welfare, and in due course she will need supplies. With the primary control system down she will have to leave the room.'

'Yes, but will we be able to get out?' Ana asked.

'Most probably, yes,' Juilla Tia answered. 'It would depend on her behavioural program, which she said was something called Golden Afternoon. I am not familiar with it, but in all likelihood it doesn't allow her to leave us on our own. If so, we need only wait until she runs out of one or another resource. Once outside we must scatter quickly. She will not be able to catch us all, and whoever escapes can fetch help.'

'The ones who get caught are going to get spankings, like you did, aren't they?' Que-Li asked.

'I'm afraid so,' Juilla Tia answered, and winced. Eight bottoms shifted uneasily in eight nappies.

'It will presently be midday,' Juilla Tia went on, 'which was time set aside for meals, then as now. I think we can safely assume that no viable food source will remain functional, or it may even be that the children would be taken to the refectory at meal times. In either case, we should have an excellent chance of escape.'

'And meanwhile?' Chi-Mai asked.

'Meanwhile we do nothing to annoy her,' Juilla Tia answered, with a quick glance back towards Nanny. 'We have some idea of what constitutes bad behaviour according to her program. From her treatment of me, I suspect the Golden Afternoon program is retrospective, perhaps even late Christian. If so, offences are likely to include lying, or what is perceived as lying; vulgarity, which is not an easy concept to explain; possibly cowardice, although I believe that was primarily an offence for boys. Sit quietly, and all should be well.'

The girls nodded, again casting uneasy glances towards Nanny. She was busy, her frown intense as one monitor after another failed to respond. Chi-Mai watched, struggling to think of some clever technique whereby she might help them escape, thus earning their admiration, and particularly that of Juilla Tia. Without controllers, nothing was obvious, yet as Juilla Tia had said, it seemed likely that the key lay in Nanny's control program.

She was still thinking when Juilla rose to her feet.

'I shall try a request for food,' she announced.

Nanny had returned to her place, and looked at Juilla Tia as the teacher approached.

'Have you come to say sorry, Miss Julia?' Nanny asked. 'You didn't, you know.'

For a moment Juilla Tia looked puzzled, then took hold of the hem of her tunic and lifted it to show her nappy, bending one knee as she did so.

'I'm sorry, Nanny,' she said softly.

'You are forgiven,' Nanny responded, 'and a very pretty curtsy too, although I must say, the skirts they give you nowadays are barely decent, and in black, a most unsuitable colour. Pink is the colour for girls. Pink for girls, blue for boys, a simple and sensible rule.'

'Yes, Nanny,' Juilla Tia answered. 'I'm hungry, Nanny. We're all hungry.'

'Well, you are a bold one, Miss Julia, I must say,' Nanny answered. 'So soon after a spanking, and you didn't cry at all, did you? Quite the little trouper . . . only, of course, you're not a boy, are you? No. *Penis absent. Vulva present. Female: girl. Julia. Insolent. Punished. Spanking: manual. Report: control. No connection . . .*'

Nanny broke off, staring at the ceiling with a glazed expression. Juilla Tia took a hasty step backwards. Nanny spoke again, once more calm.

'Oh dearie me . . . I am forgetting myself. Now what were you saying, Miss Julia?'

'We're all hungry, Nanny,' Juilla Tia repeated.

'Well, you are a bold one, Miss Julia, I must say,' Nanny answered again. 'So soon after a spanking, and you didn't cry at all, did you? Quite the little princess. Yes, it is about lunchtime, I suppose. Stand back, girls. Come along, Lucy, off the rug, run along.'

Nanny stood. Lui Zei scampered quickly off the rug, which had begun to shimmer. As they watched, it changed colour from the brilliant pattern of yellow, blue and red to plain white. It also rose, a low dais emerging from the floor beneath it, to form a table. Nine chairs rose around it, evenly spaced.

'To table, girls,' Nanny ordered, walking briskly towards one of the walls.

Cautiously, the girls obeyed, waiting for Juilla Tia to seat herself first, and following suit. Nanny had reached out a hand to touch the wall, but turned sharply as she saw the girls sit down.

'Girls, really!' she exclaimed. 'I am surprised at you, especially my regulars. Miss Julia, Miss Anna, Miss Lucy, we must show our little friends how we behave at Albion, must we not?'

'We . . .' Juilla Tia began, and stopped. 'Yes, Nanny.'

'So,' Nanny answered. 'What do we do before a meal? Miss Lucy?'

Lui Zei threw a worried glance to Juilla Tia, who shrugged.

'Now, Miss Lucy,' Nanny went on. 'There's no use asking your little friends, is there? And you do know the answer.'

'I . . . I'm sorry, Nanny,' Lui Zei answered, 'but I don't.'

'Miss Lucy,' Nanny admonished.

'I . . . Please, Nanny, I don't know,' Lui Zei managed.

'Well, really!' Nanny exclaimed. 'To think I should see the day! Such wilfulness! What has got into you girls today? We say Grace, as you very well know, and for your stubborn wilfulness, you must be punished!'

'I don't know what Grace is!' Lui Zei wailed.

'Lui Zei!' Juilla Tia hissed. Nanny was already standing over the table.

'What absolute nonsense!' Nanny exclaimed. 'You rude, disrespectful child! How dare you! It's the cane for you, my girl!'

Nanny's hand shot out, to snatch Lui Zei by the ear and wrench her forward across the table. Two swift

63

movements unfastened the wriggling, screaming girl's nappy, which was wrenched down, exposing her neatly rounded bottom. The other girls quickly made room as Nanny's other arm came up, a long, thin wand of what seemed to be wood extending from the palm. Lui Zei looked back, and screamed in terror as the cane lashed down across her naked buttocks, then in pain as it hit.

'What . . . Why?' Ana demanded.

'I . . . I don't know,' Juilla Tia stammered. 'Nanny's program is . . . is late Christian, I'm afraid . . . . barbaric . . . merciless . . . Grace must be some sort of ritual. Stand up, quickly.'

Lui Zei screamed again as the cane landed across her naked bottom for the second time. She kicked and struggled in Nanny's grip, writhing wildly, her fists beating on the table. It made no difference. She was thrashed, stroke after vicious stroke applied to her dancing, quivering bottom, until the smooth, pale skin was a mass of scarlet lines and blotchy red marks. All the while she screamed and fought, indifferent to the display she made of her sex, her anus also, even when she lost control of herself in her desperation and farted loudly.

Nanny stopped, suddenly, frozen in a rigid pose, cane still lifted, and spoke.

'*Override. Cane maximum exceeded. Report: maintenance. No connection* . . . Let that be a lesson to you, young lady! Disgusting!'

Nanny let go of Lui Zei, retracted the cane, pulled the nappy back up and fixed it into place.

'Now you will say sorry, Miss Lucy,' she ordered.

'Sorry, Nanny,' Lui Zei said quickly. 'Sorry.'

Nanny returned to the wall. Lui Zei stood slowly, as if unable to take in what had happened to her, her mouth wide, her hands going down and back, to touch her ravaged bottom through the nappy. She was shaking, with tears in her eyes and one long, wet track down a cheek.

Xui reached out to take her friend's hand, at which Lui Zei burst out crying, clutching at the offered fingers, gasping and snivelling in her pain and misery. The others watched in horrified sympathy, until the beaten girl's howls had died to sobs, sniffs and finally silence. All were standing, waiting as Nanny carried through whatever operation she was involved in. At length Nanny turned, and eight sets of frightened eyes turned to Juilla Tia. The teacher curtsied.

'Perhaps you would conduct Grace, Nanny,' she said. 'It . . . it would be most pleasing.'

'What a thoughtful young lady you are, Miss Julia,' Nanny said happily. 'There we are, girls, a clear example of the benefits of regular spankings.'

Now smiling, Nanny came to stand over the table. Pressing her hands together, she shut her eyes, and spoke.

'For what we are about to receive, may the Lord make us truly thankful. There we are, now you may sit down, if silly Miss Lucy is able.'

Nanny chuckled as she walked back to the wall. A panel slid open as she approached, revealing several shelves, on each of which stood a tray. Chi-Mai had sat, rather gingerly, terrified of making any error which might lead to the agonising punishment inflicted on Lui Zei for no comprehensible reason. Nanny had taken two trays from the recess, and now placed them on the table, one in front of Chi-Mai.

It held a plate, on which rested a lump of some pale substance, four irregular, leaf-green spheres and two flat rectangles of some soft pink substance. Beside the plate was a bowl, filled with another lump, this time hidden beneath a thick, bright yellow liquid. Her nostrils twitched to both sweet and savoury smells, but she glanced to Juilla Tia. The teacher nodded. Gingerly, Chi-Mai prodded one of the green spheres with a fork.

'Young lady,' Nanny said as she once more approached the table, her tone horribly familiar. Chi-Mai froze, dropping her fork.

'Manners, manners,' Nanny admonished. 'We mustn't be greedy, must we?'

'No, Nanny, sorry, Nanny,' Chi-Mai answered hastily.

'And what is your name?' Nanny asked.

'Chi-Mai.'

'May? What a sweet name. Well, Miss May, just you wait until everybody has been served before you start. Remember, manners maketh man.'

Nanny put down the trays she was carrying and turned away. Chi-Mai breathed a sigh of relief. Her heart was pounding, and she felt distinctly damp between her thighs. She blushed, realising that she'd wet herself a little in her fear, a realisation which brought on an idea. Despite Juilla Tia's hopes, the building's control system was evidently still able to produce food. Yet the logic behind the teacher's plan seemed sound, and Nanny had said that she was short of nappies. If two more girls would have exhausted the supply, it implied that either two, or a single one, remained. It made sense, but the solution was hideously embarrassing. Besides, from the ferocity of Nanny's response to Lui Zei's failure to know a brief ritual, it seemed very likely that a wet nappy would earn a smacked bottom. The idea of being spanked was bad enough. On a bottom wet with her own pee, with the other girls watching, it was unthinkable. Yet she could make the suggestion, so long as someone else carried it out. Leaning close to Juilla Tia, she explained the idea in a whisper.

'Miss May!' Nanny's voice boomed out suddenly. 'What did I just say about manners? It is rude to whisper, as you very well know! Really! I don't want to have to warn you again, Miss May.'

'No, Nanny, sorry, Nanny,' Chi-Mai blurted out.

'Very well, but remember what happens to naughty girls,' Nanny warned. 'Now, eat up your lunch.'

Chi-Mai picked up her fork, and dropped it, her fingers trembling in her fear. She had expelled pee again as well, at the sudden shock of Nanny's voice, and her nappy felt distinctly squashy around her sex. Twice she had been warned, and it was impossible to guess what might be an offence.

She began to eat. The food was strange, the white pulp bland with an unpleasant aftertaste, the green spheres soggy and bitter, the pink substance actively unpleasant. Yet she forced herself, sure that failing to finish her lunch would warrant a third and last warning, or even the sort of sudden and ferocious caning Lui Zei had received.

Nanny stood over them as they ate, looking down with a benign smile, her great hands folded across her lap. Que-Li finished first, eating the last of her green spheres. As she swallowed, Nanny's head moved to look at her.

'One for Mr Manners, young lady. I'm afraid I don't know your name.'

'Que-Li, Nanny,' Que-Li answered.

Nanny froze, words spilling from her mouth, '*Name: search. Kali: inappropriate. Kaley: late, vulgar. Kay: accepted.* One for Mr Manners, young lady. I'm afraid I don't know your name.'

'My name is Que-Li, Nanny.'

'Pleased to meet you, Miss Kay. Now eat up, girls. Remember, we can't have any pudding unless we eat up our meat.'

Chi-Mai stuck a fork into her last piece of the pink substance, to push it into her mouth and swallow with some difficulty. Immediately Nanny turned on her. Chi-Mai shrank back in her seat, a fresh squirt of pee erupting into her nappy.

'What did I just say to Miss Kay?' Nanny demanded.

'I . . . I don't . . . I'm sorry, Nanny . . . I . . .' Chi-Mai babbled as her bladder gave in completely, the piddle running free into her nappy as Nanny came to loom over her.

'One for Mr Manners,' Nanny said. 'Really, you are a very greedy little girl. Don't you know to leave a little on the side of your plate? I'm sure you do, so there'll be no more warnings, Miss May.'

Nanny turned away, leaving Chi-Mai shivering with fear. The pee was still coming, bubbling up around her vulva and down between the cheeks of her bottom, to wet her anus. She let it, filling the nappy until she was sitting in a warm, soggy mess, with an embarrassing bulge of swollen material between her thighs. She glanced down, wondering if it was noticeable, and discovered to her horror that the nappy had changed colour, from pink to a brilliant red.

Nobody had noticed, each intent on her own worries as they ate the contents of their bowls with exaggerated care. Chi-Mai joined in, finding the substance sweet, with an unpleasantly slimy texture. She ate it anyway, careful to finish after some but before others, and leaving a little in her bowl. All the while she was in an agony of embarrassment, waiting for the hideous moment when she had to stand up and it would be revealed that she had wet herself. Nanny cleared the trays, and it came, abruptly.

'Rug time,' Nanny announced, clapping her hands together. 'Stand back from the table, girls.'

With no choice, Chi-Mai stood, the blood rushing to her face as the bulging, scarlet mass of her nappy was revealed, sticking out from beneath her tunic. Juilla Tia looked at her, and nodded in approval. Chi-Mai managed a weak smile. The table began to retract, revealing her shame to everyone. Nanny's head turned.

'Ah, has Miss May done a wee-wee?' she asked. 'Or is it something more?'

'I ... I've uri ... I've done a wee-wee,' Chi-Mai answered, her face and even her chest flushing hot in unbearable embarrassment.

'I'm a little short on nappies,' Nanny answered. 'So you'll just have to go wet for a while. Really, whatever can have become of supply?'

'Nanny?' Juilla Tia spoke.

'Yes, Miss Julia.'

'I'm sure Miss May is dreadfully uncomfortable, and I'm sure it will happen to some others too, soon. Perhaps ... perhaps we should go out and fetch ... er ... buy some new nappies.'

'Well, Miss Julia, we might very well have to,' Nanny answered. 'Not yet, I think, not just for a little wee-wee, and I do have one left. If it was the other thing, of course ... Are you ready?'

'Ready?' Juilla Tia queried.

'Ready,' Nanny repeated. 'Are you ready, Miss Julia?'

'Ready to go out?' Juilla Tia asked.

'Ready to do your dirty, as you very well know,' Nanny snapped. 'You are a rude and disobedient, girl, Miss Julia. One more piece of nonsense from you, and Mr Cane will be visiting that naughty little bottom. You may consider yourself warned. Now, rest time. On the rug, all of you.'

The girls sat down, quickly, clustering at the centre of the rug. Nanny watched for a moment, gave a nod of approval and returned to the monitors. Immediately Juilla Tia signalled to the scholars.

'As you heard,' she said, 'Nanny clearly implied that if new nappies are needed we will go out. From her speech and behaviour, I am now certain that the Golden Afternoon is a late Christian discipline program. Poor Lui Zei was punished for a failing related to religion, a barbaric absurdity I won't even try to explain. That means Golden Afternoon must be highly retrospective, even from before the invention of computers, truly

69

primitive. I suspect the term derives from the phrase "Golden Afternoon of the British Empire", and refers to a period at which brutal physical punishment was the norm, and often given for religious reasons. They were the most terrible disciplinarians, utterly barbaric! They did, however, have some primitive notions of hygiene. Cleanliness, they called it. Nanny is still hoping to communicate with the primary control system, which appears to be moribund, and so will leave us in wet nappies, like poor Chi-Mai who tried so bravely to help. I now wish you to emulate her example, but to fully soil yourselves.'

'To defecate, in our nappies?' Xui asked in horror. 'Against our skin?'

'This is no time for sensibilities,' Juilla Tia answered. 'One of us must do it, possibly two. It is urgent, believe me. As you must have noticed, her control system seems to be breaking down, which is potentially dangerous. Who has a full rectum?'

The twins giggled, Chi-Mai shook her head, as did most of the others. Only Xui spoke.

'I couldn't, not possibly. I can't anyway . . .'

Juilla Tia was about to speak, but stopped as the scholars looked around in sudden alarm. Nanny was approaching, her homely face set in a new look, one of concern. Juilla Tia went white.

'Now what's all this?' she demanded, addressing Xui.

'Nothing . . . nothing, Nanny,' Xui said quickly.

'Now don't you nothing me, young lady,' Nanny replied. 'I'm not deaf, you know. I heard distinctly. You say you can't go?'

'I can't,' Xui replied. 'I don't need to.'

'Nonsense,' Nanny answered, suddenly kindly. 'Now there's no need to be shy. We all have our little problems. What is your name?'

'Xui.'

'Well, Miss Sue, just you come with Nanny and she'll have you right as rain in a jiffy.'

70

Xui hesitated.

'Go,' Juilla Tia advised.

Xui stood, and allowed herself to be taken by the hand. Chi-Mai watched as Xui was led across the room, to the wall. Nanny stopped, the wall moved, a section extending, to form a broad bowl. At the same time a tube extruded from the wall. Nanny took the tube and attached it to her finger while Xui looked on, fidgeting and biting her lip. Nanny sank into a squat, and patted her lap.

'No!' Xui squealed. 'Not that! Not a spanking!'

Nanny's hand shot out, snatching the girl's arm.

'Oh what nonsense!' she chided. 'You're not to be spanked, my dear, just given a little enema, that's all.'

'What . . . I don't . . .' Xui managed as she was pulled remorselessly down over Nanny's lap.

'Just a little nice clean water up your botty,' Nanny went on, 'and I'll take your temperature at the same time, just to be on the safe side. Now lie still.'

'No, not up my bottom, you can't!' Xui wailed.

Nanny didn't reply. With cold, stern efficiency, Xui's tunic was flipped up. Her nappy tabs came open at a touch, to fall away from the round pink cheeks of her bottom. She was screaming, but Nanny didn't hesitate. The girl's bottom cheeks were pulled open, a blob of cream applied to the tight pink ring of her anus and one thick finger inserted into her rectum. Immediately Xui's expression turned from fear to shock, and outrage.

'She . . . she's putting water up my bottom!' she howled. 'Help!'

'Now just you hold still, young lady!' Nanny admonished. 'Or it will be spanky-panky time. You wouldn't want that, would you? And you know it's for your own good.'

Xui said nothing, merely staring in open-mouthed, wide-eyed horror as her rectum filled with water. Her legs were well apart, spread around the bowl, the big, rounded finger quite clearly up her bottom. As the water flowed in she began to pant, then to gasp, with her feet kicking and her fists clenching in response to the rising pressure in her rectum. Finally she spoke.

'Ow! Nanny! I can't stand it! I'm going to burst!'

'Nonsense, dear,' Nanny answered, and pulled her finger free of Xui's anus.

The response was instantaneous. Xui screamed as water exploded from her anus, along with lumps of solid, to splash into the bowl behind her. At that she burst into tears, great racking sobs as spurt after spurt erupted from her bottom hole. The others watched, speechless, as the contents of Xui's rectum emptied itself of dirty water, more solid and a last trickle, to leave her anus pulsing and wet, the muscles of her legs shaking with reaction.

'Let it all out, dear,' Nanny said gently.

Xui's answer was a miserable, broken sob. Chi-Mai had hidden her face in her hands, but heard the gush of her friend's urine and the heavy, damp thump that signalled Xui's final humiliation. When she dared to look again, Nanny was cleaning up Xui's bottom, applying the same sequence of tissue, powder and cream that had been used when they were first put in nappies. Xui took it with her head hung down in defeat, still crying, with the tears making a wet patch on the floor within the curtain of dark hair hanging down from her head.

Nanny put Xui back in the nappy and sent her off with a gentle pat to her bottom. She rejoined the others, no one speaking, but sharing glances of embarrassment, uncertainty or simple fear. Juilla Tia looked round at one girl after another, except Xui. Ana shook her head. Lui Zei looked at the floor, Que-Li also.

'What of you, Learned?' Mia Ki asked.

Juilla Tia threw back a pointed look.

'There is nothing there, Mia Ki,' she answered carefully. 'Be careful when you speak! Now, one of us must do it. Chi-Mai.'

'I . . . maybe, in a while,' Chi-Mai admitted, her face colouring once more.

'Thank you,' Juilla Tia answered. 'Mia Ki?'

'No, Learned.'

'Twins?'

Both Sui-Ei and Sui-Vei giggled, and nodded. Chi-Mai turned to them. They were sat cross-legged, side by side, the pink bulges of their nappies sticking out beneath their tunics. They looked calm, serene even, absolutely relaxed, and as both sighed in unison, Chi-Mai realised why. Their nappies had begun to change colour, and to swell, bulking out as the urine flowed into them, with a patch of scarlet growing from around the locations of their cunts.

Unable to look away, Chi-Mai watched as the twins' expressions changed once more, eyes closing, mouths pursing. They rose, as one, lifting themselves to their knees, to squat, bottoms stuck out, with the now scarlet nappies protruding behind. Both girls' nappies were already evenly swollen, but as their mouths came open again in a fresh sigh of relief, the material began to bulge behind, out and down as their pouches filled. A deeper red spread across their nappies.

'It is done, Learned,' Sui-Ei said.

'Stand up, be sure Nanny sees,' Juilla Tia instructed.

Both girls stood, their loads wobbling slightly in their nappies as they got up. They turned, and took each other's hands, standing so that the state they were in was quite obvious to Nanny. She gave a sigh and came towards them.

'Have you done dirty in your nappies?' she asked.

'Yes, Nanny,' they chorused.

'How very inconvenient,' Nanny sighed. 'Still, girls will be girls, and I suppose you can't help it.'

'No, Nanny.'

'And I only have one more nappy. How troublesome. Still, where there is a will there is a way. Come with me, girls, and do tell me your names.'

'Sui-Ei.'

'Sui-Vei.'

'Suzie? You can't both be called Suzie, and besides, it is a most vulgar name.'

'We are twins, Nanny.'

'So I see. Well, we already have a Miss Sue, so you shall be Miss Susan and Miss Suki. Now do lie down on the mat. You first, Miss Susan.'

The twins had followed Nanny to the side of the room, where the bowl had once more appeared from the wall, now clean, along with a thick mat of pale pink plastic. Sui-Ei lay down and, with a last nervous glance to her twin, shut her eyes.

Chi-Mai did the same, turning away as Nanny slipped the girl's nappy tabs loose. There was a squashy noise, the sound of running water, a dull thud, and silence. Cautiously, Chi-May opened her eyes, and hastily shut them again. Sui-Ei had still been rolled up, held by her ankles as Nanny dabbed at the filthy mess smeared up between the girl's bottom cheeks and over the lips of her cunt.

After a long pause, Chi-May opened her eyes again. Sui-Ei was in a new nappy, pink, as before, and the soiled one had vanished. Nanny had stood, and spoke as she turned to Juilla Tia.

'Miss Julia, you seem very grown up, if distinctly naughty. I think I can probably risk you staying dry, so let's have your nappy off, and little Suki may use it instead.'

Juilla Tia hesitated for only a instant, then bowed her head in submission and walked across to Nanny. Her nappy was removed, to leave her bare bottom peeping out from beneath the hem of her tunic for a moment before she covered it by tugging down the material.

'Thank you, Miss Julia,' Nanny acknowledged. 'Now mind, no mess, just say when you're ready.'

'Yes, Nanny,' Juilla Tia answered.

'Miss Suki,' Nanny said, patting the changing mat.

Sui-Vei lay down, closing her eyes as Nanny took a firm grip on one leg and spread them, high and wide. The tabs were opened, the bulging scarlet nappy peeled down, to reveal the revolting brown mess plastered to the girl's cunt and buttocks, and Chi-Mai shut her eyes again. Various wet or sticky noises followed, until again there was silence. Chi-Mai waited a moment, and opened her eyes to find the twins cuddled together, both now showing fresh pink nappies beneath the hems of their tunics. Nanny approached.

'Maybe . . . Nanny, we should go out now?' Juilla Tia asked hesitantly.

'Really, Miss Julia,' Nanny answered. 'I cannot imagine why you are so keen to go outside. Here in our nursery it is safe and warm, with all the things a little girl could need, the best place to be until your parents collect you.'

'But the nappies, Nanny,' Juilla Tia insisted, 'and my bottom's bare! Is that really decent?'

'Oh my, what airs!' Nanny exclaimed. 'As if it could possibly matter that your bottom is bare in front of me and your little friends. Really!'

'I'm scared I'll mess the floor!' Juilla Tia pleaded.

'Don't you dare, young lady!' Nanny answered. 'One drop of wee-wee on the floor and it's Mr Cane for your naughty bottom! Really, I do not know!'

Juilla Tia went quiet, mumbling an apology as she backed away. Chi-Mai braced herself.

'Nanny?' she said. 'I . . . I don't think I can hold on much longer, and I'm very wet. Please could we get new nappies?'

Nanny's expression changed to a frown. Chi-Mai moved back.

'Really, Miss May, how exasperating!' Nanny exclaimed. 'This is all too much. Whatever has happened to supply? Do try and hold on, Miss May!'

'I can't, not much longer!' Chi-Mai wailed.

'Oh, very well! Nanny snapped. 'Really! Well, if I must, I must. Miss Julia, it seems you shall have your wish. We must go out, but we can't have you like that, can we, with your little bare bottom showing every time you bend down. What would people say?'

'No, Nanny,' Juilla Tia said uncertainly.

'And you're still quite pink from your spanking. I wouldn't want to embarrass you,' Nanny went on.

'Yes, Nanny,' Juilla Tia answered.

'So,' Nanny said, 'here are your panties. But no airs and graces from you, young lady, just because you're in panties. I won't stand for that.'

'No, Nanny,' Juilla Tia answered, quickly taking the little white panties Nanny had confiscated earlier and slipping into them.

'We shall go out then,' Nanny declared. 'Form a neat crocodile while I quickly try supply once more.'

Nanny walked back to the monitors. Nothing appeared to happen, only for the wall from which the facilities had emerged to abruptly open a new panel, revealing a neat stack of the pink nappies. Juilla Tia sighed in exasperation, a murmur of disappointment and fear running among the girls.

'There we are,' Nanny said happily. 'As I suspected, a simple error. Now, Miss May.'

'Yes, Nanny,' Chi-Mai answered cautiously.

'Well, come along,' Nanny said. 'You may go now, and I'll have you out of that horrid wet nappy in a trice.'

'I don't . . . I don't really need to,' Chi-Mai said.

Nanny's face became stern. 'Miss May, if you've been telling fibs . . .'

'No!' Chi-Mai said quickly.

'I'll remind you that you are on three warnings, my girl.'

'I . . .' Chi-May began, and stopped, wondering which was worse, to be put through the ordeal suffered by the twins, or to take a spanking.

'Spanky-pankies, Miss May,' Nanny said, stepping towards her.

'No, I need to go, really,' Chi-Mai babbled. 'I do.'

Nanny stopped, and folded her massive arms across her chest. She was looking directly at Chi-Mai. So were the other girls, in horrified sympathy.

Chi-Mai's face was red, her hands were trembling, her stomach was a hard knot. Determined not to make her disgrace any worse, she tried to push as she was, standing. Her body refused to respond, although she could feel the weight of her waste in her rectum. She stuck out her bottom, sobbing aloud as she struggled to make her anus relax. Still nothing came. Nanny began to tap a finger on one burly arm.

Covering her face with her hands, Chi-Mai sank down into a squat, pushing out her bottom, to leave her cheeks stretched apart inside her nappy. Finally her anus started to pout. She shut her eyes, the first heavy tears rolling from beneath the lids as her bottom hole opened wide around a piece of hard, dense faecal matter. It emerged, pushed out slowly, to meet the material of her nappy, and squash out, soiling her cunt and the crease of her bottom.

Xui gasped as she saw that Chi-Mai was doing it. Nanny gave a satisfied nod. Chi-Mai's bladder let go, urine squirting out around her sex, to add to the squashy mess in her nappy pouch. She let it come, her nappy growing quickly heavier, until it was finished and her anus had closed. Hopefully, she looked up at her tormentor.

'There's a little more where that came from, I think, Miss May,' Nanny chided.

Chi-Mai buried her face in her hands with a fresh sob. She began to cry freely, and to push. Once more her anus opened. Once more there was the awful feeling of letting go of her bowels while she was in clothes, and it was coming out, easily now, and in quantity. She was crimson with embarrassment as her nappy filled, swelling under her bottom, growing slowly heavier, until a great, sagging bulge hung beneath her. It was up the crease of her bottom, and smeared over her sex, fouling her utterly, yet still it came, more and more, until she was fervently wishing she had taken the pain and exposure of a spanking.

At last it stopped, and she stood, her face screwed up in misery, the rear of her nappy obscenely fat, for all to see what she had done. Nanny gave a satisfied smile, and beckoned her towards the wall. With no choice, Chi-May went, to allow herself to be rolled up on the changing mat, her legs spread wide, her nappy tabs opened, the sodden nappy peeled down.

It was showing, her mess, filthy and brown over her cunt and bottom, just as Sui-Vei's had been. Her eyes were shut, but she knew they'd be staring, at least some of them, and heavy tears were squeezing from the sides, to trickle down over her face.

With the twins it had seemed to take moments. With her, it seemed to go on for ever. Nanny was in no hurry, removing the soiled nappy, lifting her by the ankles, wiping her buttocks, wiping her crease, her anus, her cunt, rubbing at her clitoris . . .

Chi-Mai came, with a sudden contraction of her sex and a little involuntary cry. The orgasm had come from nowhere, and her head filled with shame and confusion even as it died. One touch to her clitoris and she had come, something that usually required several minutes of diligent work with another girl's tongue, in moments, and at the most degrading moment of her life. Somewhere behind her the twins giggled.

'Miss May,' Nanny admonished. 'We'll have none of that dirty stuff. Really! Now hold still.'

Chi-Mai went limp, abandoning herself to Nanny as she was cleaned, powdered and creamed. A new nappy was put on her, tucked under her bottom and sealed into place, before she was sent back to the others with a pat on her bottom.

'You were very brave, Chi-Mai,' Juilla Tia said.

'She came!' Mia Ki accused. 'Dirty girl!'

'Sometimes one cannot help the responses of one's body, Mia Ki,' Juilla Tia countered. 'Now, I regret that as Nanny appears to have activated the supply system, the idea of exhausting her resources has become redundant. Do any of you have any other suggestions?'

'Can't we simply wait?' Que-Li asked. 'She said we'd be here until our parents collected us.'

'True,' Juilla Tia answered, 'except that we have no parents to collect us. Who knows what her program might call for in the circumstances? Certainly she won't let us go. It will be a basic function to allow us to leave, but I suspect only with an authorised person.'

'There must be something!' Lui Zei whined.

'I must find a means to retrieve my controller,' Juilla Tia went on, ignoring the panic in Lui Zei's voice.

'How?' Mia Ki asked. 'She is so fast, so strong . . .'

She trailed off. Nanny was approaching. Quickly, all nine girls sat down on the rug. Chi-Mai looked up at the huge figure, her bottom twitching in anticipation of the spanking that would come with one more mistake. Nanny stopped and sat down.

'Story time,' she announced. 'Now, what shall it be? The Brave Tale of Captain Scott? Always popular, but perhaps more for the boys. What was I reading yesterday? Can anyone remember? *Memory: file missing. Query: stolen.*'

Nanny had frozen, but moved again almost immediately, her face setting in cold anger.

'There is a thief!' she exclaimed. 'I am shocked, disgusted! Whoever has done this will own up, now, or I will be forced to spank the whole class!'

The girls backed hurriedly away. Nanny strode forward, screeching.

'Own up! The culprit must own up! I shall spank the whole class . . . school . . . dormitory . . . team . . . *Subprogram error. Classify: Albion Surity crèche* . . . Own up! The culprit must own up! I shall spank the lot of you! Now!'

'Be calm, girls,' Juilla Tia urged, her own voice breaking as the girls cowered back. 'Don't do anything to anger her. Be truthful.'

'Yes, listen to Miss Julia!' Nanny thundered. 'She is a sensible girl! She knows what happens to girls who disobey me! They get their botties spanked, don't they! And if that's not enough, those self-same naughty botties get a visit from Mr Cane, don't they! Now who did it?'

Nobody answered. Nanny's expression grew sterner still.

'Very well,' she boomed. 'If that's the way you want it. Stand still! Immediately! Form a line! Bend down! Touch your toes!'

'Do it, just do it!' Juilla Tia said quickly.

Even as she spoke she was turning, to bend down, her back to the advancing Nanny, her tunic tail lifting to show off the taut white seat of her panties. Swallowing down the lump of fear in her throat, Chi-Mai did the same, trembling as she touched the toes of her shoes. Nanny had stopped, folding her arms across her chest.

'I'm waiting, girls,' she stated. 'Anyone not in line on the count of five will get extra. One . . . Two . . . Three . . .'

Nanny stopped. All nine girls were in line, nine heads hung down in miserable surrender, eight puffy pink nappy seats and one pair of little white panties pushed up for attention. Nanny came close, behind Lui Zei, to tug open the nappy tabs and let it fall, exposing a mess of cane bruises. Lui Zei let out a frightened sob.

'Whoever the culprit is should be thinking on her crime,' Nanny said, now calm as Que-Li's bottom was stripped in turn. 'It really would be very much easier for everybody if she were to simply own up. Otherwise I will be forced to spank you all.'

She moved to Xui, baring her, and Chi-Mai, who shut her eyes as her nappy fell away to let the cool air to her naked skin. Juilla Tia's panties were twitched down.

'How will she feel then,' Nanny went on, 'knowing that because of her selfishness all of her little friends have had their botties spanked. Won't she feel awful? Yes she will.'

Sui-Ei's nappy fell away, and Sui-Vei's. Ana's followed, and lastly Mia-Ki's, to leave nine bare girlish bottoms showing beneath nine turned-up tunic skirts, nine little pink cunts peeping out between nine sets of elegant thighs, and nine tight bottom holes turned up to the ceiling.

'I do know who did it,' Nanny stated, 'but I want her to own up of her own accord. Now come along.'

There was silence, broken by a loud smack and a squeal of pain as Nanny's hand came down hard on Mia Ki's bottom.

'I shall do it,' Nanny warned. 'Spanky-pankies, all nine of you.'

A sudden flurry of smacks was delivered to Mia Ki's bottom, to leave her squealing and dancing on her toes.

'Next,' Nanny announced. 'Miss Anna. Stick that bottom up.'

Ana was given the same treatment, a dozen hard swats to her bare bottom, to make her jump and wriggle.

'Miss Suki,' Nanny declared, and set to work on Sui-Vei.

Sui-Ei followed, both twins gasping in time to each other's spanking, and moving together, in an odd little dance of pain.

'Miss Julia,' Nanny stated, and for the second time the Learned Juilla Tia was spanked, bare bottom, in front of her scholars.

81

'Miss May,' Nanny said.

Chi-Mai braced herself, determined to hold back the tears she could already feel welling in her eyes, and not to jump about in pain the way the other girls had. Nanny's hand came down on her bottom and her resolve snapped instantly. She jumped, just like the others, kicking out her legs and hopping on her toes as her bottom bounced to the twelve firm smacks. She cried too, tears rolling down her face as the spanking was administered, and after.

'Miss Sue,' Nanny said.

As Nanny spoke, Xui's bladder went, urine spraying backwards, in a long, yellow arch, to patter on the floor, as she burst into a fit of sobbing.

'Disgusting!' Nanny snapped. 'Can't you contain yourself for a minute? You will have to clear it up yourself, you know!'

Xui was spanked, with the urine still running down her legs, to leave her with a soggy nappy between her feet and a big puddle behind her on the floor.

'Miss Kay,' Nanny said quietly, stepping over the pee puddle.

Que-Li gave a broken sob, her tears starting even before Nanny's hand descended for the first smack. She got worse, bawling her eyes out, and making little treading motions in a runnel of Xui's pee as she was spanked.

'It'll be the cane if the culprit doesn't own up,' Nanny warned. 'Think of what you'll be making me do to poor Miss Lucy.'

'Please, no,' Lui Zei babbled as the huge hand came to rest on her bruised bottom.

'Admit to the theft, one of you!' Mia Ki urged. 'We must!'

'You do!' Ana answered her.

'I don't want to be caned!' Mia Ki howled. 'Admit it, Lui Zei! You've been done. Maybe she'll let you off!'

'Well,' Nanny said. 'I'm waiting.'

'It was her, it was her!' Lui Zei shouted, jumping up to point frantically to Mia Ki. 'She stole it! She did!'

'Did she now,' Nanny retorted, placing massive fists on her hips as she turned on the cowering Mia Ki. 'Well, young lady, what is your name?'

'M . . . M . . . Mia Ki,' the terrified girl answered.

'Micky?' Nanny answered, and froze. '*Name: search. Micky: incorrect gender. Penis absent. Vulva present. Female: girl. Micky. Name: search. Micky: incorrect gender. Penis absent. Vulva present. Female: girl. Micky. Name: search. Micky: incorrect gender. Penis absent. Vulva present. Female: girl. Micky. Name: search. Micky: incorrect gender. Penis absent. Vulva present. Female: girl. Micky . . .*'

The girls jumped up, backing away in fear. Nanny's voice had risen to a shrill whine. Her arms shot out, the cane extending, retracting, extending once more, her frontal pouch erupting to spill a great gush of artefacts out on to the floor: models of ancient vehicles, strangely shaped objects in brilliantly coloured plastic, tubes of crystallised matter, and Juilla Tia's controller.

Chi-Mai snatched it up, turned to throw it to the teacher. Juilla Tia caught it, pressed her thumb into the activating depression and pointed it at the doors, which swung open. Both scholars and teacher ran.

Girls

A face appeared around the edge of the study door, pale, freckled and red-haired.

'Buzz off, Thicky!' Berenice responded automatically.

Dagmar 'Bosch' Von Pauling picked up a Latin grammar, aiming it at the head, which promptly disappeared from view.

'Beasts! Rotters!' the girl's voice sounded from beyond the door. 'You'll be jolly sorry when you find out what I was going to tell you!'

'What?' Von Pauling demanded.

'I'm not telling!' Thicky's voice sounded again, this time ending in a long squeal of pain.

Thomasina 'Thicky' Plank was marched in, her arm twisted hard into the small of her back by the third member of the study, Charlotte 'Chalky' White.

'Spill it, Thicky,' Berenice ordered.

'I shan't!' Thicky answered. 'Not if you're going to be such beasts!'

She squealed again, louder than before, as her arm was twisted tighter still.

'I'll tell, I'll tell!' she babbled. 'There's a dance, at the end of term, for everyone in the sixth form.'

'We know that,' Von Pauling replied dismissively. 'There's a dance every year.'

'Yes,' Thicky went on, 'but this year, there'll be boys.'

'Boys!' Charlotte exclaimed. 'For real?'

'What rot!' Berenice declared. 'The Penguins wouldn't let boys within a mile of the place, not ever.'

'It's true, rotter, just ask your brother!' Thicky squeaked.

'I jolly well shall,' Berenice answered her.

'So it's the boys from St Barnabas, is it?' Charlotte asked.

'Yes,' Thicky answered, 'and it's fancy dress, and if you want to go you've got to put your name down on the board.'

'Interesting,' Von Pauling said. 'Get rid of her, Chalky.'

Thomasina was sent on her way with a well-placed boot from Charlotte, and the three friends gathered round.

'Boys!' Charlotte declared with relish.

'Yes, boys,' Berenice responded, 'boys we won't be allowed to do anything with except the most boring dances.'

'You're right,' Charlotte admitted, 'one step out of line and the Penguins will swish us, right there, I wouldn't wonder.'

'Don't be a sap!' Berenice answered her. 'They wouldn't swish us in front of boys!'

'They won't swish us at all,' Von Pauling put in. 'I have a plan. Bernie, your brother is at St Barnabas. You will see him at the weekend, yes?'

'Yes,' Berenice answered.

'Then you must tell him to choose the two most handsome of his friends,' Von Pauling instructed, 'handsome and also tall. Each must borrow the habit of a monk, and wear it under his costume. They must also have the right costumes, so we may know who is who. Large animal costumes will be best, a bear, I think for one, a gorilla and a werewolf. Yes?'

'Got it, Bosch,' Berenice responded, Charlotte nodding.

'We, too, must be well covered,' Von Pauling continued, 'to conceal the Penguin clothes we wear underneath. From then, timing is everything. The boys must know what we wear, and we the boys. The pairs must not dance together, or the Penguins will suspect. At exact times, separated by five minutes, each must remove their outer costume, so they may pass the door, and out, to meet behind the chapel . . .'

'For a jolly good snog!' Charlotte cut in. 'Bags I get Georgie!'

'Oh God, you're not spoony for Georgie, are you?' Berenice demanded.

'Well, no, it's not that at all,' Charlotte stammered, blushing. 'I mean, he's not bad, and he might not choose anyone else even half-decent. I mean, he might just choose his best friends.'

'It'll be Bertie Mallowdale and Freddie Bostock, I'll bet,' Berenice assured her. 'They're decent. I'll have Bertie, if you don't mind, Bosch?'

'Freddie, he is tall?' Von Pauling asked.

'Jolly tall, blond too. It'll remind you of the boys back home in Prussia,' Berenice assured her friend.

'Good,' Von Pauling said. 'Freddie, then, is mine. He must be the werewolf, as I plan to be Little Red Riding Hood. The skirts are wide, and the cape and hood will cover well. Bertie will be the gorilla, and Georgie the bear. It is a good plan, yes?'

'Witchy!' Berenice declared. 'It can't fail!'

'You're jolly bright, Bosch old girl!' Charlotte added. 'Fancy thinking all that lot up in a few minutes, eh Bernie?'

'Daddy always says the Bosch are jolly good at that sort of thing, strategy and all,' Berenice agreed. 'So what'll you go as, Chalky?'

'Goldilocks,' Charlotte replied after a moment's thought. 'I can have a hood too, and if Georgie's to be the bear, it'll be just the thing! No brassiere either, let's be daring!'

Berenice nodded, giggling in agreement and at the prospect of allowing her bare breasts to be felt by her brother's friend. Von Pauling also nodded. At that point, a subtle change in the light alerted the three girls to a presence at the keyhole. Charlotte snatched for the door, jerking it wide to reveal Thicky Plank, who was once more sent on her way by the application of a boot to her well-rounded bottom.

'How about you, Bernie?' Charlotte asked as she sat down again. 'Who'll you go as for the gorilla? Jane?'

'Don't be dippy!' Berenice protested. 'Jane's Tarzan's girl. He's not a gorilla! I'll be Florence Nightingale, she used to wear a cape, or I think she did.'

Berenice waited, full of anticipation, glancing at the clock every few minutes. The assembly hall was crowded, the girls at one end, the boys at the other and couples in the middle, dancing decorously to a sedate tune, while both monks and nuns maintained a watchful eye over their charges.

At the far end of the hall, the three boys with whom they had made assignations were clearly visible, a werewolf, a bear and her own gorilla, seated together at the back. Just to look at them set her heart hammering. It also made her giggle at the thought of becoming excited over a gorilla.

Von Pauling was to go first, at eight o'clock, followed by Charlotte at eight fifteen. Both would have a full ten minutes with their chosen boy before having to come in. Berenice, going last, would have more, if she dared. That meant the chance for something more than a snog, and if Bertie Mallowdale was as bold as Georgie made out, it might lead anywhere, anywhere at all . . .

The minutes past, each agonisingly slow, with Berenice's eyes seldom leaving the clock. At five to eight the werewolf detached himself from the other boys, to disappear behind a screen. Moments later a monk appeared from the far end, to saunter to the door and out, without raising so much as a flicker of suspicion. It was working.

'Wish me luck, yes?' Von Pauling whispered from beside Berenice.

'Good luck, Bosch,' Berenice replied.

The German girl rose, and walked confidently to the loos. Immediately a nun followed. Berenice and Charlotte exchanged worried glances, and sure enough, a moment later Dagmar Von Pauling was led out by her ear.

'Rotten!' Charlotte exclaimed.

'Jolly bad luck,' Berenice agreed, 'a Penguin going in just behind her like that.'

'Now she'll get swished,' Charlotte added.

'She won't welch, not the Bosch.'

'Not the Bosch,' Charlotte agreed.

'You going through with it?' Berenice asked.

'You bet I am,' Charlotte answered.

Dagmar had been led away towards the main school, and Berenice was left thinking of how her friend would be feeling. Dance or no dance, it would be the same old routine, dress up to make sure it hurt, knickers down to bring home the shame of it and make it hurt even more, and six across the bare bottom. Even the notoriously tough Von Pauling had been known to howl after six on the bare.

Presently a somewhat crestfallen werewolf appeared from behind the screens, to change places with the bear. Berenice waved to her brother, who gave her a thumbs-up as he slid behind the screen. Once again a monk emerged, and once again escaped without detection.

'Time for my snog!' Charlotte declared, grinning as she moved away.

Scarcely had Charlotte disappeared into the loos than a nun followed. A minute passed, and another. Then, like Von Pauling before her, Charlotte was led out by the ear. Berenice watched in shock until both nun and the reluctant Goldilocks had been led away. Dagmar Von Pauling would not have told the nuns, not for anything. Twice before the German girl had taken a dozen of the cane rather than reveal the names of her co-conspirators in girlish crime. That left a single option.

Thomasina Plank was not hard to find. She was in a rabbit costume, Berenice knew, a fluffy pink affair with huge ears, easily visible. A quick glance revealed Thomasina dancing with the werewolf, further increasing Berenice's anger. Moving to the edge of the dance floor, she waited until the music had finished, then stepped out of the shadows, to grab the giant rabbit by the arm. It turned in shock, nose wrinkling up as Thomasina's mouth came open in fear and panic.

'Got you, Thicky!' Berenice snapped. 'Now come with me, you little welcher!'

'I'm not! I'm not!' the rabbit squealed as it was led across the room to the loos.

Berenice didn't answer, pushing inside to find several other girls within, but no nuns. They gave her glances of surprise, but made no effort to stop her as she dragged Thomasina into a cubicle and shut the door. Thomasina's rabbit head was pulled off, revealing red hair and freckled cheeks.

'You welched, didn't you?' Berenice demanded. 'You listened at our study door, and you welched!'

'No, I . . . yes, yes, I welched!' Thomasina squeaked as Berenice took her by the neck, making as if to push her head into the lavatory bowl. 'Don't bogwash me, Bernie, I'll tell everything, I swear! I welched on Von Pauling, and Chalky White, but not on you, I swear it!'

'Liar!' Berenice snapped.

'It's true!' Thomasina squealed. 'How could I? I didn't know what you'd be wearing! You caught me before you said!'

'So we did,' Berenice answered. 'I still don't believe you. What did you tell the Penguins about me?'

'Nothing!' Thomasina squeaked.

Berenice pushed down, positioning the girl's head above the suspiciously yellow water at the bottom of the lavatory bowl.

'I'll talk! I'll talk!' Thomasina babbled. 'I said you were in on it, but I didn't know what you'd be wearing. That's all, I swear!'

Berenice paused, thinking. The nuns didn't know what she was wearing, but they'd be able to find out easily enough. They would wait for her to incriminate herself, and then . . .

'Get out of your costume!' she hissed. 'Now!'

'I . . . I can't!' Thomasina wailed.

'Do it!' Berenice ordered, pushing the red-haired girl's head still further into the bowl.

'I can't!' Thomasina repeated. 'I've . . . I've nothing underneath!'

'Stop squawking, Thicky!' Berenice answered. 'You'll be wearing mine! Now say you'll do it, or I bogwash you! I mean it.'

'Beast!' Thomasina shrieked as her forehead touched the mixture of pee and water below her. 'No, stop! I'll do it, Bernie, I'll do it!'

'That's better,' Berenice said, letting Thomasina up. 'Now quickly!'

Both girls hurried to undress. For Thomasina it was simple, the rabbit costume slipping off to reveal a slim, pale body, with freckles even on the tiny, rounded breasts, also bright red pubic hair. Berenice was still fiddling with the laces of her costume as Thomasina came bare, but soon managed to remove it, leaving her in the nun's habit she wore beneath. Thomasina watched, nude and shivering in the corner, frail, vulnerable, and impossible to resist.

'This is for getting my friends swished!' Berenice announced, and grabbed Thomasina by the hair.

Thomasina put up a fight, but it did her no good. Held by the hair, she was upended over the lavatory bowl and her head pushed in. Berenice was laughing as she pulled the chain, and louder still as Thomasina's scream of panic was cut off in a strange bubbling noise as the dirty water swirled up. Berenice kept her victim's head well down the lavatory, until the water had subsided, to leave Thomasina's normally carrot-coloured hair dark and wet, also filled with little pieces of loo paper. Released, Thomasina came up, her face set in a sullen scowl, water dripping from her nose and chin, to run down over her pert breasts.

'Let that be a lesson to you,' Berenice said. 'Now get in my costume, quickly.'

Both girls dressed. Berenice made Thomasina go out first, then followed, to push open the main loo door and stop dead in her tracks. The music had stopped, the dancers too. The lights were on, and all eyes were focused on the stage. There, Dagmar Von Pauling and Charlotte White stood, or rather bent, awaiting punishment.

Both had been exposed, Goldilocks and Little Red Riding Hood side by side, bare for punishment. With the cowls and the skirts thrown up it was impossible to see the victims' faces, but that was about all. No consideration whatever had been given for the girls' modesty. Their dresses and habits were so far up that each had a pair of nubile pink breasts swinging from beneath her chest. Their knickers were down too, all the way, exposing round, pale bottoms, pouted, hairy sex lips and tight pink bumholes. Beside them stood the Mother Superior, with a cane, speaking . . .

'. . . and thus to bring home the full gravity of their offence I have chosen to administer the punishment publicly, and if they find the experience humiliating, then they should have thought of that before committing such crimes. Von Pauling, prepare yourself.'

Dagmar's bottom flinched, her anus winking, a second before the wicked yellow cane landed full across her bottom. Berenice stood still, and could only watch in horrified amazement as first Von Pauling then Charlotte White were caned. Only when the girls were ordered to stand in the corner with their bare red bottoms showing to the crowd did she think to act.

The boys had been shepherded out, and she knew where they'd be. There was only one place big enough, the dining hall. Yet it was already half past eight, and with luck Bertie would have already been in his habit. If he was, he would have had to escape outside, for fear of exposure.

Every eye was on the two beaten girls' naked bottoms, nuns and pupils alike. With her heart in her throat, Berenice made for the door. Nobody saw as she slipped through, and her last glimpse of the assembly hall showed two nuns walk straight past Florence Nightingale. Thomasina didn't stop, or even turn, and to her amazement Berenice realised that the girl was not going to inform on her. That meant there was a possibility of escaping detection altogether, and with a new elation she moved quickly on.

Outside, she ran, along the edge of the assembly hall and across the lawn, to the dark loom of the chapel and around the back, to where the supporting buttresses jutted out into a deep ditch. All was black, her eyes adapting slowly to the weak orange light from far above them. She stopped, listening. A shadow detached itself from the others, blacker than black.

'I say . . .' a voice whispered, undeniably male.

'Sh! No time,' Berenice hissed.

They embraced, fur to fur, as she realised he was still in the gorilla costume, and must have escaped the same way she had, while attention was turned elsewhere. It felt wonderful, his body strong and firm against hers, despite the intervening layers of furry fabric. They began to nuzzle noses, then to kiss, pushing the animal snouts wide to let their mouths meet, open and wet and passionate.

Even as she snogged, it occurred to Berenice that there was an inconsistency in what Thomasina had said and done. If she'd given away the whole plan, the boys would have been punished as well, and why hadn't she sneaked as soon as the chance came?

She pushed the thought away. So, Thomasina had lied, it didn't matter. Revenge would come later, and meanwhile, there were more important things to think about. The gorilla that was Bertie Mallowdale had found the zip at the rear of the rabbit costume, and pulled it down. His hands were down the back, squeezing her bottom through the nun's habit. She thought of protesting, but didn't. It was too nice. In any case, his fingers were inching up her habit, and as it was bunched at the top of the rabbit legs, there wasn't far to go.

Sure enough, his hands found the seat of her knickers, squeezing her through the thin cotton, stroking her bottom, tickling the sensitive crease between. She found herself shivering in response, and sticking it out, even as her kissing became more passionate. The gorilla responded, taking a firm hold on the seat of her knickers and sliding them down, to leave her bottom exposed to the cool night air. For the first time in her life she was bare for a man, his big hands stroking her bottom cheeks, pulling them wide, and the urge to bend for penetration rose up in her head, irresistibly strong . . .

'I say,' the gorilla whispered, pulling back, 'I've a johnny if you fancy a porking?'

Berenice nodded, unable to speak. The gorilla responded with a delighted chuckle, and began to turn her round. Berenice just let it happen. She was pushed down, against the buttress, her bottom sticking out of the rabbit costume, bare and vulnerable. She imagined how she'd look, a huge pink rabbit, ears and all, with a bare girl's bum sticking out behind. She giggled. Strange noises issued from behind her, rustling, a grunt, a tearing sound that made her think of her virginity and what was about to happen to it. Strong hands took her by the hips and something hard and round pushed between her bottom cheeks.

'Not there!' she hissed as the cock probed her bumhole.

'Sorry, old top,' the gorilla answered, and fucked her.

It went straight up, tearing the thin membrane of her hymen to make her scream in sudden pain. Then it was in her and it no longer mattered. She was being fucked, a big, hard cock pumping in and out of her body, blocking the tight hole of her vagina, something she had imagined so, so often, yet which she had never imagined could feel so good.

Sadly it didn't last. The gorilla, overcome with the pleasure of having her to fuck, came inside her, grunting in ecstasy and finishing with a long, low moan. There was silence, Berenice thinking of her new-found ecstasy, then of the bite of the cane her friends had suffered, and that she'd accept a hundred cane strokes, naked in public, just for another good fucking. A voice sounded behind her.

'I say, Chalky, that was spiffing!' the gorilla declared as he wiped his cock on the hem of her habit. 'You're a jolly good sport!'

'Chalky?' Berenice demanded. 'I'm not Chalky, silly. Why ever would you think I was Chalky?'

'You're not Chalky? Charlotte White, I mean to say.'

'No, of course I'm not!'

'Well ... I mean to say ... it's what that red-haired girl told me, that we should swap costumes, and so would you, with ... with ... oh I say.'

Berenice could say nothing. The gorilla's voice, now clear, was horribly familiar.

'Oh I say,' he repeated. 'I think I've just porked my own sister.'

Named Harlot

Caleb's cock was big, dirty and smelt faintly of goat. Rosanna was indifferent to everything but the size, taking it in her mouth to suck lovingly at the thick shaft. She was on her knees, her dress pulled up to avoid soiling the material on the dirty straw beneath her. Caleb sat on a great earthenware churn, his thighs well spread, smiling as he watched her suck on his penis. The goats also watched, staring with placid curiosity from round, brown eyes.

Caleb began to stroke the dense brown curls of Rosanna's hair.

'That's my girl,' he said. 'And you'll be sure to swallow up all of what come out, won't you?'

Rosanna nodded faithfully around her mouthful of cock. Caleb settled back, closing his eyes in satisfaction. Rosanna sucked him deeper, squeezing his fat cock head right down between her tonsils, the way he liked it best. Her throat rebelled, as she knew it would, going into a series of sudden spasms. Caleb gasped, his cock jerked, and the full load of his semen was ejaculated down Rosanna's throat.

She pulled back, coughing and spluttering but trying to laugh at the same time, with bubbles of sperm blowing from her nose and around her lips. Caleb laughed too, but stopped abruptly. Rosanna looked up, to see a dry, thin face at a window, peering down at her from beneath a black cowl.

'Blessed Father!' Caleb exclaimed.

Rosanna had swallowed at the shock of seeing the priest, taking her mouthful of sperm down the wrong way. Coughs shook her body as Caleb made a hasty retreat, leaving her gagging and spitting come from her mouth, unable to breathe, let alone rise. The priest watched in silence, until she at last managed to bring herself under control and wipe away the beard of sperm and spittle that hung from her chin.

'Father Ira?' she managed.

'What have you done?' he demanded.

'I am sorry, forgive me,' she said. 'I have erred, I confess it. I will accept my penance in all humility.'

She hung her head, waiting for sentence to be pronounced. For a long period Father Ira said nothing, although she could feel his gaze on her head, and chest, where she had unlaced her bodice to tease Caleb with a show of her cleavage. At last she looked up.

'Come here, my child,' he said gently.

Rosanna nodded and rose. Walking quickly from the pen, she made her way to the rear, where the priest stood among the gnarled quince trees of the orchard. Coming to stand in front of him, she hung her head, her hands folded in her lap.

'This is a terrible thing you have done, my child,' he stated.

'I beg forgiveness, Blessed Father,' she answered. 'I was wrong to act so. I am weak, and was not able to hold back the yearnings of my body –'

'Yearnings? For such conduct?' he interrupted. 'You speak as if you were a man. You are woman, the passive vessel. You have no such yearnings. To yearn so, for a woman, is harlotry, an abomination!'

His voice had risen in anger. Rosanna didn't answer, biting her lip as she hung her head lower still, so that the tumbled mass of her hair hid her face.

'It is the duty of woman,' he went on, 'to serve man, and to take his seed into her body. This she does in meek obedience, docile and humble, that she may be got with child, and that she may answer his bodily needs. All men have these needs, my child, it is the curse of the race of Adam. A good woman has no such needs, but may answer the needs of man without sin, in certain instances.'

Rosanna nodded her head.

'Yet for a woman unmarried to answer such needs in young men is sinful,' the priest continued. 'Young men should not waste their seed, for it saps their strength and lessens the work they may do in the fields. Nor should you assist in the needs of the married men, for this is the sin of adultery.'

'I have not committed adultery, Blessed Father,' Rosanna answered.

'I know this, Rosanna, my child,' he answered. 'At heart you are a good girl. Doubtless Caleb's lustful demands overcame the weakness of your will. You have soiled yourself. Yet there can be forgiveness.'

'I thank you, Blessed Father.'

'Indeed, and in that spirit of forgiveness I am prepared to offer you a great privilege. While a young woman should hold herself apart from young men, and also from married men, she may with honour serve those who have themselves chosen a higher path. Here, such an act as you performed would be neither sinful nor indecent, but a gesture of humble appreciation for your betters. To refuse it would be an act of mawkish petulance, suggestive of arrogance and a most unsuitable pride, quite unbecoming for a young woman.'

'Blessed Father, what are you asking of me?'

'Only that which you have given to Caleb the goatherd, and . . .'

'To take you in my mouth? I could not, ever! How could you say such a thing? And you a priest!'

'I have explained –'

'Explained! You seek to trick me, with your long words and fancy ideas! To suck an old man, in order to evade a penance? That would be the act of a harlot. Do not ask such a thing of me, it is not right!'

'What are you saying?' he demanded. 'What do you know of right? I have explained all. Do you think to question me, a Blessed Father? Enough of this. Obey, at once. On your knees!'

'Never! Not to you! You are old! You are ugly! You think to gain favours by deceit, which is worse!'

'How dare you! You give your favours to some stinking goatherd! Yet you refuse me, a Blessed Father, whose feet you are not worthy to kiss? I name you a harlot, a worthless piece of filth! Now get to your task, I order it!'

'Never! You are vile! A lecher!'

Her foot lashed out, to catch one bony shin beneath his robe. He doubled up, clutching at his leg and grimacing in pain as Rosanna skipped past him, up the orchard and into her house, slamming the door behind her.

Rosanna got to her feet at the sound of a tap on the door. Expecting a customer for produce, she opened it casually. A booted foot was immediately thrust into the opening, pushing the door wide. She gasped, stepping back as two burly men in the mustard-yellow uniforms of the church protectors pushed in. Behind them came the Blessed Father Ira Tiergarde, ducking through the low doorway as she was pulled back into her kitchen.

'Father?' she queried.

'Strip her,' he ordered, 'and spread her out on the table.'

'Why? No!' Rosanna squealed, even as she was thrown backwards across the table.

She fought, kicking and scratching as rough hands tore at her clothes. Her bodice was burst, spilling out one fat breast, her skirt jerked high, exposing her naked legs, belly and the furry mound of her sex. One man held her down, her lower body naked, her legs kicking in her panic and fear, to show off the ripe, pink centre of her quim and the chubby tuck of her bottom. The other drew a knife, to slit the waist band of her dress and tear it wide. Both big breasts tumbled out as the ruined dress was tugged high, and off, to leave her nude but for boots and the stockings of coarse blue cotton that reached to her knees. The protectors took a firm grip of her arms and legs, forcing her down.

'Tie her,' Father Tiergarde ordered.

A protector leant down over Rosanna's body, grinning as her meaty breasts squashed out beneath his arm. He took her wrists, holding her splayed as his companion drew cord from his pouch. Her wrists were tied to the table legs, each wound with cord and tied off, leaving her unable to protect herself or even to shield her naked body. The protectors moved to her legs, but Tiergarde raised his hands.

'No, I like to see them kick a little.'

The men bowed and stood back, silent but attentive. Tiergarde stepped forward, to look down on her naked body in contempt, his eyes lingering on her heaving breasts, the gentle swell of her belly, the rich thatch of her pubic mound, and the plump, ripe lips of her sex.

'Why, Blessed Father?' she asked. 'What have I done?'

'Do you not recall,' Tiergarde answered, 'that at our last meeting I named you a harlot? Where then is your signal lamp? Why do no men come to me to confess their enjoyment of your body?'

'I . . . I do not understand, Blessed Father.'

'No? I think you understand very well, and seek to evade justice.'

'What justice, Blessed Father? I have done no wrong! Why should I declare myself a harlot, because I refused to surrender myself to you?'

'Not as such, no. Your refusal was in itself insignificant. As when an apple proves worm-ridden, I simply select another apple and think no more of the matter. Your crime is your attitude, the gross temerity of failing to understand your place. This is why you are named harlot.'

'No, Blessed Father, this is not justice!'

'Justice? How dare you speak of justice? Justice is what I decree, and beyond the understanding of some stupid, fat-breasted peasant slut!'

He was shouting at her, his face red with anger, and she cowered back, sure he would hit her. He didn't, but stood back, closing his eyes, to mumble a prayer before he spoke again, now calm.

'So what is to be done with you, haughty Rosanna? For certain I must ensure that you take your proper place as the village harlot. It is what I have decreed, and I will not have my authority flouted. I am even prepared to take a portion of the responsibility on myself, although the costs, naturally, you must pay. Yes, I will have a fine brass signal lamp ordered from the smith, with panels of red glass. I will also have my men check each week, to ensure that you are performing your tasks properly, which is to say, taking men in every orifice of your fat peasant body for a groat a time. And if you have not performed with sufficient zeal? Two dozen strokes of the birch rod should mend your ways, delivered on your naked body, in the village square, for all to watch. I suspect that will have those fat thighs wide apart soon enough.

'Think how you will lie there, dreading every knock on your door, wondering who it will be, and what they will demand of you. I think I will have you fix a scale of prices outside your door, announcing to all the passing world what you do. Let me see, how to value you? A penny for your hand, two for your mouth or those blubbery, peasant breasts. A groat for your cunt, and yes, a ha'penny for your stinking breech, to ensure that you are put to common usage in the most perverted

100

way. Many would take advantage, I think, of the bargain.

'Who would you hate the most, I wonder? The fat baker, Jankin, perhaps. He is rumoured to take his pleasure in sodomy, also to have a member of deformed proportion, as fat around as that of a horse. Imagine that in your fundament, Rosanna, doubtless with frequency.'

'Please, no, Blessed Father! I am no harlot. I am virgin!'

'Virgin? Do not defile that sweet word with your filthy tongue! You are no virgin, to allow the use of your mouth to man. Did I not see you? Had I caught you moments later he would have been in your cunt, and do not deny it!'

'No, I swear! He had already spent, in my mouth. You saw! There is no harm in that . . .'

'No harm! You know nothing of propriety, nothing of what is right for woman. Yes, you are a natural harlot, it is your just fate.'

'I am virgin, Blessed Father, see!'

Father Ira cocked one eyebrow up.

'You seem earnest,' he stated. 'Well, it is easy to tell.'

Even as he spoke he had moved, stalking quickly to where he could stand between her legs.

'Spread her wide,' he ordered.

The protectors stepped forward, to haul Rosanna's legs wide and high, displaying the open hole of her sex. Father Tiergarde raised one gloved hand, reaching forward to touch her. She gasped as two fingers spread the lips of her quim, to open the hole and stretch out the thin membrane of skin that proved her virginity.

'Virgin indeed,' Tiergarde remarked, peering down at the fleshy, pink opening of her body. 'I confess astonishment. How is it that you perform lewd services for every over-muscled peasant boy in the village, and yet your hymen remains intact?'

'I do not, Blessed Father! Not often, and those I have dallied with are gentle, and take only what is offered freely.'

'Nonsense. Such as they, when aroused, simply take what they want.'

'No! They have honour, and will not force a woman. They will protect me also! They will not see me made into a harlot!'

'Who will do this for you? Caleb the goatherd? He has not the courage to look me in the eye!'

'I have many friends.'

'What? When I, the Blessed Father Ira Tiergarde, have named you harlot? You know little of the world, my child. Your supposed friends will melt away like snow. Come, let us see how well your so-called friends support you. Tie her hands behind her back, and put her in a halter. No, a moment. On a whim, I find myself inclined to clemency, although she is undeserving. Here then, Rosanna, is your final chance. I will have my men release you, that you may go to your chamber, to clean and perfume your body. There you will wait, to serve me when I come for you, as you should be honoured to do.'

'No!' Rosanna shouted. 'If you want me, take me here, tied and helpless. It is the only way you will ever enjoy my body, you foul old lecher!'

She spat, her phlegm landing on Father Tiergarde's robe. For a moment his face coloured in anger, but he held back, nodding to the protectors before he turned on his heel and left the house.

Rosanna was taken by the two men. Her wrists were released from the table legs, only to be bound behind her back, with her pushed face down on the hard table top and her arms twisted high up behind her. Her boots and stockings were pulled away, to leave her nude, and a halter of rough cord was fixed around her neck. As they tied her, so they fumbled with her body, groping her breasts and bottom, rubbing at the plump mound of her quim.

Tied, she was jerked to her knees and made to clamber down from the table, then led outside. In the lane Father Tiergarde waited, smiling in amusement as Rosanna was pulled stumbling into the sunlight. Others saw, a man bearing a basket of vegetables and a girl of the village. Both stared for a moment before hurrying their pace towards the village.

Barefoot in the dirt, smarting with shame at her nudity and the injustice of her treatment, Rosanna came behind her captors, drawn by the neck to the village square. There, a crowd was already gathering, and watching in interest as she was led up on to the cloister house steps and tied to an iron spike. Father Tiergarde climbed up beside her, waiting until he had the full attention of the crowd before speaking.

'Good people. I bring before you your neighbour, Rosanna Faine, so that I may acquaint you with her sins and administer justice. Here is a woman evil indeed. She is young, fertile, the mistress of a property. Yet does she give herself to a husband, that she may bear children and that her land may be tended properly, by a man? No! Rather she disports herself, in tight clothing, displaying that which should be hidden from all men bar he who comes to own her. She drinks ale with young men, and the husbands of her betters, and pays for their labour with the favours of her body! Worse, she gives these same favours for the sake of her own bestial indulgence! It is true, I have seen her, her mouth engorged with the virile member of the goatherd Caleb! He had not tied her, nor beaten her to his will! She was willing, eager! She is lascivious, a wanton. She is nothing, less than nothing!'

He paused, listening to the murmurs running through the crowd. Rosanna caught the note of anger in the whispered comments, but it was weak beside those of righteous condemnation, recrimination and sheer lust. Not one person spoke out for her. Tiergarde continued.

'Thus I name her harlot, and available for the amusement of those men of the village unmarried, saving only those beneath the age of thirty years. As is the custom, she will be staked out for her first evening, and available to all who are entitled, at no charge, that she may be initiated into her life of harlotry. The sole exception will be the first to take her, as despite her vile habits she is virgin. Therefore, whosoever wishes to burst her hymen must pay the sum of one shilling, to myself, in lieu of the marriage tithe I would otherwise forfeit. Take her to the stake.'

He stepped down. The protector holding Rosanna's halter tugged on it, setting her staggering behind him, in shock at the suddenness of what was happening to her. As she was dragged across the square she was pleading for clemency, words that fell on deaf ears. At the stake she was tied in place, the rope fixed low to force her down on to her knees, adopting a series of ridiculous postures as she did so, to the delight of the onlookers. With her hands tied behind her back she could shield nothing, but only crouch miserably by the stake as those entitled to use her closed in. Others stood back, younger men showing sympathy yet also envy, women for the most part gloating at her misfortune. An old egg was thrown, striking her head, to run down, sticky and reeking through her hair. At that one of the protectors turned to remonstrate with whoever had thrown it, invisible to Rosanna, an act which filled her with pitiful gratitude.

Father Tiergarde's voice rose above the excited murmur of the crowd.

'The merchant Hiram Tuller is chosen!'

'Make way!' a protector called and the crowd parted.

A man in a crimson robe belted tight across his massive belly stepped through to the front of the crowd.

He was rubbing his pale, fat hands together, his red face beaming, his pig-like eyes fixed on Rosanna's body. Without troubling to speak, he pulled up his robe and stretched the flap of his undergarment wide, exposing a set of heavy, dark genitals. He stepped forward, to take Rosanna by the hair and pull her face into his crotch. She resisted, his greasy cock and the hairy sack of his balls squashed out against her lips. One of the protectors began to draw a lash from his belt and she opened her mouth, taking in the foul-tasting penis.

The crowd murmured appreciation as she sucked on the fat merchant's cock. It grew quickly, to stubby erection, the shaft wet with her spittle as her lips moved up and down. He pulled out, and pointed to the ground.

'Like a dog,' he ordered.

They were the only words he spoke to her. The protector's whip was already half free of his belt, and she turned clumsily on to her knees, her breasts squashing out in the dirt as she stuck up her bottom. She was entered, crudely, without ceremony, his cock put to her quim and shoved in. Her hymen tore, drawing a single pained gasp from her lips. He began to fuck her, his belly smacking on her upturned buttocks, her virgin blood trickling down between her thighs, warm and wet, his cock ramming deep into her body. He came, after a few dozen strokes, his sperm bursting out from the mouth of her vagina, to splash his balls and join the warm fluid smearing her inner thighs. Rosanna was made to lick the mixture of blood and semen from his cock and balls.

Before she had finished there was another cock in her vagina. A third was put in her mouth immediately the merchant withdrew, the man holding her up by the hair as he fucked her head. Both came quickly, filling her mouth with come and adding to the mess in and around her vagina. Others took their place, and more crowded in, to grope her breasts and belly, to remark on her naked body, to take bets over whether the man in her mouth or her quim would come first. Before long a finger had penetrated her anus, then a cock, as she was buggered for the first time, by a man she could not even see. He came in her rectum, and was immediately pulled back by his fellows, who laughed as her anus closed with a long fart. Immediately she was put on top of a man and penetrated vaginally, then anally as another mounted her bottom.

Others lost patience, to spunk in her armpits or over the fat, dangling globes of her breasts. She was made to suck two cocks at once, and both loads of sperm deposited in her face. She was made to suck cocks that had been in her rectum, slimy with her own mess. Men came in her mouth until there was sperm bubbling from her nose, as it was from her vagina and anus, for the rare moments they were not plugged with erect penis. She was smacked and scratched, her nipples pinched and twisted, her hair pulled. She was made to kiss and lick at men's balls and between their buttocks.

Only when a rotten egg was smeared in her face did she realise that the men had nearly finished with her. A last one came up her bottom and she was left to the women. Where the men had been lecherous, the women were cruel. Rotten eggs and decaying vegetables were pushed in her face and smeared over her body. A marrow was forced up her vagina and tied in place around her hips, to leave half its fat green bulk sticking out from her body. Horse chestnuts from a nearby tree were fed up into her bottom, one by one, until her belly was swollen with them and the last still showed, her anus gaping wide around a patch of rich brown skin. She was made to eat refuse. Her spread buttocks were painted with the word HARLOT. She was beaten, with sticks and a dog quirt. Her hair was shorn to rough, filthy stubble. Finally she was urinated over and left in her puddle of filth.

Only then did the protectors untie her. She was taken, soiled and broken, with sperm running from every orifice of her body, filthy with rotten food, dragged from the square and thrown on to the village dungheap. There, the final dignity was inflicted, one man pressing a round boot toe to her sex and rubbing until she came to orgasm.

Rosanna kissed the baker Jankin's nose, pressing her lips gently to the bulbous, crimson veined tip. He grinned, and slapped her bottom, provoking a giggle as she climbed quickly on to the bed, kneeling, to present him with the full spread of her skirts. Her dress was velvet, dark blue with a sash of dove grey. Beneath it, the lace edge of petticoats showed, above silk stockings and boots of soft grey leather.

She put her hands to her skirts. He licked his blubbery lips as she began to pull them up, his hands wrestling with the fastening on his breeches. It came loose. He pulled out his huge, crooked penis even as the full width of Rosanna's bottom came on show, the hairy lips of her sex pouting out behind, her bumhole pink and wrinkled between her big cheeks. It was a little open, and glistening, with a knob of thick white grease melting slowly in the hole.

'My, but that's a fine sight,' he drawled. 'Not many like that.'

Rosanna wiggled her bottom and looked back.

'See,' she said, 'and I'm ready too. Goose grease that is, Peter Jankin, so you may think yourself lucky.'

'Oh I do,' he assured her. 'Best thing for buggering girls, is goose grease, I always say.'

Rosanna smiled, and put her hands to her bottom cheeks, spreading them. Jankin was already masturbating, his eyes fixed on her spread bottom. His cock began to swell, a fat red tip emerging from the fleshy bulk of his foreskin, a little more with each tug. By the time he was half hard his fingers no longer met around the shaft, and well over half of it protruded from his hand. Still it grew, his balls slapping on the leather of his breeches as he readied himself, never once taking his eyes off Rosanna's anus.

She put her face down, burying it in the bed, not daring to look at the huge cock being prepared for her bumhole. Only when the bulbous head pressed to her anus did she show her feelings, letting out a whimper of reaction. As he began to push she gritted her teeth and clutched at the bedcovers. She felt her anus push in, and stretch, gaping around his cock. The pain came, a dull ache that made the muscles of her bottom and legs twitch as her ring stretched, wider, and at last to its limit, even as Jankin's cock squeezed past the reluctant muscle and on into her rectum. She was left breathless, her cheeks blown out, her eyes wide in shock at the straining feeling in her anal ring. As Jankin began to bugger her, so she began to gasp in air, a rhythmic, dog-like panting that rose rapidly to a crescendo as the full, fat bulk of his cock was forced into her rectum.

With the whole monstrous bulk in her gut, she settled her chest to the bed and reached back. Jankin began to move inside her, grunting and mumbling to himself as he buggered her, and as he did it her hand found the plump, soft swell of her sex. Briefly she reached back to touch her straining anal ring and the huge cock shaft that plugged her body. Equally briefly, her fingers slipped into her empty, well-juiced vagina. Then, burrowing between the lips of her quim, she found her clitoris and began to rub.

Jankin chuckled as her buttocks started to quiver to the motion of her masturbation. He had her by the hips, his gross belly resting on her upturned buttocks, his balls slapping on her fingers as she rubbed at herself. As her rubbing got faster and more urgent, so did her pushes, until once more it began to hurt. Still she rubbed, concentrating on the overwhelming feeling of being buggered, until at last she felt her muscles tense. She was coming, her buttocks tightening against the fat baker's flesh, her vacant quim squeezing on nothing, her anus pulsing on the massive shaft that had been forced up into her body.

Rosanna cried out in ecstasy, her orgasm tearing through her body, her bowels squeezing hard on the intruding penis. Jankin gasped, spattering phlegm over what little of her buttocks showed beneath his quivering belly. Again Rosanna cried out, her anus still in frantic contraction as the full load of his sperm was deposited in her rectum.

She went down, panting, on the bed. He was puffing, but pulled slowly out before rolling on to his back, to lie beside her, gasping for breath with his slimy cock still sticking up from his breeches. Rosanna waited, allowing him to recover his breath before she spoke. Finally Jankin rolled on to his side, to delve into his pouch.

'My, but that was good,' he announced. 'I've never met a woman who buggered as well as you do, Rosanna, nor one so eager. Now, here's your ha-penny, and the goods you were wanting are down in the hall. I've done you a dozen currant buns, as you asked, and a fine big sponge, with damson jam and cream together. Best be eating him, before he goes stale.'

'Thank you, Peter,' Rosanna answered. 'And what do I owe you?'

'Not a penny, as you well know, my pretty. Just you keep that bottom nice and plump, and that little hole nice and easy, and old Peter Jankin'll not ask for payment.'

Rosanna smiled, kissed his bulbous nose once more and bounced up from the bed. Jankin went his way, leaving Rosanna to apply unguent to her sore bottom hole before cutting herself a large slice of sponge. This she took to her window seat, eating it as she looked out across her orchard. No more than two mouthfuls had gone down when she heard a cart drawing up outside. The door opened again, to reveal first a protector, then Father Tiergarde.

'Blessed Father,' Rosanna said quickly. 'I had not thought your tithe was required until tomorrow, but I will have it ready if you wait but a moment.'

'I will take my tithe in due time,' he answered as two further protectors entered behind him. 'For now, I have come to put an end to this.'

He waved his hand, taking in the rich furnishings of Joanna's house, the heavy drapes with which she had covered her walls, the lamps of silver and horn, the beaten copper utensils that hung above the settle.

'Why, Blessed Father?' she questioned. 'Am I not degraded, as you sought? Am I not banned from worship? Do the women of the village not spit on me as I pass?'

'Yes,' Tiergarde answered, 'and their menfolk shower you with gifts and shelter you from the public humiliations which otherwise would be your lot. How long since you were whipped or put in the stocks?'

'Many months, Blessed Father.'

'Many months, indeed, and it has been longer still since your head was shaved or your cunt crammed with dung. I see now that to make you a harlot was no punishment, not for you, even with the prospect of nightly visits from such as Jankin. You are too low even to have the decency to accept your place with humility. Instead you have gained from it, sought favours and goods. Strip her, spread her out.'

'If you wish me naked, you need merely ask,' she answered. 'There is no call for force.'

She began to lift her skirts, but the protectors chose to ignore her offer, grabbing her, to hold her tight around the waist. They pulled up her dress, tearing it, and one of the rich petticoats she wore beneath. Her sash and bodice were slit, her breasts flopped out, before she was spread out on the table in the ruins of her fine clothing, naked and panting, her face red with anger and fear. As the men hauled her legs wide to show off her sex, Father Tiergarde came to stand over her.

'So what is to be done?' he said. 'I might make you a beggar? No, for such are honoured in the holy texts. That would never do. I might sew up the lips of that pretty cunt, and have you parade in the streets with your skirts pinned up, to show your shame. You would merely continue to use your mouth and breech in your sordid trade. No, Rosanna, I have better fate for you.'

He drew a parchment from his robe, pulling it open to show her the black and white marks of writing, and a rounded seal depicting the sacred symbol entwined with another she did not recognise.

'This document,' he stated, 'declares you insane and binds you to the care of the cloister house, which is to say, my own. You become my responsibility, in effect my property, for which act of charity I am awarded an additional stipend of twelve crowns a year, by the by. What happens there, is up to you. You may live as a servant of sorts, chained, yes, also naked, but washed, well enough fed, and with the comfort afforded by a sleeping mat, at least so long as you behave yourself.'

'If you want me, rape me!' she spat. 'I can't stop you.'

'No,' he answered. 'When you come to me, it will be crawling on your belly. You will beg for my touch. You will plead for what you now refuse in your arrogance and pride. To suck on my member will be an honour so great you cry in gratitude as you swallow my seed.'

'Never!'

'Oh you will, be sure of it. For now, you may entertain my servants here before you are brought to the cloister house. And make the best of it, their cocks will be the last you enjoy for quite some time.'

He turned on his heel, walking casually from the house. Even as the door closed she had been taken by the hair, to have her head pulled around and a fat cock pushed at her mouth. As she took it in she was turned, on to her knees. A second protector climbed into the table behind her, to pull up her ruined clothes. His cock settled between her buttocks, and he began to rut in her crease. The third took her wrist, placing it on his penis, to make her masturbate him.

Fearful of their whips, she did her best as they used her, sucking with all the skill she had learnt in her months as village harlot and keeping her bottom up to best advantage. If the protectors noticed, they didn't show it, using her body like that of a doll, tugging at her and turning her to get their cocks in. The first to come did it in her mouth, keeping his cock jammed in deep as she gagged on the meaty head and her gullet filled with semen. By then, the man behind her had his hard cock in his hand, and was rubbing it over her sex and anal area, occasionally prodding at one slimy hole or the other. He was also masturbating, and he came in the greasy dimple of her anus. The third had been laughing as his cock grew in her hand, and groping her breasts. No sooner had the man behind her climbed down, than he took the place, plunging his cock up into Rosanna's anal passage, to come inside.

With sperm dribbling out at front and rear, she was stripped naked and put in a halter, to be led through the streets towards the square and the cloister house. Many of the village women were about, whispering behind their hands or openly taunting her. Some threw mud, or worse, one scooping up a double handful of horse dung to plaster it in her face and over her breasts, to the delight and encouragement of other onlookers. The protectors took no notice, other than making sure to keep far enough away not to risk getting their clothes soiled. By the time she reached the cloister house she was filthy and steaming, with a dozen women following behind in the hope that she would be staked out for public humiliation.

Instead she was dragged in through a gate in the high wall that hid the cloister-house garden. Within, she was taken to the rear and her hands untied. She was helped into a pond with a well-placed boot, and watched as she scraped the filth from her body. Wet and shivering, she was led to a rear door, down a narrow flight of steps and into a cellar. There, sipping wine as he leant on a barrel, Father Tiergarde was waiting.

He didn't acknowledge her, admiring the gleam of candlelight through the red liquid in his glass as she passed, but followed as the protectors dragged her through an inner door. Beyond was near darkness, which dissipated gradually as her eyes grew accustomed and the protectors lit oil lamps and candles. Nothing pleasant was illuminated, only a great iron cage, a lit brazier and a device of rusty chains supporting a meat hook above a heavy chair, towards which Rosanna was dragged.

It was bolted to the floor, and iron manacles were attached to hold the neck, wrists and ankles of anyone sitting in it. None of that attracted her attention, nor the chains above it, but a fat peg that rose from near the edge of the chair. It had been carved into a grotesque representation of a cock, the head of ordinary size above a narrow neck, thick folds of foreskin, a second neck and a shaft thicker still, thicker even than baker Jankin's cock. It was smooth, apparently worn with use, some parts nearly black, others, where the victims' penetrated holes had rubbed, showing glints of rich red-brown.

'Here is an interesting device,' Father Tiergarde stated from behind her, 'a relict of times when we had a little more difficulty in imposing our authority hereabouts. My predecessors would bring a man down here, along with his wife, if he had one, and perhaps a daughter or two, if any were of marriageable age yet still virgin. According to the records, the mere threat of being put

113

on the phallus in front of his family was seldom enough
to make a man pliable. More effective was watching his
daughters lowered on to it until their hymens burst.
You, with your well-used cunt, might perhaps be able to
sit on it with no more than moderate pain. Which is why
it is not going up your cunt. Impale her, anally.'

'No, please!' Rosanna begged, writhing in futile
struggle against the strength of the protectors.

They dragged her to the machine, and on to it,
ignoring her pleas and screams. Her wrists were tied,
bound tight together and hauled above her head. Two
protectors lifted her, as another reached high, to pull
down the meat hook, which he thrust through her
bonds. She was placed on the seat, the hideous phallus
sticking up between her thighs. Her legs were pushed up,
and held tight in place. Her calves were wound with
rope and tied to her thighs, they in turn to her waist,
leaving her cocooned in rope with her sex spread wide.

A protector went to grip on a loop of chain, and to
pull down. Rosanna screamed again as she was lifted,
her full weight on her wrists, with her breasts quivering
and her feet jerking back and forth in the tight bonds.
As she rose, so she came forward, the head of the
phallus brushing her sex. A protector came to grip her
body, adjusting her, until the smooth wooden bulb was
against her anus. She writhed her body, struggling to
keep the awful thing out, but was held hard, and
lowered. Her ring gave, the head penetrating her anus
easily, with the mess of goose grease and sperm
lubricating her.

'It's in,' the protector announced, and his companion
released the chains.

Rosanna screamed as her rectum filled in one sudden,
agonising movement. Her anus had stretched wide, and
was still stretching, wider and wider, as her weight drove
her down on the spike. She screamed again at a sudden,
stabbing pain, and for one terrible moment she thought

her ring had split, even as the meat of her buttocks came to rest on the surface of the chair.

She hung, gasping and panting, spit running from her mouth, sweat prickling from her skin, half the muscles in her body twitching in agonised reaction. Her anus had become a ring of red pain, taut on the intruding phallus, which held her lower body immobile, her spread sex absolutely vulnerable. Father Tiergarde stepped forward, ducking down to inspect her engorged anus.

'Remarkable,' he observed. 'I had no idea an anus could accommodate such width. I had expected you to tear. Evidently my predecessors never encountered anybody quite so dissipated. Yet it should keep you still, which is what matters.'

Rosanna had no answer. Her eyes were unfocused, her body burning with pain, all of it centred on her straining anal ring. Beyond the priest, she was vaguely aware of the protectors busying themselves around the brazier, with an iron bucket. Slowly it sank through her battered senses that she was to be branded, and she began to scream again. Father Tiergarde watched with an amused smile, the last thing Rosanna saw before she fainted.

Her next conscious reaction was to jerk in her bonds as freezing water was dashed in her face. Blinking and shaking her head, she found the priest still in front of her, holding a thick, round-ended stick. The protectors were gone, leaving the iron bucket set up on a stand and the air thick with a strange, pungent stench. As memory returned she tried to scream, but her mouth was blocked, her jaws gaping around a wooden ball, with a leather strap holding it tightly in place. All she could do was thrash on the thick wooden plug in her anus, which only brought more pain. She subsided, her eyes wide with terror.

'So where is that haughty pride now, Rosanna?' Tiergarde asked. 'Did I not say you would be crawling on your belly to me before long? You would now, no doubt, but it would be in fear, which is not what I intend. You would not understand, even now, nor agree, but it is possible to break a woman so completely that she becomes reliant on her tormentor. That is what I will do to you. No, Rosanna, when you crawl to me, it will be in worship!'

He paused, to thrust the stick into the iron bucket, before continuing.

'When your time comes, you will know, and so will I. Meanwhile, you will come to know this chair very well indeed, and also certain other devices, several of which I have never had the opportunity to test. When not under excruciation, you will live in the garden, chained most of the time, naturally, but not entirely restricted. Indeed, you will be able to go out sometimes into the square. You will have to, in fact, to beg for scraps of food, as that will represent your sole source of sustenance.

'Naturally we will need to protect the villagers from your ravings, also from attack. You will wear a brank, to still that evil tongue, and to stop your mouth so that you can no longer indulge your vile habits. A wad of caulking tar should keep the cocks out of your cunt.'

He pushed the stick into the bucket, twisting it to draw out a thick wad of sticky, black tar. Rosanna's eyes went wide and she squirmed, pulling against her bonds, writhing her anus on the huge phallus inside it. Father Tiergarde grinned, holding up the stick for her inspection, and lowering it, slowly, towards her sex as she writhed in panic-stricken fear. Her bladder burst, urine spraying out in a high arch, to patter on the floor and hiss as it struck the brazier. The priest halted, watching patiently as she emptied herself, until the last trickle of pee had run down over her sex.

Again he pushed the stick forward, to touch Rosanna's sex. Her whole body went rigid as the hot tar squashed out against her quim, her head thrown back in a soundless scream, with her teeth clamped hard on the wooden ball. She heard his chuckle as her vagina filled with tar, and her body locked again as the stick was pushed deep in, fucking her, and wadding the caulk into her hole. He filled her, three sticks' worth crammed into her vagina, until a fat black plug showed at the entrance. More was smeared into the rich growth of her pubic hair. Yet more was wiped on to her vulva, clogging the deep valley between her lips. Finally, Tiergarde put the stick to her clitoris, twisting and pushing, laughing all the while, until once more her muscles locked in a frenzied, jerking orgasm that ended with her senses slipping away.

Rosanna squatted in the cloister-house garden, naked and filthy. A length of chain joined her manacled wrists, another her ankles. A brank constrained her head, a cage of iron bars fixed to a wide collar and fitted with a metal prong that held down her tongue, to make both speech and eating difficult.

For three months she had lived as Tiergarde's ward, begging in the village or hiding in the garden by day, curled shivering in a hut of sticks and leaves by night. When it amused him, she was tortured, or thrown to the protectors to be buggered and made to suck cocks, or used as a toy in lewd games. Her quim remained blocked, the plug causing her urine to squirt out sideways in a way that particularly amused the protectors. Despite everything, she had not gone to beg Tiergarde's favour.

She was hungry, and hoping that if she went out into the square she would be able to reach the shop of Peter Jankin, who would feed her cake soaked in syrup in return for the use of her anus. Otherwise, there was a chance of reaching safety and a meal with several among her male friends. There was also a chance of being caught by those less sympathetic, or worse, by the older women.

Listening for the sound of voices from beyond the wall, she moved to the gate. There was silence, and she lifted the latch, to push it cautiously open. Outside, the square was nearly empty, with a merchant's wagon at the far side and two young girls gossiping by the well. She stole out, glancing to either side before moving out as fast as her chains would allow her, towards the alley in which the bakery stood. Seeing her, the two girls went silent.

Rosanna fought down the shame their reaction provoked, moving on, with her chains clanking behind her. She reached the alley, only to stop as a door swung open, revealing the squat body and coarse features of the most malignant of the village matrons. Another followed, and a third, catching her as she turned to run.

'Don't be scared, little Rosanna,' the eldest said. 'We only want to feed you. That's what you come out for, isn't it? To beg scraps from ugly old Jankin? Well, we can provide just as well, and at no charge. Now come inside.'

Rosanna tried to resist, but was dragged through the door, into a long room, bare but for chairs, a long table, on which a single large bowl stood, and a bench. Rosanna was forced down on the bench, the women pulling the chairs up around the table. She looked from one face to another, one thin and bony, another as fat as a pudding, the third as withered as a raisin, each showing only cruelty.

The eldest chuckled at the fear in Rosanna's eyes, and reached out, to lift the lid on the bowl. A thick, grey-brown substance was revealed, exuding a vile reek. It was pushed close to Rosanna, the smell growing stronger.

'Your meal,' the woman announced, pulling a wooden paddle from her sash, 'appropriate for a dirty, stinking little harlot, don't you think? Now eat!'

'What have I done to you?' Rosanna pleaded.

'What have you done!' the eldest screamed. 'You ask that, when you have debauched our husbands, and our sons also? Do you know what the men of the village now ask of their wives?'

Her voice rose to a screech of pure rage as Rosanna's head was snatched by the other two women. Before she could even try to resist she was forced forward, and down, her iron mask pushing into the vile substance, then her face. She closed her eyes tight as her head was rubbed in the muck.

'Eat it! Suck it up, harlot!' a voice screamed into her ear. 'Maybe it'll teach you to offer your vile body to other people's husbands!'

Her bottom had lifted as her face was forced into the bowl, and a sudden pain shot through her as it was smacked. She gasped, her mouth filling with decaying sludge. Still her head was held in place, as she was beaten with the paddle, writhing in the mess, unable to breathe, kicking out her legs and hammering at the table top with her hands. The women were shouting, no one voice clear among the three, screaming in vengeful rage. She struggled, desperately, her head dizzy, choking, until at last she was forced to swallow her filthy mouthful. Her head was pulled up immediately, to leave her gasping for air and the three women leered down at her filthy face. Again her face was thrust into the mess, and again the beating started, her buttocks jumping to the heavy paddle smacks.

'It goes on until you've finished, harlot!' a voice screamed in her ear.

Rosanna, in desperation, sucked up a mouthful of the filth, taking in slime and solid together. She swallowed frantically, one mouthful, then another, forcing it down, only for a lump of some mushy substance to stick in her throat. Her stomach rebelled, instantly, her gorge rising, and as her head was jerked back from the bowl she was violently sick, spewing the contents of her stomach into her brank and down her own breasts. The three women stood back, looking down on her in utter disgust.

'On the floor,' the eldest ordered. 'Crawling, and stay down. If there's not to be another chance, I don't aim to waste this.'

'How? What do you mean?' Rosanna managed through her half-blocked mouth.

'You don't know?' the old woman laughed. 'Well, you will, soon enough.'

Rosanna tried to speak again, but her words were cut off as the heavy wooden paddle smacked down on to her buttocks. They set to work on her, taking turns to beat her as the others watched and laughed, until her bottom and the backs of her legs were a mass of purple bruises. Tired of beating her, they each urinated on her, over her buttocks and back, in her hair and in her mouth. When she was kneeling in a pool of urine and the mess she had been made to eat, she was forced to suck and lick from the floor. She did it, as her legs were beaten, until she could take no more, and was once again sick down her breasts. At that they stopped, laughing at her as she squatted in her own filth, until first the fat woman and the eldest were forced to sit down.

None tried to stop her as she ran out through the door, tripping and stumbling in her chains. In the square, a group of men were leaving the inn, and stared in astonishment as she staggered past. She barely saw them, thinking only of the refuge of the hovel she had built in the cloister-house garden. Nobody interfered with her, and she made it to the gate, slamming it behind her. Inside, she collapsed on to the grass, only to look up at the sound of a familiar chuckle. Father Tiergarde sat in one of the ornamental chairs, and there was a girl on his lap. She was dark-haired, small, but with a heavy chest, her features beautiful, or so Rosanna thought until she turned to show eyes bereft of understanding. Tiergarde also turned, smiling.

'Ah, Rosanna,' he said, 'what an unpleasant sight you make, and how you smell! Now run along, Lily, my pet, this is not something you should see.'

The girl jumped up, to be sent on her way with a smack on her bottom. Rosanna pulled herself up, to her knees, mess dripping from her breasts and down her belly. Father Tiergarde pulled a scented kerchief from his robe, to draw it across his face. Slowly, Rosanna stood.

'Defiant still?' the priest queried. 'Extraordinary! You really have no concept of your place in this world at all, do you? No matter, in the state to which you have allowed yourself to be reduced you are of no use anyway, and, frankly, your obstinacy no longer amuses me.'

A faint spark of hope ignited in Rosanna's mind.

'So I have arranged a final little drama,' the priest went on. 'For a trivial outlay, I have arranged for a certain hermit to visit us here, a man both wise and strange; possessed, some say. He warns of our worldliness, stating that to assuage our sins it will be necessary to make a sacrifice of the most evil among us, otherwise all face damnation. He is most persuasive, and already the villagers are seeking a victim. You have been named as the best candidate by several matrons of the town, so that only my word stands between you and an extremely unpleasant death.'

Sick fear had replaced Rosanna's hope as he spoke.

'How?' she managed over her metal gag.

'Now there,' Tiergarde went on, 'my hermit has seen fit to add a little detail of his own. Apparently, the victim must be staked out in the wilds, whereupon a demon will come to devour them. Naturally there is no demon. Such tales are for the gullible, the superstitious. However, the villagers believe, which is what matters, and may be relied on not to approach the site until it is certain you are gone.

'No, there is no beast, but in due course you will wish there was. After all, death under the claws and fangs of this imaginary creature would be quick, if painful. Death by starvation and exposure will certainly be painful, but hardly quick. Reports suggest that without food a man in good condition may last fifty or even sixty days. For you, a mere woman, and exposed to the elements, I estimate twenty-five to thirty. Then again, you might derive a measure of sustenance from snails, worms and so forth, whatever you can gather up as you crawl on your belly in the mud.'

'Why?' Rosanna demanded.

'Why?' he responded. 'You ask why? You have offended me, that is why. Your whole attitude demands retribution, and what else but death will serve? I am a sensitive man, Rosanna, sensitive to a degree beyond the understanding of your dull wits. So you must die, there is no choice. It is the price of your haughty pride, Rosanna, and your arrogance in refusing to accept your place. So, do you not wish you had shown more intelligence at first, not to mention a proper attitude of humility towards me?'

'No,' she answered sullenly.

'You lie,' he answered. 'How many cocks have you taken in your mouth? Eighty, perhaps a hundred, and time after time again. How much semen have you swallowed? Had you the mathematical ability you might calculate it, but it must be in the order of gallons. How much easier would it have been to accept me?'

Rosanna gave no answer, but shook her head.

'Stubborn to the last,' he said. 'Still, you will change your mind in the moments before death overtakes you.'

'No.'

'Now there you will find you are wrong. We priests know something of this, and be assured, in that terrible instant the full measure of your stupidity will become plain to you. Now come.'

He stepped around her, the kerchief held tight to his nose. A protector stepped forward from a hidden alcove, to take hold of the chain which linked Rosanna's wrists. He pulled, and she came stumbling behind.

In the square she was led to the steps, an excited crowd gathering quickly around her. Father Tiergarde stood a little apart, waiting until he had full attention before he spoke.

'Good people. I have thought long and hard on the matter of the dire prophecy brought upon us. In the clemency of my faith I had thought to save the mad woman Rosanna Faine. Yet if one of our village must be taken, it is clear to me that she is our only choice. I had wished to show mercy, yet who can doubt her evil? Before she finally lost her mind, was there ever a harlot more brazen, less contrite? Did she crawl to the feet of you, the worthy women of the village, begging forgiveness and punishment? No, her attitude was ever of defiance, and so I say, let it be her who is given to the demon. Do any wish to argue otherwise?'

A murmur passed through the crowd, the older women in open agreement, the younger and the men briefly doubtful before giving way to the tide of popular opinion.

'Then there is nothing further that need be said,' Tiergarde continued. 'I myself shall take her to a suitable location, that the responsibility need not fall on your shoulders. Thus, should there be guilt in what I do, in what is my decision and mine alone, I may answer before he who judges all.'

There were murmurs of appreciation as he finished. Several of the villagers reached out to touch the hem of his robe as he walked past them. Rosanna came behind, led by the protector. They crossed the square, to the forge, where the protector collected new chain, two massive staples and a great black-iron hammer. A few had followed, but melted away as Rosanna was led past her old house, down through the fields and orchards of the village, to a shallow gully. In the space beneath a single great oak, the priest stopped.

'Here will do,' he stated, seating himself on a convenient rock. 'Take off her brank. We wouldn't want her to have difficulty screaming for help, would we?'

The protector laughed and came close, to free Rosanna of the cage. Tiergarde looked at her, smiling, as always when there was fear or horror in her face.

'No final plea?' he questioned.

'You wouldn't heed it if there was,' she answered.

'True,' he chuckled. 'A shame you realise that. It would have been pleasant to hear you beg. No matter. I have better things to do in any case. Fix her to the tree, so that she can reach the stream for water, but ensure that the staples are well hammered in.'

The protector nodded, tugging Rosanna towards the oak. She pulled back, her panic rising, but was drawn in, quite unable to resist his strength. Close to the tree, he lifted the chain, placing a staple through a link, only for Rosanna to jerk on it. He turned to her, lifting the hammer, then suddenly screamed, and fled.

Rosanna twisted at the patter of stones to her rear. Water sprayed over her body as a great, black shape hurled itself into the stream, and out again, full on to Father Tiergarde's back as he lurched to his feet. He went down, in a tangle of flapping black cloak, to lie screaming on the ground, pinned beneath the creature's forelegs.

Rosanna stood frozen, gibbering with fear, her back pressed to the oak tree. The creature turned, fiery yellow eyes peering from a hideous, dog-like face, a great red tongue hanging from between open jaws. It sniffed, its black nose twitching to catch her scent, growled once, and tore out Father Ira Tiergarde's throat. Rosanna had fainted, and never saw it feed or drag the priest's mangled corpse away into the bushes.

Mother

'Hey, it's the cocksman!'

Grant looked across the bar and raised his hand to the expectant-looking men gathered around a corner table. One, a thin youth with sandy hair, was already on his feet.

'Let me get you a drink, Grant,' the youth offered. 'What are you having?'

'Lager, Greg,' Grant answered.

'How did it go?' another of the men demanded as Grant sat down.

'The usual,' he answered.

'Yeah, man, but did you get her?'

'Did I get her! What a question. No, Billy boy, I didn't get her. I got them, all three.'

'Three!'

'Fuck me!'

'Are you something!'

'Three in a bed!'

'No, Jimmy, four in a bed,' Grant answered, taking his drink. 'Learn to count and you might get somewhere yourself.'

'Four in a bed,' Billy said in awe.

'You got 'em in bed, together?' Greg demanded. 'The three you left with last night?'

'No, Greg, I dropped them off home and picked up three new ones.'

'Yeah? How did . . . oh, right. Funny one, Grant.'

'So what happened?' Jimmy demanded.

'The usual,' Grant answered.

'Yeah, but what? The details, man, the details!'

'Never give away a lady's secrets. First rule, mate.'

'Come on, Grant. You fucked 'em, yeah?'

Grant spread his hands as if in disbelief.

'He fucked 'em!' Greg exclaimed. 'He only fucking fucked 'em! Three at once! Fuck me!'

'One at a time,' Grant answered. 'I may be the cocksman, but I ain't deformed.'

'From what I hear it's close. Come on, man, what happened?'

'Oh, all right,' Grant answered. 'We left, yeah? Then it's back to my place, another bottle, a bit of music and bed. The little blonde one, she's Michelle, and Louise, her sister, they did striptease, while their friend, Gina, she's the tall one, gave me a bit on the bed.'

'Sister?' Jimmy queried. 'What, they . . . together?'

'Sure.'

'Shit! You serious?'

'Shut up, will you!' Billy cut in. 'Go on, Grant.'

'So the two little ones are stripping for me,' Grant said, 'and it don't matter if they are sisters. They're helping each other with their buttons and kissing and touching each other's tits –'

'Shit!'

'Shut up, will you!'

'– and all the time Gina's getting me ready. By the time the sisters are down naked, I am ready to go. I fuck Michelle first, doggy, till her sister starts to get impatient. So I give Louise the same. By then Gina's nude, and she goes down on Michelle . . .'

'What, like lezzies?'

'Hey, there's nothing wrong with two girls going together, so long as there's a man around. So Gina's licking Michelle's cunt and I'm giving Louise a length. But I want to fuck Gina. Those legs, gorgeous . . .'

'Yeah, in that red mini-skirt she was wearing.'

'She wasn't wearing it any more, not then. She was stark naked. So she's kneeling, with that cute little arse stuck up in the air and her face in Michelle's cunt. I've got to have her, but I don't want to disappoint Louise. So do you know what I do?'

They were watching, all attention. Grant took a swallow of lager and continued.

'I pick her up, and I sit her down, right on Michelle's face. On her own sister's fucking face! Then I get up Gina and fuck her while we watch Michelle lick out her sister's cunt. I gave Gina my first load like that, right up her cunt.'

'Nice!'

'You are not joking. So I take a breather, but they're hard at it. Dirty bitches, all three of them. Gina's still licking Michelle, and Michelle's so hot she's got her face in her sister's arse, I swear it.'

'What, like, up the hole?'

'Yeah, I saw, right in, licking like it tastes of ice cream and not shit.'

'The filthy bitch!'

'With her own sister, Jesus!'

'Yeah, well, girls get that way, with me.'

'So what did you do?'

'I fucked 'em, that's what I did. Michelle first, once I got going watching 'em, and her sister later.'

'Doggy style?'

'Yeah. Lots of different ways, but I always come doggy. Some doc I saw on the telly reckons that's the best way to make 'em take. I reckon I got all three.'

'Pregnant?'

'I reckon. I only have to look at a girl and she falls pregnant.'

'How many's that?'

Grant shrugged.

'So what you going to do?' Jimmy demanded.

128

'Do?' Grant said. 'Nothing. I knock 'em up. That's my job, done.'

'Yeah?'

'Yeah. Find 'em, fuck 'em, forget 'em. That's the rule.'

'What about the babies?'

'I keep an eye, make sure the mother doesn't do anything stupid. When they grow up, maybe they can get to know me, but looking after brats is woman's work.'

'What if they, you know, get an abortion?'

'No woman murders my kid. I won't let 'em.'

Grant took another swallow of lager, leaving the others to exchange envious looks.

'I wish it had been me,' Billy said. 'That Gina, fucking gorgeous. Do you reckon I'd have a chance, Grant?'

'No,' he answered. 'Even if you weren't an ugly runt, she's had me, so she won't want anyone else.'

'I just wish I could get 'em like you, Grant,' Jimmy whined. 'How d'you do it?'

'There's no how, Jimmy boy,' Grant answered. 'You're either a cocksman or you ain't.'

'It's all down to stuff called pheromones,' Greg stated. 'Like a smell, only you can't smell it. It's subconscious.'

'This book I got says you got to be more like 'em,' Billy said. 'You know, be into the bands they like, the right films, all –'

'Bollocks,' Grant interrupted. 'It's all in the looks. Read any magazine and you'll see. It's all they go on about. Who's the best-looking film star, who's the best-looking pop star, all the time. Fame's a pull, and money. The rest's bollocks.'

He sat back, his attention wandering as the others continued to argue. A woman had come into the bar, young, blonde, with a fresh, innocent look that immediately appealed. She glanced his way and for a moment their eyes met. She smiled.

'Excuse me, boys.' He addressed his friends. 'The cocksman has pulled.'

Grant lay sprawled on the bed, sipping beer from a bottle. The fresh young blonde, Tina, lay across him, bottom pushed out to let him fondle her, mouth wide around his cock. He had already come twice, once a quick knee-trembler with her pressed up against a wall in the alley behind the pub, again when they got to his flat. Now, stripped and willing, she was doing her best to bring him back to erection. It was working too, the soft, wet feel of her mouth around his cock and the feel of her firm, meaty young bottom in his hand rapidly turning his thoughts back to sex.

'Suck harder,' he ordered. 'I'm getting there.'

Tine gave a muffled noise and began to slide her head up and down on his cock. She moved too, lifting her body as if to swing a leg across his. Grant pushed her back down.

'Hey!' he said. 'I don't lick, not ever. And you've got spunk in your cunt, fucking gross!'

She gave another muffled grunt, managing to sound disappointed, but stayed down, allowing him to continue his leisurely fondling of her body. He took a swallow of beer, finishing the bottle and throwing it on the floor. Taking her by the hair, he began to fuck her head.

'Right in,' he demanded. 'Down your throat.'

Tina managed a grunt of protest, but no more as he forced her head right down, plugging her gullet with his now erect penis. He held it, deep, until she began to gag and struggle. Only then did he let her up, and laughed as she gasped in air.

'You bastard!' she managed. 'You nearly choked me!'

'You love it!' he answered. 'I'm going to fuck you now, so get on your knees.'

'Couldn't I go on top? I only really come that way.'

'You'll come. On your knees, I said.'

She moved, reluctantly, into a kneeling position, clasping a pillow with the full white moon of her bottom lifted for him. He took a moment to admire her rear view, with the undersides of her little boobs visible between her legs, the gentle swell of her belly and pubic mound, her open, moist sex, and the brown oval surrounding her anus. He grinned to himself, thinking how she'd look in the same position with her belly swollen in pregnancy, fat and embarrassed, with the proof of his virility showing to everybody.

He got to his knees, put his cock to her already sperm-slick hole and pushed up. Tina sighed, and started to moan as he fucked her, her buttocks wobbling and her blonde hair bouncing to his rhythm. He could smell her sex, and his own sperm, which was putting him off as well as making her sloppy.

'Sorry, doll,' he said, and pulled out, putting his cock straight to the tight brown ring of her bottom hole.

'Hey, no!' Tina protested, 'not up my bum! Ow!'

He ignored her, holding her hard around the waist as he rubbed the mixture of sperm and her own juice on to her anus.

'Oh, you dirty bastard!' she complained, wriggling.

The protest was half-hearted, her weak struggles too, done more to preserve her dignity than to actually stop herself being buggered. Soon he had the head of his cock inside her little brown bumhole. Penetrated, she gave up. The rest of his cock followed the head, forced in to the sound of her complaints and pained squeals.

'Now that is tight,' he sighed, and began to bugger her.

Tina took it better than he'd expected, clutching the pillow and making weird grunting noises, but without tears or the silent rigidity he had known some buggered girls to adopt. Not that it mattered, with everything centred on the feel of his hard cock rubbing in the soft, slimy tube of her rectum and the tight feel of her straining anus. Before too long he felt the onset of orgasm, and began to pump faster. Her squeals grew louder, and shriller, showing real pain, and ending in a scream as he spunked up her bottom. He held it in, deep up her with his front squashing out her buttocks, until his ecstasy began to fade.

'Tight,' he said when it was finally over. 'First time up the shitter?'

Tina managed a feeble nod in response. Grant laughed and put his thumbs to her bottom, to hold her cheeks wide as he eased his shaft from her hole. Tina gave a hiss of pain, but held still, collapsing on the bed only when he was free.

'You're a good fuck, thanks,' he remarked.

Tina said nothing, but put her arms out, inviting him to cuddle her. Grant took no notice, wiped his cock on the curtain and began to dress.

'So what d'you reckon on Man City and Leeds?' Billy asked, poising his pen over the coupon on the table.

'Home win, got to be,' Jimmy said.

'I don't know,' Greg put in. 'Could be a draw, what with Salentino injured . . .'

Grant tuned out of the conversation as the pub door opened to let in a blonde girl, young, with a fresh, innocent look that immediately appealed, and heavily pregnant. She glanced around, saw him and started over.

'Excuse me, boys,' he said, turning in his chair as he tried to remember who she was.

'Hi, Grant,' she said, smiling a lop-sided grin.

'Hi, doll,' he answered.

'Could we have a word?' she said meekly.

'Sure.'

'Alone, outside?'

'All right. Mind the pint, boys.'

He got up, to follow her outside. They walked a little way, their breath white in the cold air, to where the bare black twigs of a tree overhung a bench. She sat down. He remained standing, to glance back to where the warm yellow lights showed through the pub windows.

'Sorry, doll,' he said. 'I can't remember your name, not for the life of me.'

'Tina,' she said softly.

'Tina? Tina . . . Oh yeah, you were so sloppy I had to fuck you up the arse! Yeah, you were good. We were good, weren't we?'

She nodded, blushing.

'And he's mine?' he asked, nodding to her swollen stomach.

Again she nodded. There was a long moment of silence.

'So, er . . . nice one,' he said.

'What happens now?' she asked.

'Now? You have a baby, doll. You ought to know that!'

'I do know that, Grant. I mean, with us?'

'Us? There's no "us", doll, only you, and me.'

'But, Grant –'

'Look, doll, we had sex, it was good. End of story.'

'But . . . but what about baby? She'll need a father!'

'He, doll, he. I make boys. And he'll have a father, me.'

'She . . . he will? You'll marry me . . . live with me?'

'I'm not the marrying type, doll.'

He squatted down, to take her hands and look up into her eyes.

'What you've got to understand, doll,' he said, 'is that I'm a free spirit, a drifter. I can't be tied down, so don't ask it of me, or you'll spoil what we have.'

'But, Grant –'

'Look, doll,' he interrupted, 'let me give you some advice. What you want to do, is find some little dipshit, and marry him. He'll be grateful for a good-looking girl like you, even when you're pregnant. He'll give you everything you want, and the baby, a nice little flat, a house even, clothes, all the gear you ask for. And all the time you'll have the memory of me, and who knows, maybe I'll drop in sometimes . . . Hey, doll!'

She had jerked her hands from his and fled, sobbing, down the road. Grant stood for a moment, watching her go, shrugged and turned back for the pub, his mind once more on predicting the football results.

Grant paused, watching the woman coming towards him across the park. She was perhaps forty, slender beneath her leather coat, poised and elegant, her face delicate, somehow familiar, her expression cool, amused. As she walked she projected an air of confidence, even arrogance, filling him with the desire to see her on her knees, grunting out her passion with his cock well immersed in her sex, impregnating her. It made a nice picture, but not a particularly realistic one. With her age and obvious wealth she was unlikely to be as easily led as the much younger women he normally went for. Nevertheless, she was walking directly towards him, and smiling.

'Are you Grant?' she asked, as she reached him.

'Grant's the name,' he answered. 'You are?'

'Paris.'

'Suits you, sophisticated. What can I do for you, Paris?'

'That we shall see,' she answered. 'My daughter speaks highly of you.'

'Your daughter?'

'Tina.'

'Tina? Blonde Tina?'

His heart jumped at the realisation of who she was, but quickly settled. There had been no animosity in her voice, only warmth.

'Yeah, I know Tina,' he went on. 'So you're Tina's mum. Nice. I should have recognised you. So how's my baby?'

'If you mean Tina, in perfect health. So is her unborn daughter.'

'Daughter? You're sure?'

'Certain. I am a doctor by profession, Grant, a gynaecologist. I don't suppose you've seen the new ultrasound scans? Here.'

She opened her bag, to pull out a picture. Grant took it, staring in astonishment at the perfect colour reproduction of an almost fully developed, and clearly female, baby.

'Nice,' he said, 'but, er . . .'

'Don't worry, Grant,' she went on. 'She won't be making any claim on you. I managed to persuade her that you would be entirely unsuitable as a husband.'

'That's what I said, I did. I said she should marry some nice bloke, decent, dependable.'

'A "dipshit", I think, was the expression you used, apparently without irony. No, Grant, she won't be marrying a dipshit. She'll be studying at the NAA from next September. Fortunately we are in a position to provide childcare.'

'Good. Good.'

'But that is not the reason I came to find you, or not the only reason.'

'Yeah?'

'I'll be frank, Grant. My husband died seven years ago, leaving me a comfortably wealthy widow. I have no desire to marry again, least of all to the sort of men who pursue me. I want someone young, energetic, and who understands that being my lover does not give them a right to control me in any way, outside the bedroom at least. Tina seemed to think you'd be ideal.'

'I'm the man,' Grant answered, taking her arm.

'I thought you might be,' she answered, 'and there's another thing. Tina would also appreciate your attention. It's been a little hard for her since she's started to show, and she is so highly sexed.'

'Tina too? What, not together?'
'Naturally together.'

Tina stretched luxuriously, pushing out her swollen belly as she wriggled herself down on to Grant's cock. She had been mounted on him for some time, enjoying the feel of his erection inside her as she stroked oil into her breasts and belly. He had let her go on top, at once fascinated and repulsed by her swollen abdomen and heavy breasts, but completely fascinated by her mother.

Paris had behaved in a way he had only ever dreamt of, not just willing and servile, but obviously enjoying the role. She had stripped almost as soon as they had entered the house, and served his beer nude. She had sucked his cock erect for her daughter's body while he watched Tina's leisurely striptease. She had applied the massage oil, not only to his body, but to Tina's, smoothing the thick yellow fluid into her daughter's breasts, belly and bottom with every sign of enjoyment. She had even used two fingers to ease her daughter's vagina, a gesture both motherly and sensual. Grant had found the whole process highly arousing, so much so that he was having difficulty stopping himself coming inside Tina as she rode him. He held back, determined to reserve the bulk of his sperm for Paris.

'I'm going to come now,' Tina moaned. 'Fuck me, Grant, and watch me come.'

She caught up her breasts and squeezed the already swollen globes of pale flesh, as if trying to milk herself. Grant began to pump into her, bouncing her body on his, to make her bloated stomach wobble in time to his thrusts. She sighed, sliding her hands down over the fat, oily surface of her bulge, to her sex. He watched, fascinated, as she spread open her plump sex lips, to show off the pink centre, with his cock moving in her tight hole. Her finger went straight to her clitoris, and she began to masturbate, closing her eyes and returning her free hand to a breast.

Grant glanced to the side. Paris was looking, her face set in a pleased smile as she watched her daughter masturbate on his cock. Not only that, but she too was stroking her breasts and sex, the motions a mirror of Tina's. He closed his eyes, trying not to think of the two of them together, as he knew it would make him come. At that moment Tina came herself, with a long, low moan, wiggling her bottom in Grant's lap and squirming her sex on to his cock as it went through her. His teeth were gritted, but he forced himself to keep pushing until she was done. Only then, as she slumped down on his body, did he roll her to one side.

Standing, he pushed his cock at Paris's mouth. She took it immediately in her hand, and extending her tongue to clean up her daughter's juice from his cock. He watched, following the little, sharp tongue-tip each time it traced a line in the thick white juice that smeared his penis. She ate what she licked up, swallowing it down with relish, faster and faster, until she finally lost control, gulping in his whole cock, to suck eagerly on the shaft.

He nearly came as his cock head wedged into the back of her throat, but steeled himself, determined to hold back. After a last, strong suck she released him, his cock emerging clean but glossy with saliva. On the bed, Tina giggled.

'Get on the bed, on your knees,' Grant ordered. 'I'm going to fuck you.'

Paris obeyed immediately, scrambling up beside Tina to lift her bottom, her knees wide, her neat sex lips pouting and ready, her anus marked by an oval of brown flesh identical to her daughter's.

'Get up beside her,' Grant told Tina. 'Go on.'

Tina giggled, and exchanged a look with her mother, but did as she was told. Grant climbed on behind them, taking his cock in hand as he admired the two naked women. They were certainly similar, in build and colouring, both compact, and pale skinned but for a little darker flesh around their bumholes. Both showed the same crinkly blonde hair on their pussies, densely grown on their mounds and outer lips, but there only. Other than a trace of tension in the older woman's flesh, the only real difference was Tina's pregnancy. Her belly hung huge and taut beneath her, while there was a good bit of extra flesh on her buttocks and thighs. Somehow it fitted their personalities, the mother svelte, elegant and cool, the daughter, plump, bouncy and enthusiastic.

Knowing he would come in his hand if he didn't insert it, Grant put his cock to Paris's sex. It went in, easily, sliding deep into her body until his stomach met her buttocks. He began to fuck and she began to moan, clutching at the bed as she was ridden. Grant took hold of her, pushing himself into her, faster and faster, too excited to hold back any longer, his hands clutching at the neat little buttocks as his orgasm rose up in his head. Tina was looking back, watching him fuck her mother, and with that Grant came, pumping the full load of his sperm into Paris's body as he cried out in ecstasy.

'You horny fucking bitches!' he grated as his cock spasmed inside her, pumping out the sperm he was hoping would make her pregnant, even at the peak of his climax.

He sat back, against the bed end. His cock was sticking up, still hard, and once more covered with white slime. Pointing to it, he clicked his fingers. Paris came immediately, crawling over, as obedient as a dog, to set to work to clean up her juice.

'You too, Tina,' he ordered. 'She cleaned your mess up.'

To his surprise, Paris said nothing, but merely moved a little, allowing her daughter to move in beside her. Grant said nothing, but stared in amazement as the two women began to clean his cock, licking and kissing at the mixture of pussy juice and sperm. Both were eager, tongues out, sometimes touching, Tina swallowing down what she could get, Paris holding back, to make a sticky white pool in her mouth. Only when he was clean did Grant discover why. When only a little sucking was needed, Paris took his cock in hand and fed it into her daughter's mouth. Tina sucked, her cheeks bulging, and swallowed, then rolled, releasing the thick, half-stiff cock from her mouth, on to her back, mouth open. Paris immediately lay down across Grant's legs, positioned herself above Tina and opened her own mouth, to release a sticky mass of saliva, sperm and her own pussy juice, full between her daughter's lips.

Tina let the fluid pool in her mouth, until it overflowed, to run down over her lips and out of the side of her mouth. Paris made more, like a mother bird feeding her chick, letting it fall as Tina's mouth came open to take it, closing, and kissing, mouth to mouth, mother and daughter, sharing sperm in an open, sensual kiss. Grant watched, speechless, until they broke apart, Tina giggling, Paris as cool as ever.

'That was wonderful,' Paris stated calmly, 'and it's about time I had my own orgasm.'

'I made you come, yeah?' Grant answered her.

'My dear boy, you were only inside me for a few seconds,' she answered. 'You have to do better than that. Let's get him ready again, darling, and I'll do it the way you did. Lie down, Grant.'

He obeyed, his automatic protest dying in his mouth at her sudden and unexpected assertiveness. Lying full length on the bed, he watched as Paris crawled between his legs, to take his cock in her mouth. As she began to suck, as willing and servile as before, his sudden pang of unease faded.

'Do it together, yeah?' he demanded, keen to see more of their sex play and wondering how far it went.

'I want my pussy licked!' Tina complained.

'I don't do that stuff,' he answered. Paris pulled her lips up from his cock.

'Don't be a spoilsport, Grant,' she said. 'Let Tina sit on you, then we can suck your lovely cock together.'

'I don't lick cunt,' he insisted.

'I bet you do,' Paris answered him as she began to stroke his cock, 'for the right incentive. Very well, if we have to bargain, how would you like to watch Tina and me together, after I've come?'

'Yeah, sure, but –'

'No buts, Grant. She sits on your face, she and I play. I spank her, you know. Sometimes she even spanks me. Does that turn you on?'

'Not my thing.'

'Then how about licking? You can watch us in a sixty-nine, and stick your gorgeous big cock anywhere you like, in our mouths, in our pussies, even up our bottoms.'

'Fuck me.'

'It would be good, wouldn't it?' Paris purred. 'And you saw how I love to clean up for her. How would you like to put your cock up her bottom for a bit, give her a good buggering, then put it in my mouth, watch me suck it clean, come in my mouth –'

'It's a deal,' Grant answered quickly. 'You get your lick, Tina.'

Tina giggled and bounced over to him, immediately swinging one leg across his body. He swallowed as her broad white rear was positioned over his face, promising himself to leave out what he was about to do when the time came to boast of his latest exploit. Paris's mouth closed on his cock and she began to suck, even as her daughter lowered her bottom. The full cheeks met Grant's face, spreading, to squash her sex against his mouth. It also pressed her bumhole to his nose. Her anal ring had become slimy during the fucking, and his nose tip went in. Tina giggled and squirmed her bottom in his face.

He began to lick, and to his embarrassment found his cock growing in Paris's mouth, much faster than it would normally have done so soon after an orgasm. He told himself that it was because of the filthy act they'd promised if he licked Tina, and went on with his task.

'I'm going to come too, Mummy,' Tina announced.

'You do that, darling,' Paris replied, pulling off, 'first if you like.'

Wet lips closed on his cock once more. Tina began to wriggle, to press his nose ever further up her bottom hole and make it harder to lick her properly. She didn't seem to mind, and nor did his cock, hardening in Paris's mouth until it was fully erect once more. Her lips left him, with a final kiss to the engorged tip, and the bed creaked as she shifted her weight.

'I'm going to come, Mummy,' Tina gasped. 'I'm going to come!'

Tina's movements had become more urgent, her bottom wiggling frantically in his face. He could barely breathe, the flesh of her bottom and pussy blocking his mouth and nose, until he could stand it no more, and pushed at her thighs.

'No, let me, Grant, let me!' she squealed. 'Think what you can do, think . . .'

She broke off, sighing and began to wiggle more frantically than ever. Grant steeled himself, thinking of how his erection had looked in Tina's anus, and how it would look after he'd buggered her again, thick and long in Paris's mouth, her delicate features, always so cool, and her mouth gaping around a fat cock shaft, dirty with her own daughter's . . .

Tina came, crying out in ecstasy with her bottom thrust hard into Grant's face. It held, her anus pulsing on his nose, his mouth choked with plump pussy flesh. Grant was barely able to lick her and totally unable to breathe. Pain started in his lungs, rising as he began to panic. He thrust Tina aside, gasping in air, even as a mask settled over his face and the hiss of gas came loud in his ears.

* * *

141

Grant came round slowly. First he was aware of voices, seeming to come from a great distance, then of bright lights, finally of figures standing above him. Vague memories crowded in, of a strange half-waking state, of injections, a calm, soothing voice.

His vision swam into focus, revealing Paris, standing over him, dressed in a white gown. Tina was beside her mother, also in white, with what appeared to be a bundle of blankets cradled gently in her arms. Beyond was more white, and silver, also pictures, complex and meaningless diagrams and studies in the rich reds and browns of internal organs.

'He's awake,' Paris's voice came to him. 'Can you see me clearly, Grant?'

He managed to nod, then tried to move his arms, wondering why they were stretched out above his head. The effort brought the chink of metal and tugs on his wrists. He lay back again, more odd memories flooding in, of pain, and knives. He began to struggle.

'Don't panic, Grant,' Paris said calmly. 'You're chained to the bed, for your own safety as much as ours.'

'Why? What have you done?' he demanded.

'Presently,' she said. 'Meanwhile, wouldn't you like to meet your daughter? We've called her Laura.'

'I don't care,' he answered. 'What have you done to me, you mad bitches!'

'Temper, temper,' Paris chided.

'My cock, you've done something to my cock!' he screeched, looking down to where a sheet hid his genitals.

'Not at all,' Paris answered. 'He's fine, and I dare say he'll be back up some unfortunate girl's pussy in due time.'

'What then? You've done something, I know it!'

'Well,' she said, 'for one thing, you've got your wish. You have successfully fertilised one of my eggs.'

'You're pregnant by me? Look, don't take it badly, Paris. I didn't mean anything. I just . . . I just can't use condoms. They make me go limp, and I thought you'd be protected, being a doctor and everything. I . . .'

'You're babbling, Grant,' she said softly. 'Do you know what this is?'

She had released a catch on a squat container, from which pale fumes rose as the lid was opened. Taking a pair of tongs, she drew out a plastic vial.

'This,' she said, 'is a sample of your sperm, so kindly provided during our little session of love-making, and kept warm inside me until we needed it. I had some eggs extracted years ago, and it was a simple matter to fertilise one. Implanting to the mesodermal cavity was a little trickier, but then I did help pioneer the technique.'

'What? What the fuck are you talking about? So Tina's pregnant again, with our baby?'

'No, Grant,' Paris said patiently. 'Tina is not pregnant. You are.'

Tigress

'You are hungry?' Lu-Sha asked.

Meilia nodded.

'I also,' Lu-Sha agreed.

They had reached the top of a line of crags, allowing them to look out across the river valley. Below them, broken brown rock fell away, with only the occasional gnarled olive or patch of yellowing grass as vegetation. Still further down, on the flat river plain, brilliant verdant green stretched to the water, an expanse of lush grass on which the huge forms of Baluchitheria grazed.

Lu-Sha's nose was twitching, also the tip of her tail. Her thumb was hooked into the belt of the loose silk culottes which were her only garment, as if about to pull them down, a mannerism Meilia recognised as signifying excitement. Again the young tigranthrope sniffed, and this time a shimmer ran through the red and black fur of her back. Adjusting the front of her kirtle over her large, sweat-slick breasts, Meilia wished she also had fur.

'What do you scent?' she asked.

'Baluchi,' Lu-Sha answered, 'camel, the river, many minor notes, and Ornacothere.'

'Ornacothere? You are certain?'

'Certain. There is a tang, like no other beast. A male.'

'They are fast, Lu-Sha, too fast for us.'

'We must do our best.'

'It is said they have two cocks, and if they take a girl it is done from the side, with one in each hole.'

'Not so. The cock is paired, and it is only chance if both entrances are penetrated.'

'Little consolation, for the girl raped and sodomised! Is it close by?'

'Not far. It will have scented us in any case, and will know we are female. You in any case, as your cunt smells ripe, while I won't come on heat for several days. Also, your dark skin shows up among the rocks.'

'So it will come?'

'I would think so. We must separate.'

'And it will follow me?'

'Just so.'

Again Lu-Sha sniffed, immediately dropping down. Meilia followed suit, her heart hammering in her chest. Lu-Sha gestured back the way they had come.

'It is already stalking us!' she hissed. 'Quickly, stay among the crags.'

Lu-Sha was moving away even as she spoke, to disappear behind a great red boulder. Meilia moved, hurrying between the boulders and outcrops of rock, along the line of crags, and constantly glancing backwards. Nothing was visible, and she began to wonder if Lu-Sha was right, or even teasing her.

The uncertainty lasted until she reached a rocky outcrop on a rise in the land and looked back once more, across a patch of open ground she had crossed just moments before. The Ornacothere was there, emerging from a group of rocks, the great wattled neck lifting to test the air.

She swallowed hard, not daring to move, and wondering for what purpose such a hideous and lewd creature had been created. It stood taller than a full-grown man, with a bulbous body supported on powerful legs. Spindly arms extended from the torso, ending in yet more spindly fingers, while the neck rose half its height to the head, bird-like except for the size of the cranium. Feathers covered its back, otherwise it had bare skin, pink-brown mottled with purple, save for the fleshy red wattles of the neck. Worse still, it was clearly aroused, with the twin prongs of an erect penis swinging below the distended belly, all too clearly ready for the soft, wet hole between her thighs.

Meilia ran, darting off between boulders, to find that the far side of her outcrop opened to the end of the crags, a shallow slope leading down in a broad fan towards a bend of the river. There was no shelter, except for another patch of boulders to one side, impossibly far off. She went for them anyway, running as fast as she could across the open expanse of sand and rock.

Behind her, she heard the beast's squawk of joy. It was coming, she knew, although she dared not turn for fear of tripping. It was running at perhaps three times her pace, the great splayed feet slapping on the earth, the hideous penis ready for her sex. Thinking of what would happen, she spurred herself on, her mind full of images of bright-red cock shaft, penetrating her body, deep in her vagina, more than likely up her bottom hole. It was sure to bugger her, she was certain of it, and that it would come in her too, copiously, the thick yellow sperm filling her vagina, smearing her anus and the deep valley between the meaty brown globes of her bottom, leaving her slimy and vile on the hot ground, raped and sodomised . . .

Again the beast cried out, far closer, too close. Meilia turned in panic, to find it coming at her with frightening speed, the huge feet kicking up dust, the great beak wide, the double penis rock hard in expectation. She screamed and ran, back towards the rock. It came after, red eyes locked on the wobbling rear of her bottom, nostrils twitching at the scent of her sex, heedless of anything but her capture and rape.

Meilia stumbled, just feet from the boulder patch, and went down. Seeing her on the ground, the Ornacothere gave a scream of triumph. An instant later it was over her, and reaching down. The spindly hands caught her, rolling her body over, on to her side. She curled, protecting herself, only to have it squat down, full on her fleshy hip. The grotesque double cock pushed at her leg, then at the meat of her bottom, and lower, to find her sex. It was going to happen, both cock shafts prodding at the mouth of her vagina, almost in her, only for one to slip sideways, to the sweaty ring of her anus, pushing. She realised she was to be sodomised, and cried out in despair, even as the bolt from Lu-Sha's crossbow slammed into the creature's head.

'Well done,' Lu-Sha stated, drawing a knife from her belt. 'I don't think it even knew I was there. Let's eat.'

Roswell Tart

'Which is it says she saw the aliens?' Walter asked.

'That's Janet,' Colin answered. 'Over by the window. With the titties.'

'They've all got titties, Col. They're girls,' Walter said.

'The big titties. The blonde with the pony-tail, in the pink dress.'

'Yeah? She's some looker. So what happened?'

'She was on this triple date, right, with Peggy Sue, the other blonde, Betty, with the black hair and the legs, and their jocks. They went out to Misquah Woods, right, in Brad's '49 Ford, for a bit of you-know-what . . .'

'I wouldn't mind a bit of that with her, or any of them girls.'

'Yeah, right, only Brad didn't get his, or that's what I reckon. She wouldn't put out, right, he demanded his dick sucked, and she lost her cool. Anyhow, she got right out of the car, she did, and Peggy Sue and Betty with her. Brad was so steamed he drove off. Left them cold.

'So they've got to go back through the woods, right? Only it's dark and they can't hardly see nothing. Then there's this light, real bright, off in the woods, just sudden. They were scared. They froze. And these figures come out of the wood, and they ain't human!'

'Yeah?'

'Yeah. They're tall, right, with big heads, and big eyes, slanty, like a Chink's. Now, Peggy Sue and Betty, they just runs, but Janet, she's too scared to move . . .'

'I bet she pissed in her panties!'

'Could be! Anyhow, this alien guy, he speaks, real wise sounding, and slow –'

'Where'd you get all this?'

'Billy, kid who lives opposite her place.'

'That jerk! How's he know?'

''Cause he was still awake when she got home. Says he was watching the moon through his telescope. More like he was trying to peak in her window and catch her nudie. Now will you shut up?'

'Go on.'

'So there's the aliens, six or seven of them, and they tell her how they've come to visit the Earth, and they need help, 'cause their civilisations dying –'

'That's straight out of *Weird Tales*!'

'Will you shut up?'

'Yeah, sorry. So what happened? They take her clothes off? Fuck her maybe?'

'No, none of that. They just said they needed human plasma, to strengthen their race, and the very best was to be found right here in Minnesota! They'd chosen her –'

'Bullshit! How'd they know she was going to be out in Misquah Woods?'

'Will you shut the fuck up! How would I know? I just got this from Billy, right? So, they take her in the woods, right, and look in her eyes and check her teeth, and stuff, all the time the head alien's telling her to keep her cool –'

'They take her panties down? What about her bra?'

'You're a sex maniac, Walter, you know that? They didn't do nothing like that! They just asked her questions, and told her they'd be in touch, then let her go. She ran all the way home, no stopping!'

'All bullshit!'

'Yeah, that's what Brad reckoned, and he wasn't the only one. Her old man was so wild he took a belt to her ass, right there on the front porch. Called her untruthful, and a harlot, and all sorts. Billy says he saw, and that he turned her skirts up, and took her panties down and all, and gave it to her bare!'

'Billy's full of shit.'

'Oh no he ain't! He says she's got a strawberry birth mark, right on her left butt cheek. How's he going to know that if he didn't see?'

'Peeping, like you said. Probably heard her howling, and added the details.'

'Could be. Now, Peggy Sue, she backs Janet up, but Brad, he reckons the two of them met some guys from the lumberjack camp out on Eagle Park, and had a little party, just the two girls and a couple dozen men. The alien stuff's to cover up what she done, he says, and he chucked her in.'

'He did?'

'Of course it's not true!' Billy laughed. 'It'll be a hallucination brought about by methane gas rising from the swamps back of Misquah Woods, or a high electrostatic build-up in the atmosphere. It doesn't matter that it's not true. It matters that Janet reckons it's true, and boy does she!'

'How's that?' Colin demanded.

'Because,' Billy went on, 'if she believes it, there can be a next time –'

'And next time,' Walter broke in, 'it's up with her bra and down with her panties, and wheee doggie!'

'You catch on quick,' Billy answered, leering.

'So what's the plan?' Walter asked, leaning close over the table.

'The plan is,' Billy responded, 'that we get her back out to the woods –'

'We ain't aliens,' Colin objected.

'We dress as aliens,' Billy explained. 'It shouldn't be hard. All we need are some bright lights, some weird gear, helmets . . .'

'She saw their faces, yeah?'

'Don't worry. Any inconsistency I can explain. It's all bull, remember. Just leave all that to me. What you need to do is get some gear. Col, you do car repair, yeah?'

Colin nodded.

'You can pinch stuff, yeah? Silver paint, a load of that plastic sheeting you use.'

'Yeah, I can get that,' Colin answered, 'and some inspection lamps and all.'

'Great. I may need other stuff too. Walter, you do Radio Shack, yeah? Can you get the key?'

'Easy.'

'Do that. The rest I can get from electronics class and from Dad's surgery. What I'm going to do, is this. Janet's got a radio, which she leaves on the porch sometimes, an RKO High Six. I can get another the same, only fixed, so when I send a signal, it'll only pick up one frequency. One of you will have to watch and see when she's listening. Don't worry, she spends hours just lying in the hammock with it right up by her ear, near every evening. Meanwhile, I'm up at Radio Shack, and I can put out a transmission for her, alien style!'

'So what we going to do?' Colin demanded. 'Do you think she'll put out? Top only, maybe? I wouldn't even mind that, I wouldn't. Just to get those big titties out. Just to feel 'em up! Oh boy!'

'Don't come on too strong,' Billy urged. 'You'll give the game away with that stuff. Just let me do the talking, yeah?'

'Yeah, right,' Colin answered.

'But we're going to take her bra and panties, right?' Walter urged.

'You're fucking weird, you know that?' Billy answered. 'Yeah, we'll make sure we get her bra and panties, just for you. Weirdo.'

'It's not weird! Just think of those big, round titties wobbling about in the nude, and that bum, and she's all bare, and her nipples show, and when she bends over!'

'It's not weird to want them off her, it's weird to want to keep them,' Billy insisted. 'Now stay quiet, she ought to be coming soon.'

They went quiet, Walter sinking down among the ferns of Misquah Wood. Billy's plan had worked perfectly. Stealing the equipment, copying the Radio Shack keys, switching radios, the broadcast, everything had gone without a hitch. He had watched from Billy's house as Janet lazed in the hammock. She had jumped up as the sound of Elvis Presley was replaced by the bass tone of Billy's alien voice, instructing her to visit Misquah Woods the next night. They didn't actually know if she had taken the bait, but it was impossible to believe she hadn't.

Billy and Colin were bent down among the ferns to either side of him. Both looked far from normal. Suits of plastic sprayed silver covered their bodies, padded at the shoulders, tight at the waist, to change their outlines. Tall helmets adapted from welding masks covered their heads and added to their apparent height. Behind them, a generator hummed gently, ready to power up the bank of lights hidden among the trees. When on, the lights would leave them as black outlines to Janet, who would barely be able to see.

A car swept past on the road, breaking the silence, headlights briefly illuminating the trees. Minutes later came a gentle, rhythmic squeak, and a new light, which drew close, and stopped a little way down the road.

'It's her!' Walter hissed.

'Just stay down,' Billy urged.

The light moved, illuminating a bicycle, then the silhouette of a person, clearly female, before turning towards the woods. Brilliant white light sprang up behind Walter and his companions. Janet turned towards them, looked shocked for an instant, and came forward a faint smile on her pretty face.

'Janet. You have come. It is good,' Billy announced.

'Hi,' Janet managed. 'Three of you, is it?'

'It is,' Billy answered. 'It was a foolish mistake to remove our suits before. Earthly microbes have infected our companions. We three alone remain.'

Janet gave a nervous giggle.

'Our need is now urgent,' Billy said.

'And only I can help?' she answered doubtfully. 'All three of you?'

'Our entire race. Our gratitude will be eternal.'

'Well, maybe, as long as you promise it doesn't go any further.'

'You have our word.'

Janet bit her lip.

'Please help us, Janet,' Billy continued. 'It is in your country that the finest specimens of humanity are to be found. When your forefathers came here, the weak were left behind. Your freedom is also valuable, more so than you perhaps understand. Here, in the country, the finest of the fine are to be found, perfect specimens, like yourself.'

'Flatterer,' Janet answered, tilting her head to one side. 'Well, OK, but only you're to . . . you know.'

'As you wish.'

'OK, then I'm all yours, Mr Alien. What would you like to do first?'

'We need human plasma,' Billy stated. 'But first, we must be certain that you are truly human. Please remove the detachable integument you call clothing.'

'Everything? To the buff?'

'Do not be concerned. Your nakedness means nothing to us, who are of another world.'

'I'll bet.'

As she spoke her hands had gone behind her neck. Walter swallowed, his eyes fixed to her body as he realised that she really was going to strip. His cock was already half stiff in his pants, the urge to squeeze it almost irresistible. As she eased her zip open he grew harder still, and by the time she had shrugged the upper part of her dress down off her shoulders, it was a solid bar of flesh.

Janet giggled, holding her dress to her ample chest and swaying her hips gently, her eyes flicking between them. Very slowly, she began to move the dress down, showing her bra straps, a hint of smooth, pale cleavage. The first tempting rise of her breasts came on show, a little lace, and all of it, her large white cotton bra absolutely bulging with plump, soft girl flesh. Her dress went lower, revealing a little flesh and the smooth lines of her girdle, but Walter's eyes were riveted to her breasts.

She glanced down at Billy's crotch, giggled again, and turned around, to look back over her shoulder with a coy glance. Walter's mouth came open as she stuck out her bottom. It was big, straining out the seat of her dress into a round ball, and her thumbs were in her dress, pushing down. The top of a pair of big panties already showed beneath her girdle, smooth, white, and tight enough to show the twin dimples in the small of her back. More panty material appeared as she pushed, the dress sliding down over the width of her hips, and lower, to show a gentle valley in the cotton to mark her bottom crease. Flesh appeared at either hip, bulging out below the panties and to either side of taut suspender straps. She paused, winked, and pushed again. At last, the full, glorious globe of her ample bottom was revealed, meaty cheeks spilling out from the panty legs, softly rounded thighs, with a fat egg of cotton pouting out between them to mark her sex.

Walter had come in his pants. Giggling, Janet dropped the dress, to step out of it and turn back to face them, lifting her arms and pushing out one hip to show off her underwear. Not one of them spoke, and she gave Billy a smile, her eyes twinkling in the bright light as she looked up to them.

'Ready, boys?' she said, and her hands went behind her back.

Despite the mess of semen in his underpants, Walter was still staring open-mouthed. He saw the tension go in Janet's bra as the catch was released. Her breasts lolled forward, heavy and firm in the slack cups, half of one rose-pink nipple peeping out through the lace. Again he swallowed, and again as she reached forward, took hold of her bra cups and tugged them up, lifting her fat breasts, to bounce back on her chest, nude. The bra was whisked off, briefly held out at arm's length, and dropped. Janet stood topless, giggling as she showed off her breasts with obvious pride.

'There we are,' she said sweetly. 'Is that good enough for you, Mr Alien?'

'You are beautiful, perfection indeed,' Billy managed.

'And now? What are you going to do with poor little me, now that I'm all nudie?'

'You m . . . must remove your panties.'

Janet glanced uncertainly to Walter, then Colin. Her face and the upper part of her chest had begun to flush pink, and she bit her lip again as she turned back to Billy. She nodded, and very quickly pushed the big white panties down and off, revealing a rich puff of golden hair in the V between her legs. She stood again, rather less confident, her thighs together to leave her sex framed between girdle, suspender straps and stocking tops.

'Ready?' she asked.

'We are ready,' Billy assured her. 'Certain samples are required, as you know. A little blood . . .'

'Blood? Are you going to get weird on me again?'

'We will take it from your bottom. There will be no pain.'

'You've been reading those weirdo magazines again, haven't you?'

'I do not understand. Please, it is essential.'

'You are the limit, sometimes! I'd better touch my toes, I suppose. That's how my doctor has me go.'

There had been irritation in her voice, but she had turned. She bent down, her fingers reaching for the toes of her shoes. Walter's mouth was open again, with a trickle of drool running from one corner. As Janet had bent, the chubby hemisphere of her bottom had parted, exposing her every intimate detail. Her anus showed, a tiny puckered hole at the centre of an oval of pale brown flesh. So did her vulva, the outer lips plump and thickly grown with dark blonde fur, the inner pink and moist, with her clitoris peeping out from under its tiny hood.

His cock was getting hard again, and slimy with come. He could smell her, and see the white juice welling up in the mouth of her vagina, things he had only imagined before. She was shaking too, obviously nervous, but she held her rude pose, looking back, around the dangling globes of her naked breasts, at Billy.

He had withdrawn something from his suit, a large syringe, to which he was fitting a needle. Janet winced at the sight, her eyes growing round, only to shut them abruptly as Billy's hand settled on her bottom. Walter watched, full of envy as much as lust as Billy took a firm pinch of one plump bottom cheek, making the flesh bugle. Janet's bottom twitched. She gripped her ankles, her teeth gritted, her eyes screwed up tight, her breasts quivering slightly as Billy pressed the needle to the taut skin of her bottom, and pushed.

Walter saw Janet's flesh push in, and puncture, the long needle sliding into her meaty bottom cheek as she gasped in sudden pain. It had gone in deep, the thin steel shaft clearly visible in her flesh. Billy changed his grip on the syringe, and began to draw out the plunger, filling the transparent chamber with Janet's blood.

156

She took it silently, only the trembling of her lower lip and her hanging breasts betraying her emotions. Walter glanced at Billy, suddenly guilty. Billy took no notice, bending over Janet's bum, his face just inches from her open crease. The syringe was full, the brilliant light throwing red gleams in Janet's blood. Billy once more changed his grip, and drew the needle slowly from the girl's flesh. A tiny bead of blood began to well from the puncture mark.

'Thank you, Janet,' Billy stated. 'And now, an ovum. Do not be alarmed at what I am about to do to you.'

Janet responded with a sob. She was shaking hard, but to Walter's surprise she held still. Billy put the syringe down, and once more delved in his suit, to produce a brass sheaf, from which he drew an object strange to Walter. There was a long extension, like the snout of an alligator, with an open end and a system of levers and screws where the bulk of the beast's head would have been.

'Are you virgin?' Billy asked.

'You know!' Janet answered, shaking her head.

'Then there should be no pain at all as I place the speculum in your cunt,' Billy stated.

Again Walter glanced at Billy, worried by the emotional state Janet was in. Again, Billy took no notice, but placed the snout of the speculum to the mouth of the girl's vagina. Her muscles twitched, her anus winking lewdly at the three boys as they crowded closer, encouraged by her passivity. Billy pushed, his fingers trembling as he slowly eased the speculum into the tight hole of Janet's vagina, stretching out the fleshy pink mouth, until the full length of the snout was inside her. Her breathing had grown faster, and the speculum had displaced some white fluid, which trickled out between the lips of her sex as the boys watched.

Billy took hold of the mechanism, twisting, to open the speculum. Janet's vagina began to spread, stretching around the jaws as they came slowly open, showing a gaping black hole, then rich pink as Billy moved to let the light shine up her passage. She had begun to give little moans, and the muscle of one thigh was shaking. Still Billy twisted the screw, opening her hole, until they could see deep into the fleshy pink tube of her vagina, with the neck of her cervix visible at the end.

'What's that thing?' Colin whispered. 'Looks like an asshole.'

'Silence!' Billy commanded. 'This is a most delicate operation.'

Walter glanced uneasily at Janet, but she seemed not to have heard, still clutching her ankles with her eyes gently shut. There was no doubt she was reacting to her examination though, her mouth open with a strand of spittle hanging from her lower lip, and her nipples in taut erection. Billy released the speculum control, leaving Janet spread wide.

'Now, Janet,' he stated. 'It is necessary that we assess your exact temperature. To do this I will need to insert the thermometer in your asshole.'

Janet responded to the news of her coming anal penetration with a sob and a wink of the tight brown hole between her bum cheeks. Billy had produced the thermometer, and put the bulb to Janet's anus. Walter found himself smiling in dirty satisfaction as the girl's anus pushed in, then opened slowly around the little bulb, taking it, and closing on the stem. So often he had imagined sticking things up girls' bottoms, generally his cock, and he now had Janet, with a thermometer protruding obscenely from her anus, just inches in front of his face. In his pants, his cock was once more rock hard.

'A moment, Janet,' Billy stated, and stood back.

Janet was left, vagina stretched wide to the speculum, anus puckered tight around the thermometer shaft. Billy put his finger to his faceplate, indicating silence. From

158

his suit he produced a strangely elongated pair of forceps, and a camera. The camera he passed to Walter, before leaning close to Janet's bottom once more. Walter peered up the bright pink hole as Billy inserted the forceps, to touch on the pouting cervix head. Janet gave a little grunt, her cervix twitching. Billy touched again, and again her cervix twitched, the tiny central hole suddenly expanding and contracting as quickly.

'Weird!' Colin hissed.

Gently, Billy paused the rounded head of the forceps at the entrance to Janet's womb. She gasped, her cervix tightening, pouting suddenly, to tighten once more.

'No, stop!' she gasped suddenly. 'I can't take that, I really can't!'

'It is done, Janet,' Billy answered her, and nodded quickly to Walter.

'Is it?' Janet asked. 'Is it enough to say sorry?'

Walter and Billy shared a glance. Both shrugged.

'Remain still for a moment more, Janet,' Billy instructed. 'I must read your temperature.'

Walter had stepped back, and was fiddling with the camera mechanism. Billy also moved clear, allowing the light to play full on Janet's body, to show her penetrated vagina and anus, the broad white expanse of her naked bottom, her dangling breasts and her pretty face with the blonde pony-tail hanging down to one side. He blew out his breath, and pressed the camera button. At the click, Janet looked around.

'Oh, you didn't have to!' Janet exclaimed. 'You didn't need that. I'm sorry, and I'll do it.'

'Do what?' Colin asked.

'You know,' Janet answered, blushing. 'Now take this thing out of me, please?'

Billy moved forward, to ease the thermometer from Janet's anus, then to release the speculum. Walter watched as her hole closed, torn between disappointment because it was over, and expectation for what she seemed to be promising. Billy slid the speculum out, and Janet's vagina closed with a loud fart.

'Oops!' she said. 'I am sorry!'

She stood up, to stretch her limbs and rub at the muscles of her legs. The boys stood watching, Walter surprised by how calm she was, and how obviously excited, with a little smile on her face. As she turned to Billy she put her hands on her hips and pushed out her breasts.

'So how do you want me?' she asked.

Billy hesitated, but only for a moment.

'On all fours,' he ordered.

'Doggie style, wow!' Colin breathed, earning what would have been a dirty look from Billy.

Janet was blushing, but she went down, on to all fours as she had been told, with her magnificent bottom pushed out towards Billy, her ready sex and the brown area around her anus on plain view. She turned her head, to smile at Billy, then at Walter. Realising that she was really willing, Walter silently thanked Billy for making it easy to get their cocks out of the suits. Colin's already was, and it was hard, the red tips straining out from his prepuce. Janet saw it, and giggled. Billy was falling to his knees, even as he struggled to get his erect cock free of his suit. It came, and he settled it between Janet's open buttocks, to rut in her crease.

'Hey! That's dirty stuff!' she protested, and gasped as Billy's erection filled her vagina.

He began to fuck her, holding her by the hips and slamming into her body, to send ripples across the flesh of her bottom and set her breasts swinging. She was quickly moaning, and as Colin sank down by her head, she gave no resistance to taking his cock in her mouth. Walter also knelt, taking Janet's arm, to guide her hand to his cock. She adjusted her position, resting on one elbow as she took him in hand, tugging at his erection as she sucked on Colin and her body rocked to the rhythm of her fucking.

Walter was in heaven, his cock in the hand of a girl in nothing but her girdle and stockings, a girl they'd tricked into stripping, and into taking things in her vagina, even her anus. He reached out, to take hold of one big breast. He felt its weight, pinched the hard nipple, squeezed the fat, dangling globe of girl flesh, and in response she just tugged harder at his cock. He thought of all the times he'd fantasised over getting her topless. Now she was, and willingly, and doing all the dirty things he had so often thought about, and so hopelessly.

She moved, releasing Colin's cock from her mouth, to take Walter's in. He gasped, as her soft, wet mouth closed around his cock. It was like no pleasure he had ever known before, and as she began to suck on him he looked down. For one instant he took in the picture of her pretty, sensitive face with his penis stuck in her mouth, and he came again. Janet jerked back, squealing, but too late, the second spurt of come catching her full in the face. She cried out in shock and disgust, but Colin had grabbed her pony-tail, and immediately stuffed his erection back in her mouth. An instant later her cheeks blew out, her eyes came open in horrified consternation, and she jerked away, sperm erupting from her mouth, to splash among the dead leaves below her.

'You . . . you . . .' she managed, and broke off with a gasp as Billy thrust his cock hard into her body.

Her head went down as the fucking grew abruptly faster. She began to moan loudly, her mouth wide open, with the spunk dribbling slowly out. More hung from her nose and chin, thick white strands that shivered as she was fucked. Her pony-tail was shaking, her breasts bouncing and quivering in the leaf mould, now dirty with bits of soil and decaying matter.

Billy was moving furiously inside her, jamming himself in, harder and harder still. His mask came loose, and fell away, showing his face with his mouth wide and

161

his eyes fixed dementedly on Janet's spread bottom. Her head was down, her eyes closed, indifferent to everything but the cock in her body, gasping and moaning in her ecstasy. Walter watched, spellbound, still clutching his damp cock, as the blob of sperm hanging from Janet's nose broke, to fly away and catch in her pony-tail. Opposite him, Colin was already tugging at his cock.

Sure he could manage again, Walter reached out for Janet's discarded clothing, to fold her panties around his cock, and draping her bra over it, so that he was wanking into the big cup that normally held a breast. His eyes fixed on her wobbling, quivering flesh and he began to grow hard, his cock swelling in the soft panty material as he watched the girl who had been wearing them fucked. Suddenly Billy moaned. Walter began to wank harder, wondering if Janet was so excited that she'd let him fuck her, to put his cock actually in her hole, to lose his virginity to the most beautiful girl he knew, and with witnesses . . .

'I'm going to spunk!' Billy gasped. 'I'm going to spunk right up her dirty cunt!'

'No, Brad, no!' Janet squealed, and jerked forward.

Billy's cock came out of her vagina, erupting sperm even as he grabbed at it, to send a long, thick streamer out over Janet's bare bottom, soiling one fat cheek. The second went right in her crease, to lie between her buttocks and pool in the brown dimple of her anus. The third was weaker, no more than a blob, which hung from the tip of his cock until he wiped it away on her bottom.

'Brad, really!' she chided. 'You know to be careful! And as for you two! See what a mess you've made of my face! Now you've had your fun with me, all right?'

She had turned her head, and as she saw Billy her mouth came open in speechless horror. She screamed.

'Oh shit!' Colin swore, jumped up, and ran. Walter followed suit, frantically stuffing his penis back into his alien suit as he darted off between the trees.

Behind him, Janet's voice rose in furious remonstration, calling Billy a string of names Walter would never have imagined she knew. He ran on, not caring where he was going, with ferns and twigs lashing at his body. Only when he was surrounded by darkness did he stop, and sink to his knees, gasping for breath.

His hands went to his helmet, pushing it up, and off. A backward glance showed their light as a distant glimmer among the trees. Janet was still shouting, her voice was faint, but distinct, demanding to know where her panties and bra had gone. Only then did Walter realise that they were still clutched in his hand.

A grin spread over his face, only to disappear abruptly as he realised the probable consequences of his actions. Billy would tell, he was certain, but then, Janet would hardly tell her father, for fear of his belt, or Brad, or anyone . . .

Once more the grin spread over his face, only to vanish again. Lights had sprung up in front of him, two brilliant white beams, dazzling his eyes. He put a hand up, shading his face, shock, then fear welling up as a tall, misshapen figure appeared in stark black outline against the light.

Walter's jaw began to shake as the being stepped closer, extending one bony arm. A grotesque head was revealed, a high dome, with great slanting eyes, a tiny mouth, twin slits for nostrils. Walter's mouth came open in fear, hot urine gushing out into his underpants as he wet himself. He cowered back, his hand going to his mouth in raw terror, stuffing in the crotch of Janet's panties. The alien lifted its arms, to take hold of its head, and pull it slowly off.

'Hey, you freak, what you doing with my girl's panties?' Brad demanded.

Succubus

Aloysius Rheingold grasped his penis more firmly as the beautiful young girl bent across the examination table. Her hospital gown rose, exposing ripe buttocks, with just a hint of nubile cunt peeping out between. She looked back, nervous, vulnerable, her pale eyes wide and moist, full at the doctor as he raised the syringe above her naked bottom, and stabbed.

As the needle pierced the girl's flesh, Aloysius came, semen exploding from the tip of his cock to splash over the hairy expanse of his gut. His eyes stayed wide, fixed on the girl's full pink cheeks as more white fluid bubbled out over his hand, to run down into his pubic hair. His whole body had gone tense, his spine arching in ecstasy, his chest tight, and tighter still, until he cried out, the pleasure turning to pain, to agony, his vision red, then black.

The video ran on, the picture expanding to show the girl injected and the needle withdrawn, then the puncture mark in the girl's flesh, with a single drop of blood welling slowly out. Slumped down into the armchair, Aloysius Rheingold still stared.

Her injection complete, the girl stayed bent as a plaster was applied to her bottom. She stood to smooth down the hospital gown in an attempt to cover herself. It was a pointless process, as the gown was not so short that the tuck of her cheeks was left peeping out from beneath. It also tied at the back, leaving an enticing slice of creamy flesh on show, including the crease of her bottom.

Abandoning her efforts to make herself decent, she turned, thanked the doctor, and stepped from the television screen. Aloysius could only watch, open-mouthed as she pulled herself free. Her body distorted briefly, twisting and enlarging, but returned to shape as she stepped onto the carpet. She bent, to turn the video off and incidentally provide the same glorious display of bare bottom he had so recently come over. Now he merely made a gurgling noise in his throat.

'There we are,' she said sweetly. 'That was fun, wasn't it?'

'Yes,' he managed. 'What . . . what happened?'

'You had a heart attack,' she said. 'You're dead.'

'Dead!'

'Dead. Too much furious wanking, I'm afraid, not to mention the cigars, the port, and you do weigh twenty-four stone. You were in no condition to go tossing off over girls' bums. I mean, don't think I'm not flattered, but careful, or rather, you should have been more careful. Too late now.'

'But I'm not dead! How can I be? I'm talking to you.'

'A girl who stepped out of a porno video? Be realistic. That sort of thing doesn't happen when you're alive, you know. I apologise for that, actually. It was a bit overdramatic, but it's such a sweet body. Did you know she was seventeen when she made that video? Such a naughty girl!'

Aloysius began to stammer out a new question. The girl put her finger to her lips for silence, leaning forward as she made the gesture, to show two small breasts, hanging down inside the inadequate gown.

'I shall explain,' she went on, extending her hand. 'First, let me introduce myself. I'm Saritu, a succubus, which is a demoness of a sort, the sexy sort, but I

165

imagine you already know that. Normally I bring dirty dreams to tempt men into the sin of lust, women too, sometimes. For now, I'd like you to think of me as your personal guide. As I say, you are dead, and I'm afraid you have been a very naughty boy, so no heaven for you. Still, who needs it, eh? All that hymn singing, and the people you meet! Dull as ditch water, darling, dull as ditch water. Now, where we're going, that's much more interesting!'

He had taken her extended hand, more by instinct than intent, and now rose as she pulled. As she stepped towards the door he followed, numb with shock. As they reached the door he glanced back, to see his own body still in the chair, naked, right hand, genitals and belly still splashed with sperm.

Saritu opened the door, but not on to the comfortable and familiar hallway he had expected. Instead there was a rock tunnel, lit red-orange by flames. A breeze sprang up at his back, fluttering Saritu's gown as she drew him into the tunnel. Fear gripped him, and he tried to pull back. She turned her head, to shake out her mane of black hair, and smiled.

'Don't be scared,' she said sweetly. 'If you'd been very bad it wouldn't be me who'd come to collect you. Now come along. I may be small, but I'm still a demoness, and you wouldn't want to make me get cross, would you?'

There was unspoken violence in her voice, and her eyes had flashed briefly red. Aloysius followed hastily, and Saritu's face became innocent once more. Still holding his hand, she led him along the tunnel. Her tread was light and merry, almost a skip, also fast. He was forced to hurry forward, over smooth worn stone, the warm breeze always at his back, always down, until the tunnel opened to a chamber.

Saritu stopped, to give a mocking curtsy to a squat red creature only vaguely human in form, with the haunches and hooves of a goat, huge, bloated genitals, a bulging stomach and stubby horns. In response to Saritu's curtsy he took hold of his cock, to jerk it in her direction.

'Patience, I'm busy,' she responded, 'but you do like my gown, don't you? Isn't it cute? Look at the back, you can see my bum slit.'

She twirled to show off her rear view, ending with her buttocks stuck out towards the creature, her back pulled in, her gown held wide to show not just her slit, but the full round ball of her bottom. The creature pulled rapidly at his cock, which grew, hardened, and erupted a great wad of sperm over her naked buttocks. Saritu giggled prettily and stuck her tongue out, then stood upright once more, to leave the creature's semen dribbling slowly down over her buttocks and legs.

'Enough nonsense, Oobass,' she chided. 'I've brought one in for you, Aloysius Rheingold.'

'Pit of Gluttonous Fornicators, the section between the spankers and sodomites,' the creature answered, jerking one clawed thumb over its shoulder towards the red-lit mouth of another tunnel.

'I thought I'd show him some of the private hells first?' Saritu said.

'Suck my goat cock,' Oobass responded.

'Excuse me a moment,' Saritu addressed Aloysius.

She got to her knees, putting her sperm-smeared bottom on view again as the hem of her gown lifted stickily from her soiled flesh. Her sex also came on show, the lips of her vulva wide and ready around a wet vagina, her anus a dirty brown star deep between her cheeks.

Without hesitation, she had taken Oobass' grotesque penis in her mouth, and was sucking. Her cheeks were blown out, and she was making swallowing motions in her throat, making Aloysius suspect that he was coming continuously. The expression of demented glee on his face suggested the same.

The goat creature began to wank at his cock. Saritu's cheeks bulged fatter still, and Aloysius' suspicion was proven when a great gout of sperm suddenly erupted from between her lips and his cock shaft. More sprayed from her nose, into the thick black tangle of his pubic hair, until it was smeared liberally over her lower face and dripping from his balls. Still she sucked, and Aloysius saw that her vagina was leaking juice down over her sex, while her anus had opened to show a wet, pink centre. Only when Oobass took her by the hair to pull her off did she stop.

'Enough,' he declared.

He wiped his cock with a handful of her hair and let go. Saritu swallowed and rocked back on to her heels. Her lower face was plastered with sperm, and a long streamer still hung from one nostril, until her sharp red tongue flicked out to catch it and draw it into her mouth. She stood, and Aloysius saw that her belly had become a hard, round ball from the spunk she had swallowed.

'Where are you taking him?' Oobass demanded.

'Lustful Avarice,' she answered, 'and perhaps the Passages of Denial.'

Oobass made a face, expressing amusement, perhaps contempt, then began to pick his nose.

'Come along,' Saritu said, beckoning to Aloysius. 'I shall show you what happens to really naughty boys and girls, the ones who devote their whole lives to lust.'

She stepped towards a passage, Aloysius following. As before, they entered a tunnel running through solid rock and lit by flames that seemed to spring from nowhere. The breeze still blew at his back, and there was noise, echoes of moans and sobs, punctuated by the occasional distant scream or half-heard voices.

Saritu walked fast, and as she went she cleaned herself, using a finger to scrape sperm from her face, neck, bottom and legs, which she transferred to her mouth. Aloysius watched her, his emotions slowly growing, of dread, but also of lust. So often he had imagined girls as dirty as her, girls who would eat sperm with relish, and suck cock until they had to be pulled away.

'I know what you're thinking, Aloysius,' she remarked, wiggling her bottom as she spoke. 'You'd like to fuck me, wouldn't you? You like to do all sorts of rude things to me first too. You'd like to make me suck your cock the way I sucked Oobass, yes? And you'd like to spank my little bottom, and bugger it. Wouldn't that be nice, Aloysius, with your nasty big penis stuck right up my dirty bottom hole? Well, maybe I'll let you, but not yet. Here, look.'

They had reached a side passage, and as they approached Aloysius saw that it was closed off by a massive iron grille. Within, a girl knelt on the floor, naked, and chained by the neck to the grille. Her body was impossibly luscious, almost like an erotic cartoon, with a tiny waist, huge, firm breasts, and a round, cheeky bottom on tapered thighs. She was kneeling, her full red lips wide around the fat, hard cock of the man seated before her. Beyond, a line of men stretched away down a tunnel, to the limit of vision.

'What did she do?' Aloysius demanded. 'Was she a prostitute? And who are the men? Not her clients?'

'Not a prostitute, no,' Saritu answered, 'not even a she. In that sweet little body is trapped the soul of one Solomon Daniels.'

'The Porn Baron?'

'The very same. In life he had a motto "Blow Job, or No Job". Models for his magazines and newspapers, strippers and lap-dancers in his clubs, even some of his receptionists and secretaries. All of them had to go through the same routine – into his office, the door locked, breasts out and down on her knees, his cock in her mouth, sucked off and the spunk swallowed down.

The men are the ones who bought his products and visited his clubs, and so he pays for his sins even as he pays back those he exploited. It's an appropriate punishment, don't you think?'

'But how many men are there? How many girls did he push into sucking him?'

'The girls ran into hundreds. There are millions of men. Some are upstairs and mostly too holy to drop in, the hypocrites. Most come whenever they get a break from their own torments. Each is entitled to a blow-job for every product of his they ever bought.'

'That must run into millions.'

'Billions,' Saritu corrected him. 'Think of all that spunk!'

'And afterwards?'

'Oh, he has eternity in Avarice, looking for coins in a heap of shit, I think.'

'That hardly seems fair. All he was trying to do was make money.'

'Believe me, the Man hates people who liked to make money. I'll take you to see the Pit of Bulls and Bears sometime. The Bull demons are a great fuck, the Bears too, all that hair, and the biggest cocks . . .'

'Eternal damnation, for making money? That's not justice!'

Saritu shrugged, waved to the man who had just come in the damned soul's mouth and walked on. Aloysius followed, his gaze lingering as another man took his place on the chair, erect cock at the ready. Aloysius turned away with a shudder.

There was another opening ahead, closed off with a grille as before. Within, a naked man lay chained across a crude stool, shuddering to the thrusts of a huge, crimson demon whose penis was embedded in his rectum.

'Some big-shot pimp,' Saritu said dismissively as she passed. 'They take up most of the space around here, those that aren't deeper.'

170

'Deeper?'

'Deeper in hell. You go as deep as your worst sin. This is nothing, strictly outer circle. The demons from the lower pits are terribly superior. Still, we have a few imaginative little tortures. I'll show you some of the Frustrators presently. Hi, Mourdrath.'

She had waved to a demon who was cheerfully buggering another pimp, and walked on, stopping at the next grille. Aloysius cautiously peered within. Three occupants met his eye, all female. One was naked, sitting on a stool with a book in one hand and the other hand between her thighs, masturbating a plump, well-furred cunt. Beside her stood a pile of other books, all dog-eared, each cover displaying a coyly erotic tableau. The second woman was bent across a desk, her long, bright hair trailing to the ground. She was dressed in a smart office suit, but had been interfered with. The neat jacket and crisp white blouse were open, and knotted behind her back to leave her arms helpless. Her bra was up, spilling out two heavy breasts on to the desk. Her skirt was up, rucked around her waist, the white silk panties in a tangle at the level of her stocking tops. Behind her stood the third female, a demoness, not unlike Saritu, who was applying a wicked-looking cane to the woman's already well-beaten bottom.

Saritu and the other demoness exchanged nods, as one professional to another.

'Who are the women?' Aloysius demanded.

'The one masturbating wrote pornographic novels,' Saritu explained. 'She has to read each one aloud, to the total number of volumes sold. The other one gets to act out the fantasies with demons. She was the editor.'

They moved on, past yet another buggered pimp. At the next opening Saritu ran her finger along the bars of the grille and put a deliberate wiggle into her walk. Aloysius glanced in as he passed, to find a tall, thin man almost invisible among mounds of paper. He was reading, his fingers clutching the stubs of red and blue crayons, his face set in an expression of uncontrollable anguish.

'Another pornographer,' Saritu explained.

'What's he doing?'

'Reading submissions, one for every person who ever read a book he brought out.'

'That doesn't sound so bad. Why does he look like that?'

'Every single one has exactly the same plot.'

'Shut up!' the editor screamed suddenly. 'Can't you see I'm trying to concentrate!'

'Temper, temper,' Saritu chided, moving on.

'What about the rapists, the sex murderers?' Aloysius asked.

'Oh, you won't find them here, darling,' Saritu replied. 'They're far deeper. Even ordinary murderers get a lake of boiling blood, but for –'

'I don't want to know!' he said hastily.

'No? Some of the tortures are ever so clever. Still, I promised to show you some of the Frustrators. They're down here, past the Pit of Immoderate Masturbators.'

She turned down a side passage. As Aloysius entered it he caught a new and curious noise, like that of a busy public swimming pool heard from outside, but mixed with noises of human ecstasy and pain. It grew louder, until the passage opened out above a great pit, so that Aloysius had to press himself to the wall for fear of falling. Beside him, Saritu was smiling.

He looked down, at what he first took to be a great mass of writhing worms, far below, indistinct through rising steam. Only as he looked more closely did he realise that he was looking at human beings, thousands upon thousands, naked and squirming in a sea of white fluid. Most were male, but there were many women among them, and all were clutching at their genitals, jerking, rubbing, or licking and sucking at each other.

Some had fingers in their mouths or up their bottoms, others were in tangled knots, legs, arms, buttocks, breasts, heads, protruding at every angle, and all covered in the sticky white substance.

'But ... but everyone masturbates, don't they?' he demanded weakly, his eyes fixed on the scene beneath him.

'Not the holy ones,' Saritu explained. 'Abstention causes a religious ecstasy. Still, once a week is acceptable. Any more, and bang, or rather, splat.'

'It's spunk, isn't it?' he asked. 'That white stuff.'

'Spunk and cunt juice,' Saritu corrected him. 'There are about thirty per cent women down there, although most of the dirty girls go in Fornicators.'

'Fornicators. Where I'm going?'

'No. Fornicators is the main pit of the Circle of Lust. You were a pervert and a glutton, so you're in a specialist pit, Gluttonous Fornicators, and a subsection of that.'

'What happens?'

'You'll see. Don't be impatient.'

She moved on, light-footed as ever. Aloysius inched his way along the narrow ledge, back to the wall, eyes on his feet, trying hard not to look at the squirming mass of flesh beneath him. Ahead, Saritu had moved to a new tunnel, from which two others split off at low angles. She waited, watching the men and women writhe in their own juice with a pleased smile. At last Aloysius gained the lip of the tunnel junction.

'The Passages of Denial,' she said. 'The left goes to the Pit of Female Self Denial, which is for women who died virgin beyond the age of menopause, nuns excepted, or some of them anyway. They lead strings of apes, very randy apes. In the centre is the Pit of Male Self Denial, which is empty. We want the right, the Frustrators.'

'Who are?'

'Those who denied others sexual pleasure, of course.'

'I'd have thought that was a way to get into heaven, if lust is a sin.'

'They mostly thought the same. Here, for instance.'

She had come to a grille, and Aloysius peered inside, to find no rock cavern, but a large room, walled with mirrors and furnished in dark wood and crimson velvet. A stage occupied the length of one wall, on which a number of succubi danced, either nude around poles, or stripping from elaborate costumes. At the far side was a long bar, behind which two more succubi stood, topless, with furry rabbit ears extending from their heads.

Nearer, on an open floor, stood tables and chairs, with alcoves beyond. More succubi moved among them, naked but for the ridiculous ears and round fluffy tails projecting out from above their bottoms. To one side a screen showed a pair of firm, black buttocks pumping between spread, milk-white thighs. People occupied the majority of the chairs, fat, sleazy-looking men, shifty-eyed in their dirty mackintoshes, and a single woman, neat, prim in a tweed two-piece, her face set in fear and disgust.

'Who are they?' Aloysius asked.

'Incubi, mainly,' Saritu answered. 'The men that is. The only soul is the woman.'

'Just one? It seems a lot of demons for one soul. What did she do?'

'Oh, she was special,' Saritu explained. 'Don't you recognise her?'

'No. Should I?'

'You'd know her name. Forty years campaigning against every form of sexual expression you care to name, nudity too, even the most innocent naturism. Come in.'

'Can we?'

'I can do as I like.'

Saritu produced a key apparently from nowhere, and pushed it into a hole in the grille, which slid wide as she pulled. The demons within greeted her with casual salutes, one or two calling out rude suggestions, to which she replied either by wiggling her bottom or sticking out her tongue. The woman got up as Saritu ushered Aloysius in, and walked towards them, her face a mask of fury.

'Who are you?' she demanded. 'I want to see someone in charge, immediately!'

'I doubt that,' Saritu answered. 'I doubt that very much. Now why don't you just sit down and enjoy the show, Wilma?'

'Wilma? You're Wilma Morehouse?' Aloysius asked.

'Yes I am,' the woman snapped. 'And who might you be? Are you management?'

'No, I'm –' Aloysius began.

'Aloysius Rheingold,' Saritu cut in. 'Anal obsessive, spanker, sodomist and more.'

Morehouse gave a haughty sniff and stepped away from Aloysius. Saritu laughed and continued towards the bar, Aloysius coming behind, and after a moment, Wilma Morehouse.

'I don't know who you are, young lady,' Morehouse spoke, 'but I would appreciate it if you would communicate my presence here to the proper authorities. I shouldn't be here. I was a campaigner against this sort of thing, a prominent campaigner!'

'I know,' Saritu answered.

'Then why am I here? There's some sort of mistake, isn't there? I don't belong in a place like this, surely you can see that?'

Saritu didn't answer her. They had reached the bar, and the succubi tending it had come forward, to kiss Saritu, open-mouthed, hands briefly stealing to breasts before they pulled apart. One turned to the row of glittering bottles behind the bar, to fill two glasses with drinks, one amber, the other a deep red.

'Port,' Saritu said, passing the second glass to Aloysius.

He sniffed, by instinct, swirled the port in the glass and sniffed again, then sipped. It was port, and finer than any of the vintages he had drunk in life, rich and heavy, full of the scents and flavours of fruits and earth, and lingering on his palate long after he had swallowed.

'Magnificent!' he stated. 'May I dare ask if I'll be able to drink this stuff on a regular basis?'

'Not until you've served your time,' Saritu answered. 'Then you can apply for a post as an incubus.'

'I can become a demon?'

'Yes. There's a period of training first, of course, and –'

'Will you kindly pay attention to me!' Wilma Morehouse snapped. 'I wish you to speak to the proper authorities concerning my presence in this dreadful place, immediately!'

'Kiss my arse.'

'I beg your pardon!'

'Kiss my arse, I said. If you want me to speak to my Lord, you've got to kiss my arse first.'

'I shall do no such thing! Disgusting!'

'Suit yourself.'

'Young lady, I am not accustomed –'

'To kissing girls' arses? No, I don't suppose you are. You should be, seeing where you are. You can play with the demons, you know.'

'I have never heard such a filthy suggestion in my life!'

'I bet you did.'

'Enough! You will put down that drink and go to the authorities on my behalf, at once. Do you hear me?'

'Yes. Kiss my arse.'

The woman's face was red with anger, her lips pursed tight, her eyes blazing. Saritu paid no attention whatever, sipping her drink and watching a fellow succubus who was in the act of stripping out of an abbreviated sailor suit. Abruptly, Wilma Morehouse dipped down, to plant the lightest possible of pecks on Saritu's hip. She rose, humiliation now warring with the anger in her expression.

'What I would have liked,' Saritu said coolly, 'was a big, wet smacker, right on my dirty bumhole. Still, it's too much to expect you to know how to kiss a girl's arse properly, isn't it? I'll speak to someone.'

'To someone in charge?' Morehouse demanded.

'To Satan himself,' Saritu promised.

'And promptly,' Morehouse ordered.

'Within hours,' Saritu said, 'just as soon as Aloysius here is safely in his pit. Drink up, Aloysius.'

Aloysius hastily took the rest of his port into his mouth, holding it to savour the exquisite taste as they left. Only when they were well down the passage did he swallow, even then concentrating on the slow fade of the flavours until at last they were gone.

'Are you really going to intervene with Satan?' he asked.

'What, and spend the next thousand years stuck up his backside?' Saritu answered. 'No, I was merely tormenting her.'

'And should she be there?'

'Of course. She caused an immense amount of suffering, across four decades and after. The consequences of her repressions still linger now. She will be in that bar until every striptease and lewd performance she prevented has been completed, also those she prevented being seen by each individual who would have gone but for her actions. Once finished, she will be further punished, for the hardship she caused by denying work to erotic dancers, models, actresses, and for the losses of club owners, bouncers, shop-keepers, printers, photographers, distributors and many, many more. More follows, until a full requital has been made. Even when finished here in Lust she is to be sent down to Envy.'

'Envy?'

'The driving force behind her actions. The Frustrators usually go there after we've finished with them.'

'I see. So if people like her don't get to heaven, who does?'

'The secret of entry to heaven,' Saritu stated, 'is to pray a lot, not earn much money and mind your own business.'

Aloysius nodded, pondering her response. They had moved well down the passage, which was darker than the others, and colder. There were no more flames, but a dull blue-green light seemed to come from algae growing on the now damp walls.

'Some of our nastier customers,' Saritu stated, kicking a grille to evoke a moan of anguish from within. 'Look here.'

She crossed to a different grille. It was dim in the chamber, and Aloysius had to stare to make out the form within at all clearly. It was a man, naked and chained upright in a high-backed chair, iron bands circling his neck, waist, limbs and crotch. In front of him a succubus was dancing in slow, sinuous movements, to emphasise her heavy chest and rounded haunches. Aloysius could smell her sex.

'The inventor of a breakfast cereal,' Saritu explained, 'although that was not his sin. Note the little cage in which his cock and balls are imprisoned. Within are spikes, which drive into his flesh as he becomes aroused. It was his own invention, designed to cure the evil of masturbation. Thousands of boys were made to wear them, often resulting in lasting damage, both physical and mental.'

'How long is he to be here?' Aloysius asked.

'For ever,' Saritu answered, and spat.

She turned and walked quickly back the way they had come. Aloysius followed, raising the courage to ask a question as he went. When they reached the Pit of Masturbators again he spoke.

'I can understand these punishments,' he said, 'some of them anyway. But why me? What have I done to compare with their sins?'

'To compare?' Saritu answered. 'Little, or you would have earned a private Hell. As I said, your sin was essentially your obsession with girls' bottoms.'

'But girls' bottoms are meant to excite men! It's the primary sexual trigger, to a man, a woman's rear view, and if God –'

'Ssh!' Saritu interrupted. 'Never say that name, not here! We say the Man.'

'Oh, right,' Aloysius went on, glancing nervously at the stone roof of the tunnel. 'What I was saying is, if he, the Man, designed humans so that the sight of the female's bottom triggers lust in the male, why are we punished for obeying that lust?'

'Temptation,' Saritu answered. 'My speciality. You're supposed to resist it. You never even tried. Besides, liking girls' bottoms is one thing. Spanking them is another, not to mention sticking needles in the cheeks, buggering them, and other insertions – thermometers, pessaries, enema hoses, an assortment of vegetables, pens, twice, a pork sausage once. Then there was the ice stick, up that poor little carol singer you invited in to get warm. You licked it out as it melted, didn't you? Now that's going to cost.'

'Why? She loved it!'

'Sodomy, perversion, excessive lust, irreligious sex . . . Besides, most of it came out in her panties on the way home. She wasn't so happy about that.'

'But the others? All were willing, at least.'

'Fairly willing. You were a very persuasive man, Aloysius. Do you remember Jane Palmer, at your college?'

'Jane? Yes, a lovely girl. We were together for months, until I left. I'd have married her –'

'She was a virgin when you met, eighteen and innocent. She'd never seen a man's cock. By the time

179

you broke up she was not only no longer a virgin, but obsessed with her own anus. She's still alive, and to this day she can only come with something in her anus, preferably a cock. When she masturbates her first thought is to insert the handle of her hairbrush or a dildo if one is to hand. She appears on a deck of playing cards, available in Greece, with a cucumber stuck up her bottom. Did you know that?'

'No,' Aloysius admitted.

'And there are others,' Saritu went on. 'Many of the girls you buggered were sore and waddling for days, which not only hurts but is very embarrassing. Then there were the spankings and so forth. Can you imagine going into a changing room at a sauna or a gym with your bum covered in cane marks or smack bruises? Highly embarrassing, I assure you. And let's not forget some of your other little peccadilloes. How about your collection of panties and the girls who've had to walk home bare under their skirts? But this is irrelevant. You are here to requite your excess lust. Surely you don't deny that? Aloysius Rheingold, the man who sodomised forty-three different women, who indulged his strange medical perversions with a further twenty-two, who spanked a hundred and six, including seven made to line up in a row dressed as pixies? Need I go on?'

Aloysius shook his head.

'Then let there be no more complaints,' Saritu finished. 'Now come along.'

She moved out on to the ledge, skipping neatly to the far side and waiting as Aloysius made his careful way across. On reaching the far side she took his hand, to lead him back to the chamber where Oobass sat, now meditatively scratching his balls as he consulted a ledger taller than himself. They entered another passage, that which Oobass had first indicated, Saritu walking faster, and not stopping at the various grilles, from behind which came moans which might equally have been pleasure or misery, also wet, smacking sounds. Aloysius tried to look, but only glimpsed figures, twisted in erotic congress or in the throes of some less easily identifiable torment.

At last they reached the end of the tunnel, a ledge, this time broad, and overlooking a great pit. Forcing himself to look, Aloysius saw that as with the Pit of Masturbators, the floor was crowded with human beings, both male and female. All were naked, and all at least plump, some definitely fat, a few huge, great shapeless mounds of blubber. Some sat alone, watching those around them, or simply brooding. More were engaged in sexual acts, those directly below spanking one another, or applying canes and whips supplied by the few crimson demons that walked among them.

'This way,' Saritu announced, nodding to the left-hand ledge.

Aloysius moved to obey, looking down all the while, with rising hope. Further in the direction indicated by Saritu, the couples appeared to be engaged in sodomy rather than spanking, or both. One voluptuous black woman was on her knees, squatting over a man whose cock was pushed well into her anus, while another man slapped at her buttocks with a paddle. Nearer, a flesh-white girl was dancing to whip strokes as a circle of men masturbated themselves to readiness around her. Saritu stopped directly above the little group.

'It doesn't seem too terrible,' Aloysius ventured, peering down.

'It's not,' Saritu agreed, 'not by our standards anyway. The thing is that, once down there, you will find yourself in not a male, but a female body. You must then persuade the men, who were originally female, to sodomise and beat you, until the total of sodomies and beatings you yourself dished out is exceeded. Your personal total is four hundred and twelve sodomies, one thousand three hundred and thirty-two spankings and various other applications of corporal punishment. When you reach your total plus one you will return to male form. I'm to collect you for a series of enemas and medically related perversions, so I shall see you then, unless you'd care to accept my earlier offer and bugger me. It'll be your last as the male participant for a very long time.'

Aloysius had been looking down into the pit with mounting horror, and swallowed as she finished speaking. She was standing, one hip cocked out provocatively, her pose both enticing and taunting. He glanced back down, to where a fat girl with rich olive skin and huge breasts was being buggered as her chest was whipped.

'The other thing,' Saritu remarked, 'is your punishment for gluttony. If you don't stay active you get fatter and fatter and fatter. Finally you won't be able to move, much less offer yourself for sodomy. Escape is difficult.'

Again Aloysius glanced down at the huge mounds of blubber from the top of which human arms and heads protruded. His fear had begun to rise steeply, and suddenly he was determined to do anything to delay his descent, even wondering if he could throw Saritu down into the pit and escape.

'Don't even think about it,' Saritu said, nodding to something behind him.

Aloysius turned, to find a huge crimson demon blocking the ledge, trident in one hand, engorged cock in the other.

'Do try,' Saritu said, coming forward. 'I would like to be buggered by you. Your depravity is impressive, you know, among the best. Very few achieve four hundred sodomies, or pass the hundred mark for spanked girls.'

Her hand had closed on his cock, stroking and tugging gently. She came close, her flesh squashing against him, warm and resilient, her breasts pressing to his chest, her lips touching his neck, to kiss, and nibble. Her scent was strong in his nose, musky, feminine, with just a hint of earth. Despite himself he began to react, his cock swelling in her hand. She made a little purring noise and sank down, to take it in her mouth.

Aloysius shut his eyes as his penis swelled in Saritu's mouth. He was going to get hard, he knew it, and then he would bugger her, as he had so many other girls, and then . . .

'Now, now,' she chided, rising to kiss his nose. 'No bad thoughts. Take me.'

She turned, bent, her gown lifting and parting to show off the glorious globe of her bottom, naked and spread. The sticking plaster that covered her injection mark was still in place, and there was still colour in her buttocks from where she had been spanked to make her accept her inoculation. Between her thighs, her sex was moist and ready.

Her anus showed as a dark spot at the centre, sweaty and moist. It exuded a rich tang, making his nostrils twitch as he got behind her, to press his cock head to the little dirty ring. She moaned, her hole opening, as soft and ready as a mouth. His cock went in, pushed easily up, her hole receptive, yet tight, her passage slimy yet firm. He could feel her heat, and soft, mushy interior of her rectum, the contents squashing out around his penis as he sank himself in her to the balls.

Saritu groaned as Aloysius began to bugger her, a low, contented sound. She was gripping her knees, bent double, her bottom pushed out to make the best of the rounded shape, her back curved, her head back in ecstasy. He pumped hard, taking her by the hips, his cock squashing in the hot mush of her insides, faster, and faster still. He cried out, teeth gritted, struggling to control himself but incapable. His cock erupted into her gut, jerking again and again as he pumped her full of sperm to the sound of her delighted squeals and his own laboured grunting.

'I've come,' he sobbed. 'I've come.'

'I know,' she answered. 'That was beautiful. Now come on, willy out, let me clean you up, and in you go.'

Aloysius pulled slowly back, his cock easing from Saritu's anus. The little hole closed as his head left it, to squeeze out a dribble of spunk, which ran slowly down over her sex, and opened once more, to reveal the rich red tube of her rectum. He stepped back, close to the edge, as she swung round and knelt at his feet, opening her mouth for his cock. He sighed as she began to suck, her soft lips moving on his shaft, her tongue rubbing on the underside, lapping up her own mess. He closed his eyes, wondering if his cock would harden again as she sucked and lapped, sucked and lapped, and pushed.

Aloysius Rheingold screamed as he toppled over the edge of the pit. Every muscle in his body had jerked in response, and to his horror he realised that his cock had come free in Saritu's mouth, even as he heard her demented laughter from above him. He hit, his body jerking to the impact, again, and again, the flames of hell wheeling above his head, red, with the mocking face of the succubus above his own, still with her hospital gown on, but larger, also a hat.

'I've got a pulse!' a voice called. 'We've got him back. His eyes are opening.'

The nurse bending over him smiled.

Princess

Three sacks lay on the black and white chequerboard of the courtyard, at the edge of a broad pool of oil. From the sewn neck of each sack protruded a head, female, young and distinctly unhappy. All three were similar, their features soft and round, with small mouths, pert noses and large, pale eyes. Two were tawny-haired, the third darker. Within the coarse sacks, nothing could be seen of their bodies, except where a rounded haunch or the curve of a breast pressed to the material, showing that they were naked. It was also evident that their hands had been tied behind their backs. A coloured sash circled each sack, tied around the girls' waists; deep red, mustard ochre and white. Each girl looked back at the dais above them, showing fear, expectation, hatred. On the dais sat a group of nobles, the Princess Ymaea Evine-y-Dactor at their centre, robed in gold, indifferent to the emotions of the sack girls.

'I need a portent,' the Princess remarked. 'Count Naidrhac, you're clever. Give me a portent.'

The young man she had addressed bowed deeply, then threw a worried glance at the palace behind them and the jungle slopes beyond and to both sides. High on the hillside a flight of brilliant scarlet birds erupted from a stand of trees, to twist, twist once more and settle as suddenly as they had started up.

'There is your portent, Serenity,' he said quickly, 'a spray of fruit birds. Red, surely, cannot fail to win.'

185

'Red then,' the Princess declared. 'Ten pieces.'

Other bets were called, exclusively on yellow and white. A tall, sharp-faced man nodded to a captain, who in turned signalled three guards forward, each bearing a long firesting. The prods were applied to the girls in the sacks, the hot jolts sending them into spasms of pain, to the delight of the Princess and her courtiers. Desperate to escape the firestings, the girls squirmed forward, bucking and twisting in their sacks in an effort to gain purchase on the slippery marble flags.

Again the firestings were applied, to the bulges where the girls' bottoms pressed to the sacking. Again the girls writhed and twisted in their pain, slithering in the oil, rolling and kicking in their desperation. One especially violent wriggle sent the white-sashed girl over the edge of the courtyard, squealing in shock and pain as she bumped down the steps, to land in a muddy ditch at the bottom. Convulsed with laughter, the Princess was forced to clutch the arm of her throne to prevent herself falling.

A third time the firestings were applied, gently for the yellow-sashed girl, with full force for the red. Yellow jerked in pain, rolling desperately away, red going into a frantic, kicking spasm, but barely moving. Quickly, the guard prodded again, harder still, but in response the girl gave a single convulsion and lay still. Yellow, still conscious, wriggled herself over the finishing line. There was immediate silence among the nobles, broken by the Princess.

'Stupid!' she snapped, stamping her foot. 'Stupid, stupid, stupid!'

'If I may make remark, Serenity,' a tall man said, bending close to her ear, 'there is little doubt that your selection would have won had it not been for the overzealous attentions of the guard.'

'You are right, Lord Hrapit,' she answered. 'He's a fool, but she should have tried harder for me. Strip him, tie them in a sack together and throw them somewhere nasty.'

'The midden, Serenity?' Hrapit suggested. 'Or perhaps the town cesspit?'

'How should I possibly know?' she answered. 'Either will do. And Count Naidrhac, fifty lashes . . . no, one hundred, you stupid little man. Take them away.'

The three were dragged off, the count begging for mercy, the guard stolid, the girl still unconscious. Another nobleman, in an elaborate gown of gold and brilliant green, made a sweeping bow to the Princess.

'Serenity,' he declared, 'may I be the first to assure you that in view of the misfortune attendant on that foolish slattern failing to secure your deserved victory, I shall be making no claims upon your purse.'

'Naturally not,' she answered. 'How could you even think such a thing? Fifty lashes.'

The nobleman went pale, and began to babble as he too was dragged away.

'My morning is quite spoiled,' the Princess remarked. 'I've a mind to have you all flogged, unless you stop being so stupid.'

'There is a supplicant, Serenity,' Hrapit said quickly, bending forward. 'The impresario Braidic Udahl wishes to present you with a gift in the hope of mitigation of his branding.'

'Braidic Udahl? Who is he?'

'A person of no consequence, Serenity,' Hrapit went on. 'Naturally there is no reason you should recall him. He was responsible for the entertainment last week. You ordered him branded on the soles of his feet.'

'I don't remember. What is his gift?'

'It is most unusual, Serenity, a man-ape, apparently trained to the most droll antics.'

'Yes. I shall see it.'

Hrapit stood and clapped his hands. Immediately a curtain was drawn back, to reveal a portly man in red and green harlequinade, a chain in his hand, which led back to the man-ape. It was large, almost twice the height of the man, and covered in shaggy grey fur, except for its face and buttocks, both of which showed bare skin of a brilliant turquoise blue. It sported a great bulbous nose, so large that it hung down below the creature's mouth. The Princess Ymaea laughed, a sound immediately echoed by her courtiers.

'You do me great honour, Resplendent Serenity,' Braidic Udahl stated, bowing low once more.

'I accept your gift,' she answered. 'Your punishment is rescinded. Now go away.'

Braidic Udahl retreated, backwards, bowing repeatedly, until he reached the edge of the platform, whereupon he fled down the steps. He had dropped the chain, and the great grey man-ape remained, scratching placidly at its blue backside. The Princess watched it for a moment, giggled and turned to Hrapit.

'Wait until this afternoon,' she said, 'then have the man Udahl brought up here for his branding. Oh, and have his buttocks done too.'

'Most amusing, Serenity,' Hrapit replied. 'Your wit is exceeded only by your beauty, and both are unsurpassed. Sadly I suspect that even as we speak he hurries for the harbour. Your reputation for humour is well established.'

She laughed, then spoke again, looking at the man-ape.

'What do you suppose it does?'

'It is said to perform dances, Serenity,' he answered, 'in comic imitation of modern styles.'

'I shouldn't like that,' she said. 'How could I execute a Thasom's Glide or the Sea Spume Delicate, which I do so well, after seeing them parodied by an ape, and one so ridiculous? What else does it do?'

'Nothing, I fear, Serenity,' Hrapit replied. 'Not that I am aware. Braidic Udahl said it had been taught a special trick for your edification, but he refused to elaborate on the details.'

'No doubt some dull clownishness,' she stated. 'Have it killed in some amusing way.'

Hrapit bowed low and signalled to the captain. A guard stepped forward to jerk at the man-ape's chain. The man-ape reached out, snatched the man by one arm and hurled him away, to skid on the oil flagstones and disappear over the far edge. The nobles scattered as it came forward, great grey arms swinging out. Other guards rushed in with firestings but were swept aside, and the Princess Ymaea screamed as it reached her throne.

The Princess was snatched up, one-handed, screaming and beating at the great hairy chest. The man-ape took no notice whatever, but swung its rear into the throne and slapped the frantic Princess down across its lap. With two quick motions it tore her beautiful golden robe open and off, exposing underthings of the lightest silk, chemise and pantalottes. The chemise went. Two little round breasts burst free. A huge hand was thrust down the back of the pantalottes and tore up. A neatly formed bottom was exposed.

Nude and screaming, the Princess Ymaea Evine-y-Dactor was spanked. As she struggled, so her elaborate coiffure came loose, disintegrating into a cloud of pale blonde. Her arms flailed wildly, her legs kicked, up and down and wide, to show off the pink slit of her virgin cunt. Her howls cut the air, a wild screeching blended of fear and pain.

So large was the man-ape's hand that it covered the whole of her pert bottom, squashing out the soft flesh with each slap. It turned pink, then red, but only when the meaty little orbs were a bruised purple did the man-ape stop. By then the Princess lay sobbing across the beast's lap. Nude and dishevelled, she was barely recognisable, and less so for the hot, spanked bottom that stuck up above the man-ape's raised knee.

The man-ape made to release her, but stopped, sniffing the air, his great blue nose waggling, his face set in a frown of comic puzzlement. He grunted, lifting her, and took her by the legs, to turn her upside down and press his face between her thighs. His bulbous nose tip pressed to her vagina, and up, wringing a gasp of pain from her as her hymen tore. He pushed deeper, and her mouth went wide as she was fully penetrated, her eyes also, staring in horror before losing focus as the man-ape began to snuffle about in her vagina. In his lap, a fat blue scrotum now showed through the fur, and the bright red tip of a broad penis had begun to poke free of its prepuce.

Hrapit, and those few remaining others who had not fled, could only gape in horror as the man-ape pulled his nose free of the Princess's hole. A smeared ring of red on the blue flesh of the man-ape's proboscis showed where her virginity had gone. Mucus could be seen dribbling from her hole as she was turned over and sat firmly in his lap, penis to vagina.

It went in, the fat scarlet head engulfed in the flesh of her sex, in full view of her courtiers, any question of her retaining virginity vanishing as she was openly penetrated. The shaft followed, slid slowly into her body until her trim sex lips were pressed to the bloated scrotal sack. He began to fuck her, his hands clasping her waist, her hair and breasts bouncing up and down in time to his rhythm. Her eyes were glassy, her limbs slack, unresisting as she was fucked in plain view, with her cunt full of ape cock and her hot red bottom rubbing on the creature's fur.

The man-ape took his time, happily bouncing the helpless Princess up and down on his erection and making little burbling sounds through lips drawn back to reveal yellowing teeth. She was more responsive, with the beast's coarse ball hair tickling her exposed clitoris, until her doll-like body went suddenly rigid in orgasm. A gasp of shock went up from the spectators at seeing her made to come, and another as it happened a second time, to leave a grin of idiot satisfaction on her face.

The man-ape continued to jerk her up and down on his cock, faster now, with the white of her private lubrication showing at the junction of penis and vagina as the strokes got longer. He became louder too, smacking his blubbery lips together in glee in between emitting snickers and grunts of excitement. At last he came, thick white sperm bursting out around the mouth of the Princess's vagina as he thrust her body down on his cock one last time. Even as the hot sperm splashed out over his balls she cried out, brought to her third orgasm.

Having come, the man-ape lost all interest in the Princess. She was pulled off his cock and dumped unceremoniously on the ground, red bottom up, anus showing, also the gaping hole of her vagina. Her torn hymen was visible, and pinkish fluid was running down over her sex, but she made no effort to conceal the evidence of her ravishment, or even to get up.

As the man-ape shambled away to investigate a bowl of bananas, Hrapit moved cautiously in, to squat down beside her, touching her hair. She groaned in response and turned her face to his. Behind him, a squad of guards armed with more effective weapons clattered up the steps.

'Where is it?' she asked.

'We have it, Serenity, do not fear,' he said. 'It will be skinned alive, staked out on a nest of forest ants, caulked in boiling pitch –'

'Harm it in any way,' she responded weakly, 'and it is you who will suffer these torments.'

Cows

WPC Kate Hastings looked up as the police station doors slid aside to admit a man. He was tall, middle-aged, with a patrician face and a three-piece tweed suit which, while worn, had evidently once been expensive. A wealthy farmer, Kate guessed, or possibly just another of Guernsey's retired rich.

'Good morning,' he greeted her. 'Might I trouble you to call upstairs for Superintendent Woods?'

'Certainly, sir. Perhaps if ...' Kate began, and stopped as the superintendent himself appeared in the doorway that led to the body of the station. The man smiled and turned, addressing the superintendent.

'Ah, John, there you are, I was just asking this charming young lady to call up for you.'

'Sir Francis,' the superintendent answered, extending his hand. 'What can I do for you? Do come up to my office.'

'There's trouble with my cows again, I'm afraid ...' Kate caught as they disappeared through the doors.

The superintendent still had the door open, and held it as the man walked through. Kate leant forward to watch them through the glass door, wondering who the man was to be so immediately invited up to the superintendent's office without an appointment.

Another visitor distracted her, and the man passed from her mind, until a fellow WPC appeared to relieve her and to send her up to the superintendent's office. Puzzled, Kate hurried up the stairs, to find Superintendent Woods still with the man she had seen earlier.

'You wanted to see me, sir?' Kate enquired.

'Yes, Kate, thank you for coming up so promptly,' Superintendent Woods replied. 'This is Sir Francis Dalcourt. He is the Seigneur over on Lesquoires.'

Kate smiled and extended her hand to the man, trying to ignore his frank attention to the front of her blouse. Most men stared, her breasts having been awkwardly large since the onset of puberty, but there was something embarrassingly familiar about the quality of Dalcourt's attention, almost as if his interest was in some way professional. He shook her hand and nodded as he turned back to the superintendent.

'Eminently qualified,' he pronounced.

'Well, she's young,' Woods replied. 'In fact she's barely finished her probation, but she's sharp.'

'I'm sure she'll do admirably,' Dalcourt stated.

'Sir?' Kate enquired.

'I'd like to offer you a case,' the superintendent explained. 'Sir Francis has been having some difficulty with er . . . poachers, I suppose you'd call them.'

'Interfering with my cows,' Dalcourt explained. 'Yachtsmen, I think. They think it's funny, damn them. And as for the cows, they don't say anything, of course, but just look away and whistle between their teeth.'

Kate managed a nervous laugh at the joke.

'It's not so funny when I stand to lose money, believe me, my girl,' Dalcourt answered her.

'No, sir. Sorry, sir,' Kate said quickly.

'Think nothing off it,' Dalcourt answered. 'I'd be very grateful if you would come over and assist me. John says he can spare you.'

'It would be a useful opportunity,' the superintendent advised. 'You have already mentioned an interest in CID, and if you perform well it will certainly help in that direction. You'll be in plain clothes, and it will be an opportunity to demonstrate your ability to be discreet, on more than one level.'

'Very discreet,' Dalcourt added.

'I can be discreet, sir,' she replied. 'I'd like to accept, if you don't think it's a task for somebody more experienced?'

'No, no, you are ideal,' Dalcourt insisted, glancing once more at the overfilled front of her blouse. 'As to the details, I shall explain when we arrive on Lesquoires.'

Kate caught hold of the iron ladder, to pull herself up from the police launch and on to the quay. Above her, cliffs rose steeply on three sides, broken only by the mouth of a tunnel and the harbour entrance through which the launch had come. To gain access a boom had been lifted, and its operator now stood above her on the quay, a large, solid man who was extending a hand.

'Kate Hastings,' she said.

'Lewis,' he answered. 'Sir Francis's stockman.'

'Pleased to meet you,' she said. 'I'll be with you in a moment.'

She turned back to catch her two bags as they were thrown up. Lewis watched, making no effort to help. An old tractor stood on the quay, and he climbed into it, gesturing for her to follow. Before she was properly in her seat he had started off, steering the tractor into the tunnel mouth. A light passed, and another, before the bore of the tunnel shifted and they emerged from beneath a low granite bluff, into a sheltered bowl of land with trees to either side of the road.

'It's ever so pretty,' Kate remarked.

Lewis nodded as the trees to one side gave way to an open field, a field in which perhaps two dozen naked people were standing in a group. All were women, most young, some older, a few slim, the majority voluptuous if not actually fat. Two things united them. All had curly brown hair, and all had large, heavy breasts. All, in fact, looked rather like her. Beyond, another group occupied a second field, these blonde, but with even larger breasts.

'I didn't know there was a naturist colony on Lesquoires,' she said. 'You certainly keep it quiet.'

'No naturist colony here.' He laughed. 'Those are some of our milkers, Devons, those near ones, with the curly brown hair. Those others, the big blonde sorts in the next field, those are Swedes and Danes, good producers, but not so sweet.'

'Sorry?' Kate queried.

'The Swedes and Danes,' he answered, speaking as if addressing a rather slow-witted child, 'produce more, perhaps twenty-five per cent more, on average, but it's not as sweet as the Devons'.'

'More what?' Kate demanded. 'What's sweet?'

'Milk, of course,' he said.

'Milk?' Kate demanded. 'These women produce milk?'

'The best girl's milk in the Channel Isles,' Lewis responded. 'Which is the same as saying the best in the world.'

'But . . . what . . . like farm animals? Cows?'

'Cows. Exactly.'

'But . . . you can't do that! You can't treat women like farm animals!'

'Every one of them's here by her own free will,' he assured her. 'You can check their contracts if you don't believe me. Five years at a time we sign them up, and there's a few on their fourth round.'

'Five years? Stuck out in a field, like a cow?'

'Don't be foolish, girl. They got barns, for the winter, and if the weather turns nasty.'

'But naked, and . . . and being milked! It's so degrading. No woman could want that.'

'No? But there they are, which shows how much you understand about your own sex, my girl.'

Lewis laughed and Kate found herself blushing. Angry and embarrassed, she went silent, looking away from the naked women, only to see yet another group as the last of the trees ended. These were black-skinned, and if anything more fleshy than the others.

'Caribbeans,' Lewis stated, apparently oblivious to Kate's cold silence. 'Jamaican mostly, with a few Virgin Islanders thrown in. Good rich milk, and plenty of it.'

Kate stared fixedly ahead, and as the tractor rounded a bend three long, low barns came into view, set among a grove of oak and large hawthorns. The roof of a larger shed showed to one side, and chimneys of grey stone beyond the trees. Where the track forked, Lewis drew the tractor up beside a stone gateway.

'Sir Francis'll be waiting for you,' he announced bluntly as she jumped down. 'I'll catch you at feeding time then. You'll know when the bell rings.'

The tractor moved off, barely giving Kate time to put her bags down, and leaving her to puzzle over his parting remark. He had nodded towards the barns as he spoke and, sure enough, beyond the largest building was a concrete tower, supporting a cage inside which the outline of a large bell could be made out.

She shrugged, putting aside the question in favour of the sense of moral outrage that had been rising steadily inside her. Her job obliged her to help Sir Francis Dalcourt, but it did not mean she had to accept what he was doing, and she had every intention of letting him know that.

The house proved to be a long, two-storey building of grey stone, set in a natural bowl of land and surrounded by yews which seemed as ancient as the building itself. The scene carried the same sense of privilege and self-containment Sir Francis had, which added to her dislike.

An elderly and obese butler opened the door for her and she was ushered into a room panelled in dark oak, with many bookcases lining the walls and several fine pieces of furniture standing on a fine but old rug. Sir Francis was seated behind a great desk, and rose politely as she entered.

'Sherry, my dear?' he asked, indicating a tray on which several decanters stood. 'Madeira perhaps, I have a particularly fine Sercial. I could send Judson for a little cheese perhaps. Girl's cheese, naturally. We're self-sufficient in all dairy products –'

'No, thank you,' she interrupted, 'and before we go further, Sir Francis, I would like to say that I consider what you are doing here to be morally indefensible.'

'Nonsense, my dear, nonsense. Do sit down, won't you.'

'Please don't patronise me, Sir Francis. I realise that what you are doing is within the letter of the law, and therefore I will do my best to provide whatever professional assistance is required. Personally, I object.'

'To what, exactly, my dear?'

'To the keeping of women as farm animals, of course! It's monstrous!'

'Monstrous? Hardly that, my dear girl. I assure you that our standards are among the highest in Europe –'

'These are women, Sir Francis!'

He smiled and steepled his fingers, a condescending gesture that sent Kate's anger higher still.

'Let me ask you a question,' he said. 'Do you believe that our society represents the only acceptable way to live?'

'No, of course not –'

'And do you believe that every human being is an individual, and should have the right to make individual choices?'

'Yes, of course I do, and you are denying it to these women –'

197

'Not at all, my dear. Each woman here has read our prospectus, and agreed to accept both the benefits and obligations of her tenure as a cow. There is no small print. There are no hidden clauses.'

'No woman –'

'Now, let me stop you there. "No woman" is a phrase I have heard before, generally uttered by those too dull to see outside their own skulls. You, I feel sure, are more intelligent. How many human beings are there on this planet, Kate? Six billion, give or take. Half are women, or slightly more, I believe. So we have three billion individuals. Do you really suppose those three billion minds all work the same way, all want the same things?'

'In certain ways, yes, all want freedom, dignity –'

'Freedom, dignity? Come, come, Kate, you are being simplistic. You, a policewoman, are surely not going to claim that our society is entirely free? Can you walk naked through the streets of St Peter Port?'

'No, but no . . .'

She trailed off. She had been about to say that no woman would want to. It was not true. Only the year before a group of determined naturists had demanded the right to go where they pleased without clothes. More than half had been women.

'You see, Kate,' Sir Francis went on, 'not all women want what society tells them they should want. My cows come here for a variety of reasons, but the principle one is security. Here there is food, shelter, all the basic needs of life –'

'But not of civilised life!'

'Of life, Kate. What we call civilisation, other than in the technical sense, is simply a set of largely arbitrary social codes the imposition of which we accept. They change, with time, with place, and with few exceptions the majority simply go with the flow. However, can you think of any person who is completely content with every aspect of society?'

'No, I suppose not.'

'Yet few protest. Could it not be argued that those who reject the restrictions of society are in fact the stronger?'

'Yes, maybe . . . but there must be law, Sir Francis.'

'Oh, certainly, against murder, rape, theft, many things. I am thinking more of the petty, unwritten rules we impose on ourselves, and allow to be imposed on us by the media. Here, on Lesquoires, the rules are merely different –'

'And imposed by your contract!'

'Which is voluntary.'

'Which is perverted!'

'Nonsense.'

'It is not nonsense! Your contract even denies women the choice of what to wear!'

'And yours doesn't? You normally wear a uniform, do you not, Kate? I imagine John Woods might have something to say if you turned up for duty casually dressed.'

'My uniform serves a purpose. Come on, Sir Francis, I see you ogling my chest, you know. You get off on having them naked, don't you?'

'Naturally I do.'

'You admit it?'

'Of course. To deny it would be a lie, and to lie would diminish my self-esteem. Think what you will of me, Kate, but I am neither a liar nor a hypocrite.'

'I suppose not, but . . . but why humiliate them? Making them go naked outdoors! Keeping them in fields!'

'It improves the milk.'

'It improves the milk?' Kate repeated in incredulity.

'It does, no question of it,' Sir Francis answered. 'Now, why it does, that is not so clear. Agriculture is never an exact science, least of all in its most rarefied manifestations. Despite the best efforts of scientists the exact factors governing the quality of the world's great wines remain elusive. They are there, make no mistake, and detectable, but we lack full understanding. The same is true of girl's milk. As you doubtless saw, I have three herds, each of which gives milk of a distinctive type. The Devons give their milk sweet and creamy, the Caribbeans richer still but not so sweet, the Swedes and Danes lighter than either but with an individual scent, herbal. All that may be explained by breed, and yet, if a Devon is introduced to the Swede and Dane herd, her milk becomes lighter. If a Caribbean is introduced to the Devon herd her milk becomes sweeter.'

'The soil?' Kate suggested, the detective in her rising to the question despite her feelings.

'So one might suppose,' he answered. 'But why? The soil is a fine wind-blown loess over granite and shale. It hardly varies between the three fields, and in any case, while they eat some clover, along with blackberries and perhaps the occasional field mushroom in season, that's no more than a minor element of their diet. I prefer to think the effect is related to pheromones, similar perhaps to the way the menstrual cycles of women in a group will converge.'

Kate found herself blushing at the casual way he had spoken of something so intimate and feminine. Sir Francis had pursed his lips as he finished speaking, and was looking out of the window, his attention presumably on the problem of milk flavours.

'You were going to explain my assignment, sir,' Kate ventured.

'Ah, yes, quite,' he answered. 'The thing is, Kate, that as you can imagine, what we do here tends to attract a good deal of prurient interest, and while we do our best to be discreet, rumours do occasionally get out. The very inaccessibility of Lesquoires is enough to deter the merely inquisitive, but recently we seem to have attracted a more determined visitor. Lewis, whom you met, has found footprints, and also cigarette stubs. We fear the stock is being interfered with.'

'Interfered with? Do you mean peeped at? Molested? Raped?'

'No. If intercourse is taking place, and we must assume it is, it is entirely consenting.'

'Then I'm afraid I don't see the difficulty, sir.'

'The difficulty, Kate, is that if a heifer becomes pregnant, she'll be out of production. Unprotected sexual intercourse is strictly against the terms of the contract. These people take milk too, which is blatant poaching.'

'You could provide condoms, sir.'

'What, and have the filthy things littering the fields? Besides, providing them is one thing, ensuring they're used is another. Worst of all, semen gives the milk a fishy taste, which could ruin our market.'

'A fishy taste?' Kate demanded in disgust. 'Why?'

'Don't be naive,' he answered. 'By swallowing it, of course. Feed affects the taste of milk, and it's very important to get it right. Garlic is disastrous, asparagus worse, and too much of anything should be avoided. We use a mash of potatoes, sugar beet, carrots, with a little port and honey, and one or two other ingredients I'm not at liberty to divulge. The result is famed Europe-wide, and justly so. Our milking process is also quality-orientated. You're lucky on Guernsey, but on the mainland they now collect every other day, so you might not get Monday night's milk until the Thursday morning, even the Friday. That would never do on Lesquoires. We milk each evening and first thing in the morning into a refrigerated tank kept at precisely three degrees centigrade. Lewis takes a refrigerated container to St Peter Port, and up to La Villiaze to be flown out. The milk's at Eastleigh and Cherbourg well before noon, and in London and Paris by lunchtime. Our prices are correspondingly higher than our competitors',

201

and so it is essential that we maintain our reputation, as I'm sure you'll understand.'

Kate was barely listening, but thinking of naked girls, on their knees in the long grass, sucking men's cocks and swallowing what came out. She grimaced.

'I also suspect that the testosterone in semen reduces production,' Sir Francis went on. 'So, as you see, it's a serious matter. I suspect Frenchmen, probably local fishermen rather than yachtsmen, as with the tides around here it's a damn tricky business coming close into shore at night.'

'I would agree,' Kate answered. 'Have you or Lewis seen anyone?'

'No,' he replied, 'although we've both spent a lot of time waiting. They always seem to know when we're about, and where. The other night, for instance, we stood guard at Queslinque Bay, down below the Devons' field, which is probably the easiest place to climb up, and damned if the beggars didn't get in among the Caribbeans!'

'I see. And what do the girls have to say?'

'Nothing. They refuse to talk, any of them, or if they do, it's to deny it. They stick together, you know, a sort of bovine mafia, and anyone who breaks ranks . . . Well, I won't disturb you with the details, but suffice to say they seldom if ever break ranks. They'd also be in breach of contract if they admitted to it. No, I even suspect they've worked out some way of signalling the poachers.'

'Couldn't you just keep them in the sheds?' Kate suggested.

'They like to sleep out on warm nights,' he answered, 'and any break in routine affects production. Besides, when it rained the other night we took them in. I'm sure somebody got into the Devons' shed. We can't lock the sheds, it's against fire regulations. I'm damned if I see why I should either. This is my island, and I want to be able to go about my lawful business in peace.'

'So you want me to catch these ... er ... poachers?' Kate asked.

'My dear girl!' Sir Francis answered. 'I realise you don't approve of me, but please allow me some credit. I wouldn't dream of sending you single-handed against perhaps half a dozen burly and excitable French fishermen!'

'So what do you want me to do?'

'To infiltrate the Devon herd.'

Kate stood in the field, naked. It had taken a lot of persuasion and a phone call to Superintendent Woods to make her agree, but eventually she had given in to the inevitable. Even then she had insisted on going to a private room to undress, to the obvious amusement of both Sir Francis and the butler, Judson.

Nude and blushing a furious scarlet, she had been taken down to the field by Sir Francis, with first the Caribbean girls, then the Swedes and Danes watching her as she passed their fields. At the gate, Sir Francis had sent her in with a familiar pat to her bottom, earning him a dirty look.

The Devons were at the far side of their field, but looking at her. She began to walk towards them, all the while resisting the urge to cover her breasts and sex. As both Sir Francis and Lewis had been at pains to point out, any show of modesty risked her exposure as an infiltrator, as would her opinions. So she smiled, her walk happy, almost a skip, as if it was the most natural thing in the world to have her bare boobs bouncing on her chest in the open air.

Most of the girls – or cows as she knew she was supposed to think of them – were lying down. As Kate drew closer, she realised that their breasts were not merely large, but plumper and rounder than normal, quite clearly engorged with milk. Most had erect nipples, and one or two were touching their breasts in apparent discomfort. As she drew closer, she became aware of their scent, distinctly feminine, and also distinctly milky.

Only one cow got up as Kate approached, a tall, solidly built woman of perhaps thirty-five, with massive white breasts and straining nipples on which flecks of pale fluid could be seen. Kate smiled and extended a hand. The big woman ignored it, but reached forward to kiss Kate, full on the mouth. Despite a jolt of discomfort, Kate forced herself to respond, even allowing her lips to part a little. The woman drew back, nodding in apparent approval.

'I'm Daisy,' the woman said.

'Buttercup,' Kate answered, getting the humiliating name she had been given out with some difficulty and adding a new black mark against Sir Francis for not giving her a pet name suitable for both humans and cows.

'Think of me as your mother,' Daisy said, 'and we'll get along just fine. Keep your place in the herd, which is bottom, wait your turn and don't go making eyes at them from the house. Got that?'

Kate nodded.

'Good,' Daisy answered, gesturing to a plump girl with breasts large and swollen even by comparison with the others. 'Now this is Holly, who'll be keeping an eye on you, and needs a companion, just now. She's overproducing. And this is . . .'

All twenty-two women were introduced, Kate nodding to each in turn and trying to find some way of telling them apart. No two were exactly alike, but with their brown curls and abundant figures, the majority could have passed as sisters, or mothers and daughters, without difficulty. With the introductions finished, Kate walked round to Holly, who took her a little way aside, to where they could look out over the sea and down into what Kate reasoned was Queslinque Bay. The cliff was steep, a long slope thickly grown with sloe and bramble above perhaps twenty feet of sheer rock, and her immediate thought was that only a lunatic would try to climb it in the dark, whatever the inducement.

'You can't actually fall,' Holly said, 'but it's pretty spiky if you go in the bushes.'

'It looks it,' Kate admitted. 'So er . . . Daisy's in charge, yes? I wasn't told anything about that.'

'The farmers let us sort it out among ourselves,' Holly explained. 'Daisy's on her fourth round, and she's not as bad as some. Now that Rose, who runs the black herd, she's hard. She makes the young ones drink her you know what if they get out of line. Daisy'd never do that, and she spanks with a cupped hand, so it sounds worse than it is.'

'Spanks?' Kate demanded in horror. 'Spanks what? Our bums?'

'Of course, silly.' Holly giggled. 'But only if we're naughty. Farmer's out of sight now, so before I go on I'd be ever so grateful if you could do me my favour.'

'Sure, no problem. But what's this about spanking? I wasn't told about that either.'

'Oh, don't worry about it. Daisy will watch you for a few days, just to be sure you're not going to be uppity. If she thinks it's needed, she'll spank you, just to set an example, but it's really nothing to worry about.'

'Nothing to worry about!'

'No. You've been spanked before, haven't you?'

'No, I have not!'

'No? Well I never . . . Look, don't let Daisy know that, or she'll do it just to make sure you know how it feels. Now if you could, please?'

'What's that?'

'My milk. I'm bursting.'

'I'm sorry, I don't understand.'

'Oh, you poor thing, you're not even in yet, are you? It gets awfully sore before milking, and I'm dripping already. If I'm not suckled soon I'll go spare.'

Kate's mouth came open in shock as she realised what Holly wanted. The fat girl's huge breasts looked as if they were about to burst, and the distended nipples were wet with milk. Why Holly couldn't simply squeeze them, or suck her own nipples, Kate wasn't sure, but to refuse would look suspicious. Worse, it might even lead to her being made an example of by Daisy, and being given a spanking. Sucking another woman's breasts was desperately embarrassing, but nothing compared to taking a spanking, and a public one at that. She was going to have to do it.

Fighting back every ingrained instinct of her upbringing, she moved closer to the fat girl, leant forward, and took the big nipple into her mouth. Holly responded by taking Kate's head, to cradle it in her plump arms. Reasoning that if she was going to do it, she might as well be comfortable, Kate adjusted her position, allowing Holly to cuddle her.

Kate began to suck, tentatively. Immediately her mouth filled with milk, warm and rich, sweet, but a taste sharper than cow's milk. Holly sighed in pleasure and pulled Kate closer in. Kate began to drink.

Despite her best efforts to push it down, Kate found that a wonderful feeling of comfort was building up inside her. Her head was resting on pillows of fat, female flesh, her mouth was full of fleshy nipple and the taste of girl skin and milk. It was impossible not to feel good about it. Soon her tentative motions had changed to proper suckling.

Holly showed no reserve whatever, purring as Kate fed on her. She was also stroking Kate's hair and the nape of her neck, which was not merely comforting but shamefully erotic, the more so because she was so aware of her nudity. She was sure the other girls would be watching, and the way she was curled into Holly's lap gave a fine view of her bottom from the rear, with her sex lips and anus showing.

She dared not cover herself, or stop, but could only carry on, praying that the sexual response of her body would not be obvious. Yet she knew how easily her sex juiced, and how abundantly. Nor did there seem to be any end to Holly's milk, each suck filling her mouth, if anything more quickly than before.

In the end, it was Holly who stopped it, pulling Kate's head gently away from her breast.

'Best not be greedy, darling,' the fat girl advised. 'Farmer might notice at milking. Still, there's another to be done.'

As Holly spoke, she had curled an arm around Kate's legs, and now pulled, showing remarkable strength as Kate's position was adjusted to get at the other nipple. Kate was now lying half across Holly's body, head pillowed in the crook of one fat arm and against the big girl's bulging belly. It also left Holly's other arm draped across Kate's hips, the hand resting lightly on her bottom.

Kate began to suckle, and as she did so Holly began to stroke, only not just Kate's hair, but her bottom too. Kate stiffened, but forced herself not to pull away, despite her appalling embarrassment at having her bottom felt. Despite the embarrassment, there was no denying the sense of being soothed, and that having her bottom stroked made it worse. Holly's caresses were gentle, more so than those of any man. It was doing dreadful things to Kate's sex, and her nipples, which were poking into Holly's flesh in a way she was certain would be noticed.

'Nice, isn't it?' Holly sighed. 'Would you like me to diddle you?'

Kate shook her head in frantic denial.

'Don't be shy!' Holly giggled, and pulled Kate into her.

Kate gasped, almost choking on her mouthful of milk as Holly's fingers found her sex. For a moment she tried to pull back, but Holly held on, gently but firmly, her fat fingers burrowing into the damp flesh of Kate's sex, to find the clitoris. Kate was held, still wriggling, into Holly's body, and masturbated. The orgasm came quickly, shamefully quickly, but before it did Kate had surrendered herself. Her hands had gone to Holly's breast, squeezing the fat globe of flesh as she mouthed at the nipple. She was swallowing, over and over, to taste the milk. Despite Kate's surrender, Holly held tight to bring the feeling of being comforted to an exquisite peak, part of the sheer, overwhelming joy of suckling at the breast as she was expertly brought to orgasm.

As she came, Kate's whole body locked tight. Holly giggled in pleasure to feel the orgasm go through Kate's body, and squeezed tighter still. Kate's face was smothered in fat breast flesh, just as she was coming, to bring the orgasm higher still, higher than she had ever known. At the peak she was squirming herself into Holly, sucking and biting at the engorged nipple, and pushing her bottom out on to the girl's fat fingers as they manipulated her sex.

At last the orgasm broke, but even then Kate stayed where she'd been put, shivering in Holly's arms, her head a whirl of embarrassment and shock, satisfaction and gratitude. Holly held her, stroking her hair and whispering to her, until at last Kate found the courage to look round. The other cows sat as before. One or two had obviously watched, and smiled back at Kate's nervous half-smile. Most hadn't, but Daisy had, and met Kate's eye, nodding.

Kate stayed beside Holly for the rest of the afternoon. At first, her guilt and embarrassment at the way she had become aroused and allowed herself to be publicly masturbated was so overwhelming she could barely speak. The experience had been so strong, and so soothing, that it was impossible to actually feel she had done wrong, which only made her guilt worse. She could only imagine the reaction among her colleagues or friends to such blatant lesbianism, or any lesbianism at all. While officially tolerated, it carried a heavy stigma. The cows were different.

Within minutes of Kate's orgasm, two of the cows who had been watching had mounted less senior members of the herd. In both cases the smaller or younger female had been told to lie down and spread her legs, so that her partner could climb on top to rub pussies, in a gesture combining sex with a show of dominance. All four girls had come, either under their partners' obviously practised fingers, or by simple friction. Another of the biggest women simply took a smaller one by the hair and pulled her down, first to her breasts, then between her thighs, holding her as she sucked and licked. The young girl had soon been masturbating.

Kate's feelings softened as it became apparent that both suckling and sex play were normal among her fellow cows, if only when they were certain that neither Sir Francis Dalcourt nor Lewis were watching. The tractor could be heard and, to be sure, they had an arrangement with the Swedes and Danes, whose field was higher and looked over the lane and the black girls' field. At any time one girl in each herd would be alert, standing, and signal the others simply by sitting down in a distinctive posture, with her arms wrapped around her knees.

Kate listened as Holly explain, realising both why the style of the girls' milk tended to converge to the herd style, and that there was a good deal more organisation among the herds than the farmers expected. Each had a hierarchy, headed by a mother, and with the smaller or more placid girls taking more servile roles. The bonds between them were strong, and Kate quickly came to realise that the secrecy Sir Francis found so irritating was imposed not by fear but by loyalty.

As the afternoon passed, the suckling grew more frequent, but also of shorter duration, the girls keeping themselves right at the edge of pain. They also became more irritable. The sex play stopped, and twice Daisy had to threaten spankings to maintain order.

When the bell finally rang, they moved quickly for the gate, with Daisy in the lead. Kate stayed by Holly, uncertain what she was supposed to do when her breasts were not producing milk.

'Should I come with you?' she asked.

'Oh yes,' Holly answered. 'They'll want to get your milk in as soon as possible.'

'Good,' Kate answered, trying to sound enthusiastic and wondering exactly what being brought into milk would involve.

Lewis had come to open the gate, holding it wide as the girls trooped out, and watching the movement of breasts and rumps with casual but unconcealed pleasure. Kate ignored him, but felt the prickle of male eyes on her skin as she passed, restoring her awareness of her nudity to its earlier level.

Holly was closer to Lewis as she and Kate passed through the gate, and was sent along with a pat to her ample rump. He then closed the gate and followed them, making Kate yet more self-conscious as she tried to walk without her bottom wiggling more than was absolutely necessary. Despite her fears, he kept his hands to himself, even when the herd stopped to let the Caribbeans out of their field.

Between the hedges of the lane, the milky smell grew stronger, and stronger still as the three herds were marshalled into the largest of the barns. As the last in line among sixty or so cows, Kate found herself herded into a long pen at the centre of the building, along with Holly and most of the Devons. The Danes and Swedes had been first in line, and were already being prepared for milking.

To either side of the barn stood stainless steel tanks, six in all, each the same, with a set of gauges and controls at one end and a row of five pieces of identical apparatus along the front. Each apparatus consisted of a coiled hose of transparent plastic, running from the tank to end in twin cups, the purpose of which was obvious. Lines of stools stood in front of the tanks, and on these the girls sat, ample bottoms spilling over the sides. Each girl, either on her own or helped by Lewis or Sir Francis, would fit the suction cups over her breasts, before twisting a toggle at the point her tube divided.

The milking stations closest to Kate were occupied by Caribbeans, and she watched in mingled fascination and shock as they milked themselves. With the cups held across her breasts, each girl would adjust her toggle, which evidently turned the suction on, as the plump brown breast flesh would immediately be sucked into the cup, filling and sealing all but the front. The girls' nipples could be seen, pulled out into the tube, with milk beading briefly before it began to squirt out against the plastic and run down the tube.

The machines sucked to a slow rhythm, not unlike that Kate had used when suckling Holly. The result was to draw the girls' nipples in and out, the stiff black buds extending with each suck, and spraying milk as they did. That the sensation was pleasurable was obvious. The girls responded differently, but each well, with sighs, or gentle moans. Some held their breasts up, one fat brown globe in each hand. Others used an arm to support their breasts, leaving the other free to stroke their bellies or thighs, even to rub at their pussies.

Kate watched open-mouthed as the girl nearest to her masturbated. It was done casually, plump black fingers burrowing into a yet plumper and blacker pussy, to snatch and rub at her clitoris while her milk bubbled and squirted from her breasts. When she came it was with no more than a gentle sigh and a wiggle of her meaty bottom on the stool beneath her. Nobody took the slightest notice, busy either with their apparatus or their own pussies.

It was clear to Kate that before long she would be put on a milking machine. As before, there was nothing she could do, while it was plain that the farmers could not be seen to give special treatment. So she waited, nervous and embarrassed, as the black girls were milked just feet in front of her.

Her turn came sooner than she expected. The black girl who had masturbated called for Lewis. He came over, to take hold of one full breast and inspect the nipple as it was sucked on, then nod. The girl immediately turned her toggle and gently eased her breasts from the machine. They were left clearly less swollen, but with the nipples straining to erection and the area of flesh which had been within the suction cup pulled out into a bowl-shaped mound.

Free of the milking machine, the black girl rose and smiled at Kate. Lewis was still standing by, and took Kate's arm, pulling her gently forward. Kate went, glancing in resignation at the patch of pussy juice the black girl had left on the stool before sitting in it. She made a face as she felt the wet between her bottom cheeks and against her own sex, but stayed put as Lewis reached to pull the apparatus out from the milking machine.

'I can do it, thank you,' Kate said, her voice loud above the throb of the machines.

'It's not so easy as it looks,' he called back. 'Now come on, no fuss.'

Kate sighed as he casually took hold of her left breast, cupping it to squeeze out the nipple, then pinch the sensitive bud between finger and thumb. She gasped as he began to manipulate her, but came quickly erect.

'Good-sized udders,' he remarked, 'and good teats as well, for a new one. I reckon we'll have you in milk before the fortnight's out.'

Kate didn't reply. Her mouth was pursed in annoyance as he casually brought her other nipple to erection, handling her right breast as he had the left, without the slightest consideration for her personal space or dignity. With both her nipples hard, he took the cups, pressing one and then the other over Kate's breasts. She took them, ignoring the butterflies in her stomach as she held herself to the milking machine and Lewis reached out for the toggle.

'Twist clockwise for on,' he instructed, and did so.

Kate gasped as her nipples were sucked out into the machine. Both had distended, suddenly, to nearly twice their natural size, the rose-pink flesh sucked into the tube with a jolt. Another followed, a third, the milking rhythm setting in, to leave her panting and clutching at her breasts. Lewis chuckled.

'You'll get used to it,' he assured her, 'you all do. Oh, and feel free to frig your fanny if you've a need. There's no standing on ceremony with us.'

He left her with a slap to her bottom where her cheeks bulged out over the edge of the stool. She turned, meaning to give him a dirty look, but found herself smiling instead as she realised that Holly, several of the other Devons and the black girl beside her were all watching.

'You new?' the black girl asked.

'In today,' Kate managed, gasping the words out over the sensation of having her breasts sucked. 'Kate ... I mean, Buttercup.'

'Robinson,' she answered, 'a little joke of the farmer's.'

'Hi,' Kate responded, glancing further down the line to where Lewis was helping a buxom blonde adjust her toggle. 'Lewis, does he ... I mean, he seems very familiar.'

'Does he fuck us? No, well, not often, and when he does he uses these thick condoms. He won't let you give

213

a blow-job, neither, or Francis. Spoils the milk, they say. No, if they want you, they'll take you up the ass.'

'My . . . my bum? Oh my God!'

'Yeah, if you let them catch you alone, they'll take you somewhere nice and quiet and put you in a halter, kneeling, so they can get at your bum. They use our own butter to grease our assholes, you know. Plenty of it, pushed in with a finger, and whoops, up goes a cock. They don't care how tight you are, neither.'

'Oh my God! That's awful. I mean, how could they, up our bums!'

'You've never had it up the butthole?'

'Never!'

'Then you have a shock coming! I'm done. See you around, yeah?'

Kate managed a weak nod as Robinson began to detach herself from the milking machine. Suddenly her bottom felt a lot more prominent, while the light tingle where Lewis had slapped her seemed far more intense. Her bottom hole was twitching at the thought of him pushing his cock into it, after buttering her ring until she was loose enough to take him. It didn't bear thinking about, but she couldn't stop herself.

Robinson had said it so casually too, as if being buggered was not just a reasonable thing for a girl to expect, but something she should look forward to. Not only that, but it was hard to imagine the earthy Lewis being sensitive about it. He'd just grease her and push his cock up, indifferent to her reaction, indifferent to any mess he made. He wouldn't care, just enjoy her bumhole because it was tight and hot around his cock and because she was a girl with her buttocks spread in front of him, naked and buggered in the warm grass. She'd be watched too, by the other cows, as he rammed his erection in and out of her slimy anal ring, to come deep in her rectum, to leave her dripping with mess, and masturbating . . .

She stopped, pulling herself back from the edge a moment before her hand slid down between her thighs to find her sex. It wasn't going to happen. She was a police officer, not a cow. She could not be casually buggered, and she was not going to masturbate in front of him either, never mind Sir Francis and sixty or so women. It didn't matter how many of the others did it. There was no obligation, and she would hold back.

To keep her hands busy she made a show of adjusting her breasts, lifting them in her hands and peering at the distended nipples as they were sucked on. It was the sensation of being milked which had brought her to the edge of losing control as much as what Robinson had said about Lewis buggering girls, and she tried to concentrate on something else.

She had been accepted, and if it had been at quite a cost to her dignity, she could at least take professional pride in her acting. After all, it was no worse than dressing as a prostitute in order to catch kerb crawlers, which she had done with no more than a trace of embarrassment. Being strapped nude to a milking machine was no worse than strutting along an ill-lit alley in a PVC mini-dress, and the one didn't make her a real cow any more than the other made her a real prostitute. On the other hand, pretending to be a prostitute hadn't led to lesbian sex and the best orgasm of her life.

It had been good too. Holly, who was now strapping herself into the milking machine beside Kate, had been so tender, so understanding of Kate's emotions, more so than any man. Then there had been the sensation of suckling, the taste of Holly's milk and the feel of warm girl flesh, skin to skin, her face pressed to one enormous boob, her mouth full of nipple, fingers busy in her sex . . .

'How do you feel?' Holly asked.

For a second time Kate snapped back from the edge of disgracing herself.

'Strange,' she replied. 'A bit dizzy.'

'Naughty?'

'Yes. I can't help it.'

'Of course you can't, darling. You're a natural cow, you know.'

Kate managed a smile. It was impossible to resent the remark, so obviously intended as the highest of compliments, and delivered with simple honesty. In fact, Holly was impossible to resent, despite having held Kate still to stop her getting away during the masturbation. Holly had known what Kate truly wanted, and provided it. Kate shivered at the memory, and turned away as the fat girl sighed with pleasure in response to the suction.

Another Devon girl was now on the opposite side, one of the slimmest, but with breasts little smaller than Holly's and exceptionally large nipples. She already had the suction cups on, with a good two inches of pinky-brown flesh sucked into each tube and milk squirting plentifully. She also had the tube pulled fully out from the machine, to make a loop which she had pressed between her legs.

Having once spent a guilty few minutes with the hose of a petrol pump squeezed tight between her thighs, Kate knew exactly what the girl was doing. The sucking of the machines produced a slow rhythm, just right for a girl's breasts. The electric motors that powered the machines produced another, a juddering vibration which carried up the pipes, just right for a pussy. Kate turned her face stolidly to the front.

She listened to the girl beside her coming, meanwhile trying to ignore the sucking sensation at her nipples and the gentle vibration coming up through her stool. It was hard to resist, and part of her mind was telling her not to be silly, and to pull the tube in between her legs as the other Devon girl had done. Nobody was going to mind. It was tempting. The wet patch under her bottom was no longer entirely the fault of the black girl who had used the stool before her. Her clitoris was itching to be touched. It would be so easy ... and she was doing it, the tube pulled towards her, her bottom slipping forward in the pool of pussy juice.

'That's probably enough for your first day,' a voice spoke right in her ear. 'Wouldn't want those pretty nipples sore, would we?'

Kate jumped in shock, looking back to find Sir Francis leaning over her. He extended his hand, twisting her toggle to the off position as the blood rushed to her face. He gave a knowing chuckle and stepped away, leaving her sitting confused and vulnerable in her puddle of excitement.

'He's right, you know,' Holly remarked casually. 'The skin will crack if you overdo it. The best thing is to rub a little milk in every so often. Take the cups off and I'll give you some.'

'Thanks, I'll be OK,' Kate answered, tugging at one of her suction cups.

'Not like that,' Holly said. 'Here, I'm nearly done, let me.'

Kate nodded gratefully. Her breast flesh was visible through the suction cups, and was distinctly pink, especially her nipples. They ached, much as they did after being rubbed during sex.

'They are sore,' she complained, as Holly turned to her.

'Watch how I do it,' Holly instructed, taking a pinch of Kate's breast to get hold of the lip of a suction cup.

The cup was peeled off, then the second, to leave Kate with both breasts topped by low red bulges, each in turn topped by a still redder nipple. Exposed to the air, they felt sorer still, and she winced as she touched them.

'Here,' Holly said, squeezing one fat breast to bleed out a last drop of milk, which she let run into her cupped hand.

Kate let it happen, telling herself that it was good for her cover and also her skin as Holly smoothed the warm milk on. Her nipples had stayed hard, and grew harder still under Holly's caresses, turning her thoughts back to the urgent state of her sex. For a moment her lust threatened to overcome her prudishness, but all around her the girls were finishing and moving towards the door of the barn. Holly too was looking anxiously over her shoulder, and stopped stroking in the milk just as Kate was trying to pluck up the courage to ask the fat girl to masturbate her again.

'Supper,' Holly stated, 'we don't want to lose our share.'

Thinking of potatoes, sugar beet, carrots, port and honey mashed into a paste, Kate had to hold back a sigh. Holly got up and hurried across to the door, fat bottom wobbling behind her. Kate followed at a more relaxed pace, reaching the door behind all the other girls and just as Lewis was starting to pull it shut.

'You're good, I'll give you that,' he said quietly as she passed. 'I wouldn't know myself.'

Kate didn't reply, wary of the girls in the yard. The three herds were separating out, each heading towards a particular hut. Kate followed the other Devons, into a long, low space that smelt of hay, boiled vegetables and the ever-present milky tang. The floor was concrete, with hay piled to either side and a long zinc trough at the centre. Holly was already kneeling by the trough, and Kate joined her.

'Does the food just go in the trough?' she asked.

'Yes,' Holly answered, 'but you can eat with your hands if you like.'

'Thanks,' Kate answered, 'what about washing and stuff?'

'There's a trough at the end,' Holly answered, jerking her thumb towards the far end of the barn.

Kate looked, but could see no evidence of sanitary facilities, let alone anything that might provide privacy.

'In front of everyone else?' she demanded.

'Sure,' Holly answered. 'Don't be shy. We all have to do it.'

Kate nodded and swallowed, thinking of the prospect of squatting down to pee where sixty other women could see her, or worse. Already her bladder felt full, but she decided to hang on until nightfall, when the dark would give her the privacy she wanted.

Lewis appeared at the door, a large zinc pail in either hand. The girls made way, allowing him to slop out the contents into the trough, and crowding back in as he passed. Kate looked in disgust at the lumpy, orange mess in the trough, and hesitated. Holly showed no such reluctance, scooping up a double handful of the mash, which she began to mouth up with obvious relish. Kate followed suit, taking a little and tasting it gingerly, only to find that it actually tasted quite pleasant, fresh and well seasoned, if unusual in flavour.

She began to eat, delicately at first, then faster. One or two of the girls had simply put their faces in the trough, coming up smeared with food, but smiling happily. After a while Holly followed suit, bending down with her fat pink bottom stuck up in the air.

'More like a pig than a cow, isn't she?' the girl opposite Kate remarked, nodding to Holly.

Holly looked up, bringing her food-smeared face out of the trough. The other girl giggled and winked at Kate.

'Who's a pig?' Holly demanded.

'Oink! Oink!' the girl replied.

'I've had enough of you, Bramble,' Holly warned.

'As if you'd dare!' Bramble taunted.

The next instant she had been grabbed by the hair and jerked forward, off balance, squealing in shock an instant before her face was pushed into the food.

'I'll show you who's the pig!' Holly spat. 'Eat it!'

The girl was struggling as her face was rubbed in the food, trying to push herself up with her arms and making little kicking motions with her feet. It did no good, and she was held firmly in place until she started to eat the swill. Holly laughed, reaching out to plant a firm smack on her victim's raised bottom.

'Spank her, Holly!' another girl called.

'Yeah, spank her hard, until she's eaten her dinner up,' another added.

'I'm going to,' Holly assured them, planting another spank, to make the unfortunate girl jump on her knees. 'Come on, Bramble, eat up, this doesn't stop until you've finished!'

Holly began to spank harder, setting the girl squirming and making odd bubbling noises in the swill she was desperately trying to eat. Despite herself, Kate was soon giggling at the sight, along with the other girls. The laughter encouraged Holly, who scooped up a handful of the food, to slap it between her victim's bottom cheeks. The girl's struggles became more desperate still, but Holly held on, adding a second handful, full on the girl's sex. Two messy fingers went into Bramble's vagina, briefly pumped in and out with a loud slopping noise before Holly went back to spanking.

'I'm going to do it this time, Bramble, I am!' Holly declared.

The girl went wild, writhing in Holly's grip, beating her fists in the mess of food in the trough, her fat breasts and reddened bottom jiggling in panic. Holly held on tight, rising, to step over the trough, a foot to either side. The other girls moved hastily back, wide-eyed and giggling as the fat girl sank into a squat over her victim's body.

Kate's hand went to her mouth as she realised what Holly was going to do. She too scrambled back, only just in time, as a great gush of yellow pee exploded from Holly's sex, over Bramble's head and into the trough below. Bramble went into hysterics and the urine sprayed out into her hair, thrashing crazily in the mess to send bits of mash and droplets of piddle in every direction. Holly just laughed, rubbing her desperate victim's face in the now filthy mess.

'Now eat it!' she ordered, and began to spank the hapless Bramble once more.

Bramble shook her head in frantic denial. Holly answered with a slap to Bramble's pussy. Still Bramble refused.

'Eat!' Holly ordered. 'Eat now or . . .'

At once Bramble was eating, mouthing at the mess of cow food and piddle as if it was the finest food imaginable. Holly laughed, shifting her weight and squatting lower, to direct the jet of urine full into the girl's face. Yellow pee exploded across Bramble's face as it was pulled up out of the slimy mess, only to be dunked once more. Holly held the quivering girl in the mess as her pee died to a trickle. Bramble was still trying to eat, and when her face was pulled up again her mouth stayed open, full of yellowish pulp, her eyes closed with mess, a mixture of urine and mucus dribbling from her nose.

'Say sorry,' Holly demanded.

'I'm sorry, Holly,' Bramble snivelled. 'I'll be nice, I promise!'

'Good,' Holly answered.

Bramble's head was dropped back into the filthy slurry. Holly climbed off, to leave her victim to lift herself up and scamper away to the far end of the barn. Kate could only gape open-mouthed at the fat girl, who had seemed so gentle and motherly, yet had just forced another woman to drink her urine, and threatened worse.

'You weren't . . . you know, going to . . . on her head and . . . and make her eat it?' she asked.

For a moment Holly looked blank, then laughed.

'No,' she answered, 'Bramble hates it up her bum. Last time she was cheeky I'd threatened to stake her out so she got it.'

'Stake her out? To be buggered! Who by, Lewis?'

'Not Lewis, no. She wouldn't mind Lewis so much, he's only got a little one. He gives us chocolates if we let him too. No, for Sir Francis. His is huge, and he'll only give you a spoonful of honey.'

'Well at least he doesn't make you eat his you-know-what. I heard from another girl, in the milking shed, that some French fishermen made her suck them all off, one by one, and eat it!'

'That's just a story! That was Robinson, wasn't it? I saw you were talking to her. She's always making up horror stories. You don't need to worry about strangers getting at us, no one's even tried while I've been here. There's only one man who'll make you eat his spunk, and . . .'

She stopped abruptly, the happy look on her face changing to apprehension. Kate looked around, to find Daisy behind her. The big woman was looking stern. Kate moved quickly out of the way as Daisy raised one leg, placing a foot on the trough to make a knee. Holly's hand went to her mouth.

'Across my knee, Holly,' Daisy ordered.

'Oh, Daisy, please, no, not in front of Buttercup . . .'

'Across my knee,' Daisy repeated.

Holly made a face, but went forward, and down, across Daisy's lap to lift her fat pink bottom into the air and leaving her huge breasts hanging free at the other end. Seeing that there was going to be a spanking, the other Devons began to gather around. Some showed touches of arousal, others trepidation, but all were clearly amused by the prospect of watching the fat girl spanked. Daisy waited, holding Holly firmly in place, until the entire herd was ready.

As the girls gathered Holly made little whimpering sounds. She was shivering too, her ample bottom and fleshy reams at her waist quivering in reaction to her fear. Kate found herself sympathising, and also scared, but she could not turn her eyes away, and knew she wouldn't. She had never seen a girl spanked, never mind naked, and it was impossible not to watch.

'Are we ready?' Daisy asked.

Holly responded with a louder and yet more miserable whimper. Immediately Daisy cocked up her knee. Holly squealed as her legs came apart to show off the fat pink lips of her sex, and once again as Daisy's hand landed at the centre of one huge buttock, to send ripples out through the flesh. Another smack was delivered, and a third, before Daisy set to work.

Kate put her hand to her mouth as the spanking began in earnest, horrified yet fascinated, with her own bottom twitching in both sympathy and anxiety as the fat girl was beaten. Daisy did it hard, landing the slaps on every part of Holly's bottom and upper thighs, also noisily, the smacks ringing out around the corrugated iron shed, along with her victim's cries.

Holly took it badly, her legs kicking out and her fat bottom wobbling as she was spanked, in time to the slaps of Daisy's hand. There was no attempt to hold herself in at all, squealing and begging for mercy as she was beaten, or to keep herself to herself, her thighs and bottom cheeks parting to provide a display of plump pink cunt and puckered anus.

'See what you get for not watching your mouth,' the girl next to Kate remarked. 'Imagine that was you.'

'I am,' Kate admitted. 'Does it hurt very much?'

'Yes,' the girl answered with feeling.

Finally Daisy let go of Holly's waist. Immediately Holly rolled off, to land hard on her bottom, which drew laughter from several of the girls and a last pained squeak from her. She was snivelling and miserable, her chubby face stained with tears, but to Kate's surprise she made no effort to rise, but lay back on the floor. Daisy rose though, grinning, to straddle Holly's prone body, bottom to head. Kate realised to her horror that the big woman intended to sit on her friend's face.

Daisy went down, spreading her bottom in Holly's face. Kate could only gape as she realised that Holly was being made to lick Daisy's bottom hole. She watched, unable to tear her eyes away as the fat girl was made to clean Daisy's anus, licking at the tight ring. Daisy masturbated as her anus was licked, very casually, occasionally moving to press her sex to Holly's mouth, but always going back to the anal position, until at last she came.

Holly kept licking, tonguing at Daisy's anus in full view of the watching girls, and Lewis too, until the orgasm was finished. Even then Daisy spent a moment sitting at rest on Holly's face before climbing off. Holly pulled herself up into a kneeling position, to wipe her mouth, then rub at her red bottom, and crane back over her shoulder in a largely futile effort to inspect the damage. Kate came closer, gingerly, worried that Holly might want to take out her humiliation on her own bottom. Holly managed a wry smile and Kate answered it, then spoke as Daisy walked away.

'You poor thing!' Kate sympathised. 'And what was that for? I mean, if she didn't want you to punish Bramble, why didn't she stop it?'

'It wasn't for that,' Holly said quickly.

'What then?'

'Shh!'

'Yes, but I don't want to get spanked myself, or sat on!'

'You won't, not spanked anyway.'

'Sat on? Who . . .'

She was interrupted by a rushing sound, and turned, to catch a spatter of water and food across her legs and bottom as Lewis aimed a hose into the trough. Holly had stepped quickly back, and Kate followed suit. Lewis gave them a grin and quickly flicked the hose at them, spraying their faces and chests. Kate squeaked in alarm and retreated further. She was feeling extremely vulnerable, thinking of bare bottom spankings, public humiliation and having another woman's bottom sitting in her face.

'Another fine night,' Lewis announced as he turned the hose off. 'You'll be sleeping outside.'

There was a pleased murmur at the news. The girls began to move towards the exit, lining up behind Daisy as before. Outside, the light was beginning to fade, with the sun already behind the high cliff which sheltered the house to the west. The Swedes and Danes were already in the lane, Sir Francis leading a tall ash-blonde on a halter at their head.

'Snowdrop'll have a sore bumhole in the morning,' Bramble remarked from beside her.

'It'll be you one day,' Holly answered.

'Don't!' Bramble answered, then squeaked as Lewis pinched her bottom.

Kate moved quickly forward, out of range of his fingers. He grinned and gave her wink, then slapped Bramble's bottom as the herd began to move forward. The Caribbeans were moving already out into the lane, and Kate saw Robinson slip in among their ranks as they passed the fork in the track. The other black girls moved to let her into their ranks, and the herds moved on down the lane, separating as they reached their respective fields.

Holly seemed to have got over her spanking, chatting merrily as the herd settled down in the long grass. Kate barely noticed, her mind working on her problem and rapidly approaching a solution.

'What's the best way to get on with Daisy?' she asked, breaking into the flow of Holly's talk.

'She gets what she wants,' Holly answered. 'If you're thinking of sucking up to her, be careful. You'll just end up with your tongue up her bum.'

'I was thinking more of a present,' Kate went on. 'Something from the house maybe. Wine maybe?'

'Ssh!' Holly hissed, and went on in a whisper, 'Don't do it. You'll get in trouble. She gets everything she needs. We pay, so if she takes you into the bushes to suck a cock, just do as you're told.'

Kate nodded, wondering if she should simply return to the house or wait until morning milking. With dusk it was going to be easy to slip away, and it would all be over. She'd be able to take a hot bath, use the toilet, for which she was getting desperate, and best of all, put her clothes back on. The prospect was very enticing indeed, but there was no denying it also came with a measure of regret. To stay might allow her to learn more. It would also allow her another chance to suckle Holly, perhaps to be masturbated, and so release the sexual tension that had been building up in her ever since milking time.

It was not yet dark enough to be sure of leaving unobserved, and she decided to hold back, telling herself it was the sensible, rational decision. She knew it wasn't. Beside her, Holly had stretched out in the grass, as had many of the other girls. Kate bit her lip, fighting the urge to simply cuddle into Holly's soft embrace, sure she would be accepted, but too guilty to try.

She was still trying to overcome her inhibitions when she caught a movement at the top of the field in the corner of her eye. A figure had emerged from a dark hole in the hedge, obviously female, although petite by the standards of the cows. She stayed ducked low as she approached, and Kate saw that she was a black girl, small, but heavy breasted, obviously one of the Caribbeans.

The girl went straight to Daisy and sank down beside her, to whisper in her ear. Daisy answered with a nod, looked straight at Kate, and spoke.

'Looks like the farmers have set a police snoop on us, girls. Buttercup, or rather, WPC Kate Hastings.'

'It's not true!' Kate answered automatically. 'I'm not police.'

'Yes you are,' Daisy answered.

'I'm not!' Kate protested. 'I'm a cow, like the rest of you!'

'That's not what I hear,' Daisy answered. 'Get her.'

Kate jumped back as the nearest of the girls snatched for her hair, tripped on an out-thrust leg and went down, sprawling across Holly. Strong hands immediately took hold of her and she was rolled on to her back. Holly straddled her, and another girl, almost as big.

'Are you?' Holly demanded, her voice full of hurt. 'Are you really?'

'She is,' Daisy answered. 'No mistake. When she came over this morning and went to the house, it wasn't to sign her contract, it was for Francis Dalcourt to brief her.'

Kate made to speak, but stopped. Every single girl was looking at her, their expressions reading betrayal and sadness, Holly's especially.

'Keep her still,' Daisy commanded. 'Bramble, Poppy, get the twine from the gate.'

'Don't do anything you might regret,' Kate managed, struggling to hold her voice even.

'I won't,' Daisy answered her. 'You can count on it. Shut her up, Holly.'

Holly moved, swinging herself around to lower her huge bottom on to Kate's head. Kate moved just in time to stop her face going in between the fat girl's buttocks, but still found herself half smothered in bottom, and unable to do more than mumble. Unable to see, crushed beneath them, she felt her panic start to rise.

It got worse, as she felt twine put to her ankles and twisted around them. She began to fight, struggling frantically to stop herself being tied. It made no difference. Her ankles were lashed. She was rolled over, squealing for help and struggling frantically as her hands were tied tight behind her back. The girls' response was to wad her mouth with grass and tie it in with the last of the twine. At that, she lost control of her bladder, wetting herself in the grass in full view of her persecutors. They simply laughed, watching the arch of urine as it sprayed from her pussy to patter down on the grass.

She was left to finish, then picked up by Daisy and slung over one shoulder, still mewling through her gag in her panic, and carried up the field to the lane. There, they crouched down in the shadow of the hedge. Other black girls joined them, including the enormous Rose. Kate was dumped on the ground as Daisy thanked Rose for the tip-off. Blonde-haired Swedes and Danes also appeared, the most massive approaching the other two herd mothers, to speak in whispers. Eventually they parted, Daisy returning to Kate.

'Looks like our luck's in,' the big woman crowed. 'Francis has taken Snowdrop indoors to bugger her in comfort. Lewis has got Robinson down at the dock for the same treatment. So you, my girl, are going to be taught a sharp lesson.'

Daisy chuckled as she once more picked Kate up. The women now walked quickly, speaking in low, excited voices, up the lane to the barns. Kate writhed, trying to throw herself off Daisy's shoulders, only to get her bottom smacked and two fingers inserted into her vagina for her pains. They reached the milking shed, Daisy carrying Kate to the rear, where a sour, decaying reek struck her nose.

She tried to turn round to see what was happening as Daisy stopped and took a firm grip on her thighs. An instant later an agonising pain exploded across her bottom. Her whole body jerked, her breasts bouncing high, her legs kicking out. Girlish laughter greeted her display of pain and a second jolt of agony hit her bottom. She went wild, wriggling and kicking, as they set to work on her, her curls flying out around her head, her body bucking up and down. Daisy held on tight, indifferent to the smaller woman's struggling body, except to laugh.

It stopped, Kate slumping down on her captor's back, sweaty and exhausted, her bottom a throbbing ball of pain. She had no idea who had beaten her, or what it had been done with, only that it hurt crazily and left her hot and dizzy, also defeated. Even when Daisy's fingers once more slid up into her vagina she made no effort to stop it, allowing herself to be explored without so much as a token kick.

'Soaking,' Daisy announced, 'a tart, policewoman or otherwise.'

'In she goes then,' another woman answered and Kate was heaved high into the air.

It came as a total shock. There was a sudden movement, a burst of laughter and then she was in some foul-smelling, lumpy substance, her bottom well down, the surface already coming up over her breasts as she sank.

She kicked out in terror as her face started to go under, only to immediately hit her feet on the bottom. The girls laughed again, watching as she struggled in the slops, with bits of vegetable peel and congealed milk dropping off her breasts and belly as she sat up. She tried to stand, her body pulling out with a sucking noise.

'Stay down,' Daisy ordered.

Kate sank back into the slops, her bottom squashing out in the mess and a lumpy object she hoped was a piece of carrot pushing into her vagina. Daisy was grinning down on her, her expression more amused than anything. Reaching down, the big woman selected a large, half-rotten carrot from the slops, holding it up to Kate's face.

'Stick your arse out,' Daisy ordered.

Kate obeyed, struggling into a kneeling position, her bottom lifting free of the mess with a thick, sucking noise. Daisy laughed at Kate's easy compliance and walked around the tub. Kate shut her eyes in miserable resignation as the rounded, rubbery tip of the decaying carrot was pressed to her anus. Her hole was slimy, and it went in easily enough, and up, hurting only when the fat neck stretched her anus beyond its normal width.

As Daisy let go, Kate allowed her bottom to sink back below the surface, keen to deprive the girls of the sight of the fat carrot end sticking out from between her buttocks. She squatted low, her breasts hanging in the sludge, hoping that by utter submission she would keep her punishment to a minimum.

'Sit up, tits showing,' Daisy ordered.

Kate obeyed, lifting her breasts free, the cool air immediately reacting on her nipples, to make both pop out. Someone laughed.

'Who's full?' Daisy demanded.

Rose answered, then the big blonde woman, and several others. They began to come forward, and Kate could only watch in horror, squatting further down in the filth as the huge black woman came to stand over her and spread the lips of her sex. The urine caught Kate full in the face, to spray her features and soak her hair, to run down her neck and on to her breasts, with Rose laughing as she pissed. The blonde woman followed, and others, Kate no longer able to see, her eyes stinging with urine, her hair sodden. With the grass gag in, it was impossible to keep her lips shut, and her mouth was soon full of it, the acrid taste strong in her throat. Still they kept on, one after another, emptying their bladders over her, until the urine was bubbling out of her nose, her stomach was full of it, her fat breasts dripping.

Even when the last had finished it was not the end of her ordeal. She was taken by the hair, and pulled into some unseen woman's crotch, to have her face used to masturbate on. Several did it, some also groping her breasts, even pushing their hands down below the

230

surface of the muck to grope at her pussy. Most came, against her nose or chin, the others laughing to see.

They finally left her, giggling together as they walked away. Kate squatted down in the swill, filthy, stinking and, to her utter horror, more aroused than she had ever been short of orgasm. She wanted to masturbate, desperately, while she was still in the filthy slop bin, covered in rancid milk waste, rotting vegetables and piddle. She fought the need desperately, even glad her hands were safely tied behind her back so that she couldn't get at her pussy, and instead concentrated on getting out of the slop bin.

It was low but with her ankles tied all she could hope to do was roll herself over the edge so that she would fall to the ground. She waited until she could open her eyes, then tried moving, only to force the lumpy object beneath her fully into her vagina. It was too much, her penetration the final, filthy detail. She postponed her attempt to escape and began to squirm her aching bottom in the filth, agonising shame filling her head even as she struggled to get friction to her clitoris. It worked, a piece of some unknown muck squashing up between her thighs and against her pussy. She began to buck her bottom up and down, her fat breasts bouncing and splashing in the muck as she jiggled herself in frantic masturbation. The thing in between her legs began to disintegrate, bits of it squelching and oozing up between her sex lips, and she was coming . . .

Only to stop as a black figure loomed out of the darkness. It was in clothes, male, and big, fat, neither Sir Francis, nor Lewis. Kate swallowed in sudden fear, squirming away as fat hands reached out for her head, pulling her close, to take the knot behind her head and tug at it. She relaxed, allowing the man to undo her gag, and pull the straw from her mouth, only to immediately replace it with an erect and extremely large penis.

Kate's eyes had gone wide in shock, but she was lost. Even as her mouth filled with bloated erection, she had begun to masturbate again, rubbing her sex in the muck. Once more her tits began to bounce, splashing filth in all directions. Again she began to squirm her bottom about, in a lewd jiggling motion she knew would seem ridiculous, yet was the only way to get the friction she so desperately needed. She was sucking cock too, an eager little slut, knowing her mouth was shortly going to be spunked in, and wanting it. Already her man was groaning, and she went into a frantic wriggling motion as he took hold of himself to masturbate into her mouth. The slapping of fat breasts in sludge grew louder, the sucking, squashy noises of her bottom and thighs moving in the slops faster and faster still, and she was coming, her whole body locking in one glorious, perfect orgasm even as her man erupted his cock into her mouth, filling her throat with hot, thick sperm, until it burst from her nose and out around his shaft, to spray back across his balls and clothes.

Kate collapsed, sinking back into the slop bin, dizzy, weak, for one instant perfectly satisfied, the next burning with guilt and shame. Suddenly her situation was anything but erotic. She was merely filthy, covered in refuse and piddle, with sperm running out of her mouth and hanging from her nostrils, on her breasts too. The man took no notice at all, ambling off into the darkness, not even troubling to thank her. Kate made to call out to him, but thought better of it.

An hour later she had climbed out of the slop bin, abraded her bonds on a piece of rusty iron and washed herself down with the hose Lewis had used earlier. Wet and shivering, she made for the house, and upstairs.

Sir Francis was in his room, naked but for a pair of purple socks, his erect cock deep up Snowdrop's bottom hole. Both looked around as Kate pushed open the door.

'I have your man, Sir Francis,' she announced. 'The butler did it.'

Fantasy Worlds in Erotica

One of the greatest pleasures of writing is to be able to create one's own worlds.

I am not referring only to science fiction and fantasy, but would argue that to write fiction is to create a world. Even when set in what is supposed to be the real world, all fiction is subjective, at least to some extent. It expresses the author's viewpoint, and stresses those things she or he considers important, either personally or in terms of the development of the work. Anything considered unimportant, or inconvenient, can be glossed over, or more frequently, simply ignored. For the author not to do this risks spoiling the work, by making it dull or pedantic. On the other hand, too much of it can easily jar, making the story implausible, and so spoil the reader's enjoyment another way.

A simple example may be taken from detective fiction. Inspector Morse is presented as set in the real world, a fictional Oxford no more arcane or eccentric than the reality. Some years ago, a punt with two skeletons still on board was discovered in a system of abandoned sewers beneath Christ Church College. Reality or Inspector Morse? It could be either. Nevertheless, the world of Inspector Morse is not our own, the most obvious difference being that Oxford does not produce one or more convoluted murder cases per week. Not in reality, but for the series plot to work it has to.

Take any genre and the same is true: chick-lit, romance, horror, sci-fi, fantasy, and, of course, erotica. In every case, the reader is asked to suspend their disbelief to a lesser or greater extent. For the writer, the question then becomes – to what extent can the reader be expected to suspend disbelief?

There is no simple answer to this, unfortunately. When creating a fictional world a balance must be found, but where? Readers are individuals, with different tastes. Certainly it is impossible to please everybody. Also, one person's acceptable fact or self-evident truth may be another's impossibility or absurdity. God? The rock on which all existence is founded, or a laughable concept fit only for fools and primitives?

Then there is the matter of the reader's own perceptions and experiences, particularly in worlds that approximate the real. I was once called a liar to my face after describing how some friends and I had driven a three-seater carriage through London pulled by a four-in-hand team of pony-girls. We did it, but he simply would not believe it, because it lay outside the boundaries of his experience. It is inevitable that an equally elaborate erotic set piece in a novel will meet with similar snorts of derision from the unimaginative.

All an author can hope to do is establish a balance that works for them.

When setting out to write a novel, the nature of the world to be created must be among the first decisions. When writing erotica, or pornography if you prefer, it is essential to make your world a viable setting for sex scenes. To achieve this, the simplest thing to do is create a place where the normal rules of society do not apply, usually a remote country house or an island. Thus ordinary 'real world' women, or men, may be trained to sexual slavery or indulge in whatever fantasy the author enjoys. De Sade did this, and Pauline Réage in *Story of O*. Since then it has been redone so often that editors begin to gibber when yet another example lands on their desks. There are exceptions, with the real world settings used far more skilfully, by authors such as Penny Birch and Lucy Golden, although even then factors such as pregnancy and sexually transmitted diseases are conveniently forgotten.

I prefer to take a step further into fantasy, or several steps. So far, across twelve novels, I have created four principal worlds. Each has its distinct, internally consistent rules, which I believe is important, no matter how far the world is detached from reality. Each world should work, according to its own rules, and once set, those rules should not be broken. This allows the greatest possible scope for imagination, while hopefully not leaving the reader incredulous.

Each world also reflects my own fantasies, rather than being tailored to market demands. Aside from straightforward sex, many sexual or sexualised objects and practices appeal to me. The whole cycle of female reproduction: male orgasm, impregnation, pregnancy, lactation, all are highly sexual. In the right circumstances, just about any female bodily function can be sexually arousing. Messy things also appeal, semen, pee, mud, more or less anything wet or sticky, both for the hell of it and for the sexual humiliation it can provide. Then there is the deliberately bizarre, particularly in terms of strange beasts or demons. On a cerebral level, tension is important to me, and loss of control due to the strength of sexual desire. There is also an appeal in the grotesque, and extreme contrasts of beauty and ugliness.

On the other hand, many popular sexual practices and fetishes do not excite me. Male submission has little appeal. Foot worship and the whole constellations of fantasies based on it have even less. Transvestism I do not even pretend to understand. Torture for its own sake I consider irrelevant. I seldom mention such things at all, and never in detail, for the simple reason that if I did, my heart would not be in the writing.

My first world, and that which comes closest to reality, is the world conceived for *The Rake* and including the other two Henry Truscott novels, *Purity* and *Velvet Skin*. *Devon Cream*, *Peaches and Cream* and the short stories *The Beast Strap and the Birch* and *A Lady in Church* also belong to this world.

Essentially it is an eroticised version of history, and was created to exploit my love of corporal punishment, pregnancy, lactation and good, dirty sex. Despite this, the plots never stray far from real events. For instance, Sir Joseph Snapes's eugenics theories may seem insane by the standards of our time, but they are taken from genuine late-eighteenth-century ideas. From the existence of the theory it is a small step to imagining him attempting to actually cross women with chimpanzees. Far fetched? Don't you believe it.

It is also sanitised, but only slightly, and then only when reality would spoil the erotic element. When describing a pretty girl I don't include details of her smallpox scars. There is poverty, injustice, inequality, etc, all of which can be used to add detail and tension to erotic scenes. There is also pregnancy, which is often avoided in erotic novels, but which I include, and not only for the sake of reality. For me being pregnant is intensely sexual, and the possibility of impregnation during sex adds to my pleasure.

There is a measure of compromise with character. I refuse to give historical characters modern morals, particularly when it comes to giving heroines and heroes politically correct attitudes to gender, race or class. Henry Truscott does not give Suki a place as maid because she's a poor, lost black girl, but because he wants to roger her senseless. On the other hand, he doesn't go around setting fire to peasant cottages so that he can flush the women out and rape them, which is something genuine eighteenth-century rakes did.

Another area I compromise on is language. I have researched genuine Devon dialect from both the eighteenth and nineteenth centuries. It is almost incomprehensible. To a lesser extent, the same is true of London slang. I therefore pick and choose, including genuine words and expressions to give a flavour of period, area and class, but without being pedantic. I also avoid overused expressions such as 'Lawks a mercy'.

The result, I would like to think, is a historical setting sufficiently convincing not to irritate the reader but flexible enough for the plot and erotic content to work.

The second world can be called Kora, and is the setting for *Maiden*, *Captive*, and *Innocent*, also *Princess* from this collection. Kora is an unashamedly derivative fantasy world, complete with goblins, trolls, mighty heroes, avaricious merchants, and, of course, beautiful girls. The influences are Lewis Carroll, Tolkien, Howard's *Conan*, Jack Vance and John Norman's *Gor*.

An important thing about Kora is that it carries a strong element of pastiche. This is something two separate reviewers managed to miss completely, to my astonishment. Did they really think I was being serious?

Maybe it's just my perverted imagination, but I find the idea of half-willing sex with a group of over-endowed goblins both arousing and funny. When I read *Jabberwocky*, I don't fantasise about being rescued from the monster, but about being caught and fucked by it. (OK, you can lock me up now.) Then again, I always hate it when the macho slave trader offers the poor moppet he's caught the choice of slavery or death, then laughs at her when she chooses slavery, thus proving she is a slave at heart. In *Maiden*, Elethrine and Talithea demand death, only to be told they're far too valuable. Thus Kora was created mainly to explore those sexual fantasies spawned by the fantasy genre but also to send up aspects of it.

Because Kora is an erotic pastiche of an established genre, it is acceptable to follow the conventions of that genre, those I wish to anyway. Everybody conveniently speaks the same language, despite living in completely different cultures thousands of miles apart. This is an unrealistic but useful plot device, which I use to avoid unnecessary complexity and exposition. For the same reasons I use simple plots involving a journey or quest, another well-established and convenient plot device. In contrast, I do try not to make the characters think the way we do. Each culture I create is separate, with its own moral and social values. Modern, Western values are unknown, much less seen as an ideal.

An advantage of a fantasy world, especially one not designed to be taken too seriously, is that the author can get away with things which could be considered unacceptable in a real world setting. I support every individual's right to fantasise over what they please so long as they harm nobody. Yet when writing erotica it would be irresponsible not to take into account the fact that there might just be some lunatic out there prepared to put my fantasy into reality. When the world itself is complete fantasy, this ceases to be an issue. After all, where would they get the goblins?

Kora is light-hearted and escapist, intended to amuse as well as arouse. If you like your heroines to end up as the hero's grovelling and obedient slaves, forget it.

My third world is Susa. It is the setting for *Tiger, Tiger* and *Pleasure Toy*, while in this collection there is the short *Tigress*. Susa is less derivative than Kora, owing something to Mervyn Peake, Jack Vance and others, but a great deal more to the ancient human obsession with creatures half-man, half-animal. This is the most personal of my creations, and my favourite, created to explore my fascination with the sexual aspects of fur and beasts.

While fantastical in that the setting is purely imaginary, Susa is also rational. There is no magic, and everything has an explanation. Thus the strange creatures which inhabit the world are the creations of genetic engineering, although such advanced techniques are long forgotten. The tigranthropes and suanthropes are humans endowed with the characteristics of tigers and pigs respectively. Other animals, such as the giant baluchitheria used as riding beasts, are extinct species retrieved by genetic manipulation.

Other than the sheer joy of writing in a world entirely of my own creation, the main pleasure of Susa for me is to create and experiment with imaginary moral and social systems and their erotic consequences. For Susa I have created elaborate social, political and economic structures, the function and interaction of which provides the drive for the stories and in turn the erotic detail.

As with my other work, I try to make my characters think and act in ways appropriate to their setting rather than according to contemporary Western thought. I have heard it argued that this dilutes the power of the erotic scenes, and that sexual writing is only really effective when the reader can easily associate with the characters. Personally I think this merely shows lack of imagination. I have no more difficulty empathising with Tian-Sha in *Tiger, Tiger* than Elethrine in *Maiden*, Eloise and Henry in *The Rake* or Lily and Nich in *Deep Blue*.

I would hope that my Susa novels can fascinate as well as arouse, perhaps occasionally even make people think a little.

My fourth major world is that of *Deep Blue* and *Satan's Slut*. It is contemporary and contrasts reality with fantasy. Thus, unlike the others, the rules of society are our own, and the majority of characters think and act in ways familiar to us. Sexually, these characters are deliberately prosaic, as is their setting, to create a stronger contrast with those few characters who very definitely do not belong to the real world.

Thus there are two levels to this world in terms of erotic content. Superficially, it is involved with straight-forward eroticism, power-play, domination and submission, just basic sex. At a deeper level are much stranger fantasies, which would probably be too weird to stand alone, sex with demons and the desire to be enfolded by a colossal octopus.

In many ways, this is the easiest world to write. Speech is contemporary, and there are few considerations of language and culture. The characters tend to be derived from people I've met and are therefore easier to flesh out. Likewise, the settings are mainly real places, so easier to describe. Only when it comes to the interactions between the ordinary and fantastical characters does this become difficult.

Deep Blue is currently my fastest selling book, which probably owes more to the descriptions of the thoroughly unpleasant Ed exploiting the meek and intellectual Lily than to the octopus sex, but it would be nice to imagine otherwise.

For the future, I intend to produce at least one more novel set within each of these four worlds. Henry Truscott has probably had his day, but his father will be making an appearance in due time, in a story derived from the exploits of John Arscott, complete with dwarf. There will be a third girl's milk novel. Kora could run and run, but I think it is a mistake to try to extend a series indefinitely, so will be bringing the saga to an end with a fourth and final novel. Susa will certainly produce a third novel, maybe more. Neither *Deep Blue* nor *Satan's Slut* really allow for sequels, but there will certainly be others set within the same world.

In the collection you will presumably have just finished, I have set short stories in several new worlds. *Black Tide* (from *New Erotica 5*) and *Named Harlot* both come from the same setting, a gothic/medieval world of malign priests and complicated tortures much darker than my other creations. I am beginning to really enjoy this world, and will certainly be expanding on it in the future. Another world worth at least one full-length novel is the Hell of *Succubus*. The possibilities are endless. Among the others, *Mother*, *Virtual Tramps* and *Virago* all belong to possible futures, with their detachment from our own reality in direct proportion to how far ahead in time they are set. *Roswell Tart*, *Girls*, *Cows* and *Mistress Perfection* are all set in parodies of the real world, containing a deliberate element of the ludicrous, and hopefully recognisable to the reader.

I hope you have enjoyed this book, and that this essay has added to your appreciation. Feedback and opinion are always welcome.

NEXUS NEW BOOKS

To be published in November

PLAYTHINGS OF THE PRIVATE HOUSE
Esme Ombreux

When Olena, nubile and much-appreciated guest at the secretive flagellant community that is the Private House, is kinapped, Supreme Mistress Jem Darke and her lover Julia, chief of the guards, are unusually at a loss as to what to do. But Talia, the fey, submissive but resourceful leader of the forest people, who live a bucolic but perverted life on the House's large estate, has evidence that leads to Madame la Patronne, Jem's rival in the arts of dominance. Jem, Julia, Talia and her lover Anne agree a plan of pursuit. Their actions lead them straight into deep sexual waters: how far will they be required to submit to Madame la Patronne, whose imperious sexuality knows no limits. And even if their tormented odyssey brings them to Oleana, will she even want to return?

ISBN 0 352 33761 3

CRUEL TRIUMPH
William Doughty

Alice is Steve's demon dominatrix, and red-hot lover and friend. After a few years of trust, commitment and fantastic sex, the couple are invited to a very special party at the sumptuous home of the successful, dominant and *very* perverted Kurt. Alice's interest is piqued, and Steve learns the hard way that he does not know the extremes of Alice's sexuality quite as well as he thinks he does. Just how far does Alice's newfound taste for submission extend beyond the realms of SM fantasy into reality? And will Steve lose Alice to the assertive Kurt, or will he find the strength within himself to give Alice what she *really* wants?

ISBN 0 352 33759 1

THE HOUSE AT MALDONA
Yolanda Celbridge

There's a hidden world deep in the heart of southern Spain where the bizarre rituals of the Inquisition have survived to this day. A strange, some would say perverse, society of women has formed the House of Maldona. Like the Knights Templar of old, their lives are governed by a strict set of rules and a hierarchy based on discipline. When Jane, an adventurous young Chelsea girl, travels to Spain to look for her friends, she finds instead the welcoming arms of Maldona's lesbian elite. Becoming involved in their strange games and ceremonies, she is to discover shocking things about herself and her ancestors.

ISBN 0 352 33740 0

If you would like more information about Nexus titles, please visit our website at www.nexus-books.co.uk, or send a stamped addressed envelope to:
Nexus, Thames Wharf Studios,
Rainville Road, London W6 9HA

NEXUS BACKLIST

This information is correct at time of printing. For up-to-date information, please visit our website at www.nexus-books.co.uk

All books are priced at £5.99 unless another price is given.

THE TORTURE CHAMBER	Lisette Ashton	☐
	ISBN 0 352 33530 0	
UNIFORM DOLL	Penny Birch	☐
£6.99	ISBN 0 352 33698 6	
WHIP HAND	G. C. Scott	☐
£6.99	ISBN 0 352 33694 3	
THE YOUNG WIFE	Stephanie Calvin	☐
	ISBN 0 352 33502 5	

Nexus books with Ancient and Fantasy settings

CAPTIVE	Aishling Morgan	☐
	ISBN 0 352 33585 8	
DEEP BLUE	Aishling Morgan	☐
	ISBN 0 352 33600 5	
DUNGEONS OF LIDIR	Aran Ashe	☐
	ISBN 0 352 33506 8	
INNOCENT	Aishling Morgan	☐
£6.99	ISBN 0 352 33699 4	
MAIDEN	Aishling Morgan	☐
	ISBN 0 352 33466 5	
NYMPHS OF DIONYSUS	Susan Tinoff	☐
£4.99	ISBN 0 352 33150 X	
PLEASURE TOY	Aishling Morgan	☐
	ISBN 0 352 33634 X	
SLAVE MINES OF TORMUNIL	Aran Ashe	☐
£6.99	ISBN 0 352 33695 1	
THE SLAVE OF LIDIR	Aran Ashe	☐
	ISBN 0 352 33504 1	
TIGER, TIGER	Aishling Morgan	☐
	ISBN 0 352 33455 X	

Period

CONFESSION OF AN ENGLISH SLAVE	Yolanda Celbridge	☐
	ISBN 0 352 33433 9	
THE MASTER OF CASTLELEIGH	Jacqueline Bellevois	☐
	ISBN 0 352 32644 7	
PURITY	Aishling Morgan	☐
	ISBN 0 352 33510 6	
VELVET SKIN	Aishling Morgan	☐
	ISBN 0 352 33660 9	

Samplers and collections

NEW EROTICA 5	Various ISBN 0 352 33540 8	☐
EROTICON 1	Various ISBN 0 352 33593 9	☐
EROTICON 2	Various ISBN 0 352 33594 7	☐
EROTICON 3	Various ISBN 0 352 33597 1	☐
EROTICON 4	Various ISBN 0 352 33602 1	☐
THE NEXUS LETTERS	Various ISBN 0 352 33621 8	☐
SATURNALIA £7.99	ed. Paul Scott ISBN 0 352 33717 6	☐
MY SECRET GARDEN SHED £7.99	ed. Paul Scott ISBN 0 352 33725 7	☐

Nexus Classics

A new imprint dedicated to putting the finest works of erotic fiction back in print.

AMANDA IN THE PRIVATE HOUSE £6.99	Esme Ombreux ISBN 0 352 33705 2	☐
BAD PENNY	Penny Birch ISBN 0 352 33661 7	☐
BRAT £6.99	Penny Birch ISBN 0 352 33674 9	☐
DARK DELIGHTS £6.99	Maria del Rey ISBN 0 352 33667 6	☐
DARK DESIRES	Maria del Rey ISBN 0 352 33648 X	☐
DISPLAYS OF INNOCENTS £6.99	Lucy Golden ISBN 0 352 33679 X	☐
DISCIPLINE OF THE PRIVATE HOUSE £6.99	Esme Ombreux ISBN 0 352 33459 2	☐
EDEN UNVEILED	Maria del Rey ISBN 0 352 33542 4	☐

- - - - - ✂ -

Please send me the books I have ticked above.

Name ....

Address ....

....

....

.... Post code...................

Send to: **Cash Sales, Nexus Books, Thames Wharf Studios, Rainville Road, London W6 9HA**

US customers: for prices and details of how to order books for delivery by mail, call 1-800-343-4499.

Please enclose a cheque or postal order, made payable to **Nexus Books Ltd**, to the value of the books you have ordered plus postage and packing costs as follows:

UK and BFPO – £1.00 for the first book, 50p for each subsequent book.

Overseas (including Republic of Ireland) – £2.00 for the first book, £1.00 for each subsequent book.

If you would prefer to pay by VISA, ACCESS/MASTERCARD, AMEX, DINERS CLUB or SWITCH, please write your card number and expiry date here:

....

Please allow up to 28 days for delivery.

Signature ....

Our privacy policy.

We will not disclose information you supply us to any other parties. We will not disclose any information which identifies you personally to any person without your express consent.

From time to time we may send out information about Nexus books and special offers. Please tick here if you do *not* wish to receive Nexus information. ☐

- - - - - ✂ -